"Why didn't you say something while we were being robbed?"

Jed set cold, blue eyes on Hannah's face. "Because I didn't want everyone there to end up dead."

He was right, of course. Not that she would *tell* him so. "Well, thank you," she said softly. "I am particularly pleased to see my mother's brooch here. Everything else can be replaced, but that . . ." She choked back the tears that threatened. She was not normally so sentimental! "Well, thank you."

Hannah wondered if a kiss on the cheek was in order, simply as a thank-you. She leaned slowly and hesitantly toward Jed, her eyes on that hairy cheek of his. She stopped long before her lips came near it.

"You're welcome," he said gruffly, and then he squirmed.

Had no one ever thanked him before?

"I wish I could convince you," she said softly. "I know with all my heart that Baxter is innocent."

Jed retated his head slowly to look at her. His eyes narrowed suspiciously. "Don't try that old trick on me." he grumbled.

"What old trick?"

"A pretty girl batting her eyelashes at me isn't going to make me change my mind," he said with a shake of his head. "You can pout and quiver all you want, but I'm too damn old to fall for that one."

Dear Romance Reader,

Last year, we launched the Ballad line with four new series, and each month we'll present both new and continuing stories set everywhere from medieval England to the American West—the kind of passionate, romantic stories you love best, written by the most gifted authors. At the back of each book, we'll tell you when you can find subsequent books in the series that have captured your heart.

This month, rising star Martha Schroeder returns with the final book in her *Angels of Mercy* series. In **A Rose for Julian,** a young nurse with a painful past agrees to care for a nobleman's wounded son—but never imagines that she will come to love him, too. Next, Linda Devlin offers the next installment of *The Rock Creek Six* with **Jed.** What happens when an independent man and a stubborn woman must work together to solve a crime? Teamwork, of course—the married kind!

In the last entry of RITA-nominated author Elizabeth Keys's atmospheric *Irish Blessing* series, the youngest Reilly sibling believes she's immune to the family Blessing because she's a woman. But one kiss from a certain man changes that immediately—and she vows to show him the power of *this* **Reilly's Heart.** Finally, Kathryn Fox concludes her adventurous *Mounties* series with **The Third Daughter,** as a new mounted officer makes a business arrangement with a local ranch, and finds that he wants something far more personal from the rancher's oldest daughter—her love. Enjoy!

Kate Duffy
Editorial Director

The Rock Creek Six

JED

Linda Devlin

ZEBRA BOOKS
Kensington Publishing Corp.
http://www.kensingtonbooks.com

ZEBRA BOOKS are published by

Kensington Publishing Corp.
850 Third Avenue
New York, NY 10022

All Kensington titles, imprints, and distributed lines are
available at special quantity discounts for bulk purchases for
sales promotion, premiums, fund-raising, educational or in-
stitutional use.

Special book excerpts or customized printings can also be
created to fit specific needs. For details, write or phone the
office of the Kensington Special Sales Manager: Kensington
Publishing Corp., 850 Third Avenue, New York, NY 10022.
Attn. Special Sales Department. Phone: 1-800-221-2647.

First Printing: December 2001
10 9 8 7 6 5 4 3 2 1

Printed in the United States of America

One

The stagecoach hit a rut in the road, and for a few terrible seconds it seemed to Hannah that the primitive conveyance, which was filled to capacity with six suffering passengers, flew through the air. It landed with a thud, and she gripped the seat tight to avoid being thrown into someone's lap. She gripped the head of her cane more tightly, too, though that wasn't likely to be of any assistance if she found herself airborne.

Bertie was seated quietly beside her. It gave Hannah some comfort to know that if she did have the misfortune to land in someone's lap, it would most likely be that of her maid and companion, and not one of the unsavory men who were seated on the opposite bench.

"I plan to write a strong letter of protest to the stage company once we arrive in Rock Creek," she said through gritted teeth, as she made a futile attempt to remove some of the dust from the silver-gray camel hair skirt of her traveling dress. The matching silk sash was most likely ruined, as was the gray felt hat she'd discarded days ago, after the first surprising jolt of the stagecoach. "This journey has been the most unbearable experience of my life. The food at the last stop was inedible, the coffee was cold and thick, the dust and heat are insufferable, and I believe our driver is approximately one hundred and two years old. A few of these bumps in the road could be made easier, I am certain, if we had been assigned a driver with a more skilled touch."

Bertie, bless her meek soul, muttered a weak "Yes, ma'am." Everyone else ignored her.

Well, everyone but the disgustingly filthy man who sat directly opposite her. Bearded, long-haired, and covered with a layer of Texas dirt, he lifted his head and peered beneath the rim of his foul, misshapen wide-brimmed hat to glare at her with narrowed, glittering, hard, very blue eyes. How rude!

Bertie was the perfect traveling companion, in Hannah's estimation. She was neat—as her own dark blue traveling dress attested to—quiet, well-mannered, and humble. With her fair hair and deep brown eyes she might have been called attractive by some, but as her eyes were always downcast and her fair hair was always severely contained, that attractiveness was not a distraction.

She glanced at the young girl who sat at Bertie's left side, out of curiosity and also as an excuse to take her eyes off the bearlike man who continued to stare so audaciously. She was a pretty, dark-haired girl by the name of Irene Benedict, and she didn't appear to be more than sixteen years old. It was abominable that she was traveling unescorted! It was distressing, as well, that she was inappropriately dressed for traveling. While her pale pink dress was young and feminine and lovely, it was best suited to a casual party or an evening at home, not traveling in mixed company. It was certainly not suitable for December, no matter how balmy the weather.

Seated directly across from Irene was an elderly lady, a Mrs. Reynolds, who'd joined their party at the last stop. She was going to visit her son in Rock Creek, she'd said, to see the latest addition to the family, her first granddaughter. Her son, who owned one of the ranches near Rock Creek, had four sons, but this was his first daughter. She very proudly showed them the small pastel quilt she'd fashioned for the child.

Next to Mrs. Reynolds, wedged between the older woman and the rude, scruffy bear of a man, sat a portly gentleman who sipped frequently from a flask he stored in the inside pocket of his checkered coat. He'd introduced himself as Mr. Virgil Wyndham and then added "gambler" with a wink in her direction, as if she might find that occupation delightful. All things considered, Hannah considered herself fortunate to have her seat between the window and Bertie.

When she glanced again at the man before her, his eyes were closed. Hours ago, when introductions had been made, he'd mumbled Jed Rourke, with no further explanation offered. Perhaps he had no occupation; he looked rather like a mountain man, in his worn denim trousers, threadbare cotton shirt, and leather vest. He'd been wearing a long buckskin coat and carrying a rifle when he'd joined them, but those items were now stored beneath the seat, along with his saddlebag—all he carried with him. No baggage, no trunk. Yes, he appeared to be a wandering wild man. Surely no gentleman with a suitable profession would allow his beard and hair to grow in such an untamed manner, or possess such a well-worn hat.

Mr. Rourke, whatever he might be, had been trying to sleep for the past two hours but was apparently having no luck. Those steely eyes never stayed closed for long.

Between the bumps and the dust and the heat, how could anyone sleep?

Rose better have a damned good reason for summoning me to this godforsaken place, she thought, not for the first time since her interminable journey from Alabama had begun.

Her irritation at the current situation came and went, but in truth Hannah knew her sister had to have an excellent reason for sending the summoning telegram. After all, it had been twelve years since her sister had run off with that good-for-nothing shopkeeper, and in all that time there had been no requests for help. There were letters, of course, and since their father's death three years earlier there had been several invitations for Hannah to visit and see the children, but this . . . This was very different from a friendly invitation.

Come at once. I need you. Could the telegram have been more cryptic?

Perhaps Rose was ill and needed assistance. The very idea gave Hannah an unpleasant chill. Maybe Baxter's general store was failing and they needed money. Hannah frowned as she stared out the window. That was probably the reason for the telegram. Everyone came to Hannah Winters for a loan when they found themselves in a bind. Some gentlemen were even so witless as to ask her to marry them in order that they might have ready access to her late father's fortune, the substantial sum that was now hers. Foolish men.

"Hang on, folks!" The driver yelled his warning just a moment too late.

Hannah grasped the seat and the gold head of her ebony cane as the coach ran carelessly over yet another rut. Yes, it was probably money Rose needed. Perhaps she thought it would be easy for Hannah to refuse by telegram but difficult to refuse the same request face-to-face.

Rose doesn't know me anymore, Hannah thought with a hardening of her heart as she watched the most desolate, ugly landscape she'd ever seen fly past. Beyond the window was rock and dirt and dust, the barrenness broken, here and there, by a few stunted and scraggly bushes that were more brown than green.

"Why on earth does anyone *choose* to live here?" she muttered.

Everyone ignored her except, again, the oaf across the way. He didn't open his eyes, though. "There's beauty most everywhere," he muttered. "Only sometimes you have to look real hard for it."

She was glad his eyes were closed, so he wouldn't see her blush. Hannah Winters didn't need any man to tell her, in a subtle or not-so-subtle way, that she wasn't pretty. She'd known it all her life, and she had accepted the fact years ago. Her hair was too red, her nose was slightly crooked, her chin was pointed, and her eyes were a very ordinary gray. Growing up side by side with Rose, who had their mother's blond hair, vibrant greenish blue eyes, and angelic face, Hannah had been forced to face the sad fact of her plainness from a very early age. She wasn't beautiful, even if the kindest eyes looked "real hard."

"Oh, I know what you mean," Mrs. Reynolds said, her voice lively. "When I first came here I thought the very same thing, that this was the ugliest place on earth. But once you've seen the sunrise or the sunset you just know this land has been blessed."

Still without opening his eyes, Jed Rourke smiled. It was difficult to be certain, with that drooping mustache and scruffy beard, but yes . . . he definitely smiled.

Maybe he hadn't been talking about her, after all.

Hannah looked out the window again, trying, really trying, to see beauty in the rocky landscape. She failed miserably; already she missed the green of Alabama.

Movement caught her eye, and she dismissed her displeasure at the desolate nature of the landscape and her unexpected bout of homesickness. There was nothing between the last station, a miserable town called Ranburne, and Rock Creek but this sadly neglected roadway, so what might she have seen out there?

Suddenly a single rider, with a black bandanna covering the lower half of his face, shot from behind a boulder, followed by another masked rider on a dappled horse. Each of them brandished a weapon.

"Bandits," she whispered, a moment before she was startled by the explosion of a gunshot from the other side of the stagecoach. Bertie and Irene whimpered, Mrs. Reynolds emitted what might have been a weak, short scream, and the portly drunk slunk low in his seat and cowered. The large, hairy man, Mr. Rourke, was immediately alert.

"How many?" he asked as the stage began to slow.

"Two on this side, at least one on the other," Hannah said. Mr. Rourke didn't have a good view, seated as he was with his back to the driver, so she felt it her duty to keep him informed. "Masked and armed," she added.

He spread his legs and reached between them and beneath his seat to pull out his saddlebag. His hands moved quickly and efficiently, opening the leather bag, withdrawing a six-shooter, and checking to make sure it was fully loaded before the stagecoach came to a complete stop. He barely had time to conceal the weapon at his spine before the door flew open and the passengers were instructed, with the silent motion of a gun, to disembark.

Hannah was first to step from the coach, refusing to take the offered hand of the bandit who waved a gun in her direction. She hesitated long enough for Mr. Rourke, who was squirming and trying to inconspicuously adjust the six-shooter he'd hurriedly jammed at his back, to make sure his weapon was safely hidden beneath his leather vest. Out of the corner of her eye she saw him nod once, and only then did she step down, leaning on her cane for support as her feet hit the hard road.

"Heathens," she muttered loud enough for the bandits to hear. There were four of them, all armed, all masked. One dragged the stagecoach driver, a miserable, sickly looking old man, to the ground, while the others impatiently herded the passengers off the conveyance.

The four bandits were all dressed in typical Western fashion, in denim trousers, badly scuffed boots, and dirty shirts, along with the requisite wide-brimmed hats and heavy gunbelts. They were masked with bandannas, black on one face, red on two, and a bright yellow on a very tall, very thin outlaw.

She glanced at Mr. Rourke, waiting for him to make his move. Perhaps he was a quick-draw artist and could take all four men before they even knew what was happening. For a long moment she held her breath and waited anxiously. Her heart even skipped a beat in anticipation.

But Jed Rourke stood meekly with the rest of the passengers, while two of the bandits began to paw through their belongings, taking whatever struck their fancy. They were looking for cash, but seemed delighted with the jewelry they found. Hannah pursed her lips and bit her tongue. Most of the pieces they gloated over were hers, taken from the tapestry bag she'd stored beneath her seat. They tossed Rourke's buckskin coat onto the ground, barely giving it a second glance, but they seemed pleased with the rifle they pulled from beneath that coat. Rourke grumbled a curse as they admired it.

Mrs. Reynolds was visibly shaken, and Irene sniffled once or twice. Bertie, meek as she was, had the good grace not to humiliate herself by sniveling like the drunk who stood beside her. Mr. Rourke, quickly if grudgingly abandoning his rifle to the bandits, yawned and shifted restlessly on his big, booted feet as he readjusted the dust-covered hat on his head.

Perhaps he was right to keep calm in this situation. It didn't look as if the bandits planned to harm anyone. As long as that was the case, it would be foolish for Mr. Rourke to initiate gunplay.

Hannah sighed in disgust and resignation. It infuriated her to know that perfectly able men chose thievery as a profession, but she knew that everything the bandits were so gleefully taking could be replaced.

Satisfied with what they'd found, the masked men loaded their saddlebags with stolen goods. One impatient thief guarded the passengers. Even with his bandanna and a wide-brimmed hat worn low, Hannah could tell he was fairly young. And mean. He seemed to delight in making the detained passengers stand in a straight line, and in harassing the more distraught victims of this holdup. Walking before them like an inspector, waving that weapon in a dangerous fashion, he looked them all up and down.

The elderly driver was rubbing his head as if it pained him. He hadn't said a word—they'd been instructed to maintain silence while the thieves went about their work—but Hannah suspected one of the brigands had hit the poor old man over the head. The young watchman laughed at the old man in a way that was hideously disrespectful. The driver ignored the taunt.

Standing before Hannah, the outlaw gave her a quick once-over. He was either trying to intimidate her or he was searching for pockets that might contain a valuable they'd missed. In any case, he was an insolent bandit. Her traveling dress was plain, but it was constructed of the very best materials and would tell anyone who knew anything about fashion that it was quite expensive. She didn't expect this oaf would recognize the fact.

"Coward," she said when his eyes rose to meet hers. Pale eyes above a red bandanna flashed at her.

Mr. Rourke, who stood beside her, groaned, but the bandit didn't seem to take offense. He merely smiled and moved on. Since Jed Rourke was a powerfully built man and stood a good head taller than the young bandit, he wasn't subjected to an impertinent examination. The outlaw moved on to Bertie.

"You ought not to be so scared," he said. "Why, as long as you behave yourselves we ain't gonna hurt nobody. Just think of the story you can tell your friends when this is all over with." He moved on to the drunk, curling his lip in disgust.

He called Mrs. Reynolds "Granny."

In a voice that wavered ever so slightly, she bravely answered him. "If you have a grandmother, Junior, she would surely be ashamed to see you now."

Hannah couldn't help but smile.

And then he reached Irene, at the end of the line. The poor girl bowed her head and sobbed.

"Now, now," Junior said in a voice that was a mixture of glee and solace. "Don't cry, sugar." He reached out and touched her face, wiping away the tears. "Ain't nothing to cry about, I promise you. Oh," he mumbled when she tried to gently move her face out of his reach, "you're a pretty one."

Hannah took a step forward, but a hand snaked out and very firmly grabbed her arm, then yanked her back into line. She glared up at Jed Rourke and with a swift jerk freed her arm from his grasp.

Junior cupped Irene's chin and forced her to look into his face. She sobbed loudly, once, which only delighted the coward who tormented her. "I think I'll take you home with me, sugar."

"Take your hands off her," Mrs. Reynolds insisted indignantly.

The grin disappeared. "Shut up, Granny."

This time Hannah moved quickly, stepping past Rourke while his eyes were on the bandit and Irene. She raised her cane and smacked the lascivious brigand across the back of his thin legs. He howled loudly and nearly dropped to his knees. He caught himself, though, and spun around with his weapon raised, and Hannah found herself staring down the barrel of a loaded pistol.

"She's a child," Hannah said calmly. "Leave her alone." Her mouth was dry and her heart beat much faster than was healthy, as she peered over the barrel of the weapon that was aimed at her nose, but she was determined not to let the thief see her fear.

"You hit me with that damn stick," Junior said with righteous indignation, and then he reached out and snatched the cane out of her hand. He cocked the hammer of his pistol back with his thumb.

Her father had always told her that one day her quick tongue would get her into trouble. On occasion she'd silently agreed with him, but she'd never expected that a few hotly spoken words would lead to her violent death. Still, she wouldn't take back what she'd said. She wouldn't apologize for doing what she could to protect an innocent young girl.

She was so intently focused on the bandit and the gun she didn't realize that Mr. Rourke had left his place in line until he stepped quickly into view and his six-shooter touched Junior's neck.

"Put it down," Mr. Rourke said calmly. "I really, really don't want to shoot anyone today." There was a weary quality to his voice, but that voice was hard, too. Inflexible. Hannah had no doubt that Mr. Rourke would shoot the outlaw if he had to.

Junior apparently didn't doubt it, either. The barrel of his weapon swung unthreateningly to the side. "I wasn't really going to shoot her."

One of the other thieves, who'd been intent on collecting his booty, finally realized what was happening. "What the hell?" he shouted, raising his gun as he came around the front of the stagecoach.

"Miss Winters," Rourke said coldly and without so much as glancing at her, "stand behind me, please."

She moved to do as he asked, reaching out to wrench her cane from the robber before she skirted around Rourke. Standing behind him, she gave thanks that he was such a large man. For the moment, at least, she was well shielded.

Without being instructed, the other passengers followed suit until they all stood behind Jed Rourke.

"Now," he continued wearily and calmly, "this little episode has just gotten out of hand, don't you think? Nobody's been hurt, and nobody needs to get hurt. You take your loot and get out of here, and we continue on our way. What do you say?"

Mr. Rourke sounded relaxed—calm and completely in control—but the situation remained perilous and strained. He held a weapon at Junior's throat, but the three robbers he faced were all armed.

"I want your gun," the bandit in the black bandanna said, and as he spoke the others fanned out. "Hand it over."

"I can't do that," Rourke said with a shake of his head. "You've already got my best rifle."

Three firearms to one; it was hardly fair. Once the two outlaws who were moving to the side were in position, the passengers would be surrounded. Jed Rourke might very well kill Junior, and perhaps he'd even fire off another shot at the outlaw in the black bandanna . . . but by then several of the passengers would be dead or wounded.

Hannah took a deep breath, straightened her spine, and stepped around Mr. Rourke. "I don't think you understand fully what happened here." She addressed the black-bandanna bandit in her most sensible voice. "Your associate made an improper suggestion to our young friend and frightened her terribly."

"Miss Winters . . ." Mr. Rourke began, his voice low and tight.

She waved a silencing hand in his direction and continued. "Surely you don't blame Mr. Rourke and me for trying to protect her. She's just a child, after all." She glanced at the bandit who'd frightened Irene, giving him her most glacial stare. "Even though it's apparent he's little more than a child himself, he . . ."

"Rourke?" one of the men asked, eyes narrowed suspiciously as he looked the mountainous man up and down. "Did she call him Mr. *Rourke?*"

All four of the bandits stared at the tall, gruff man.

"Can't be *that* Rourke," another one said in a low voice. "Jedidiah Rourke is seven feet tall, mean as a snake, and wouldn't be caught dead riding on a stagecoach. If that were Jedidiah Rourke we'd all be dead by now."

The other bandit nodded in agreement, but they continued to look at Mr. Rourke with undisguised awe.

Hannah allowed herself to study Jed Rourke, as well. Who was he? A famous bandit himself? An outlaw? He stood there without response to their suppositions, looking nothing but weary and bored.

An arm snaked around Hannah's waist and jerked her back. She'd foolishly lost track of one of the bandits, the tall one with the yellow bandanna, and he'd sneaked up behind her! *Coward.*

The brush of a gun barrel against her temple drove away every other thought.

"Now," a gritty voice whispered, so close she could feel the touch of hot breath, "I don't care which Rourke you are, you let him go or I blow the lady's brains out right here."

Irene and Bertie and Mrs. Reynolds all cried openly. The gambler stared at the ground. The driver cradled his head and mumbled something about "fool women."

Jed Rourke lost his calm facade. He began to mutter, letting loose a flood of the most vulgar language she'd ever heard. The six-shooter he'd been holding to Junior's neck popped up to point harmlessly at the sky, and he gave the outlaw a gentle shove.

"Drop the gun and kick it over here," the voice near Hannah's ear demanded.

Rourke cursed again as he obeyed the outlaw's order and kicked away his weapon.

The young hothead argued his case with Black Bandanna. All Hannah heard was his continued insistence that he be allowed to kill them all. If she allowed herself to curse aloud, she'd borrow a few of Mr. Rourke's choice words right now.

Fortunately, cooler heads prevailed. The leader of the gang—at least she assumed Black Bandanna was the leader since he did almost all the talking—ordered Junior to mount up and start riding, and a moment later the outlaw who held Hannah released her, shoving her toward the others. It was with the greatest luck and skill that she avoided falling headlong into Jed Rourke.

He didn't look at her. . . . In fact, all eyes were on the bandits. Mean as a snake? Seven feet tall? What Rourke were they talking about?

The thieves had everything they needed and wanted, and everyone was safe. Hannah decided to be grateful that no one had been hurt.

"Get the horses," the leader said to the men who remained, and as he held a weapon on the prisoners, his companions complied, beginning the process of loosening the bonds on the animals who pulled the stage.

"You're not going to strand us out here," Rourke said softly.

It was hard to tell, with that black scarf hiding the lower half of his face, but Hannah was almost certain the bandit smiled. "Yep." His eyes were on Hannah as he spoke. "You turned out to be more trouble than we expected, so it is tempting. I don't abide unnecessary killin', but, by golly, I don't have to make things easy for you, neither."

"Let me have my Peacemaker, then, or my rifle," Rourke said sensibly. "We'll have a long walk ahead of us, and it'll be dark soon. You know what kind of critters live in these parts."

Hannah shivered. Was he speaking of critters like the ones they faced now, or other dangerous animals?

"Can't do that," the man said with a sigh. "Sorry."

The four horses cooperated meekly as they were freed from the constraints that had bound them to the stage.

At last the three remaining outlaws mounted their horses, which were heavily laden with stolen goods. They led the traitorously cooperative stage-coach steeds as they galloped away.

When they'd rounded the big boulder and disappeared from sight, Hannah turned to the rest of the group to see that all eyes were on her. Mr. Rourke, in particular, stared most audaciously.

"Are you happy now, Miss Winters?" he seethed, his voice soft.

"Surely you're not blaming *me* for this fiasco," she asked, raising an indignant hand to her breast.

"Oh, no," he said, his voice rising slightly. "I'm only blaming you for the fact that we have no horses and no goddamn weapon!"

She lifted her chin. "There's no reason to be vulgar, Mr. Rourke."

He took a single step toward her, eyes narrowed and hands balled into large fists. Suddenly Hannah was certain she had more reason to fear this man than she had the masked bandits who'd taken her money and jewelry and threatened her life.

Two

Vulgar? Jed suppressed the urge to show Miss Winters what vulgar really was. He kept his mouth shut. There were three ladies present. Three ladies and one aggravating, meddling, loud-mouthed, nose-in-the-air, redheaded harridan.

"Miss Winters," he said through clenched teeth, calling upon every ounce of self-control he had left; there wasn't much. "All you had to do was stand still and keep your mouth shut, and right now we'd be on our way to Rock Creek in that stage." He pointed for emphasis. "But no. Instead of *riding* to Rock Creek, poorer but no wiser, we're stranded miles from town!"

"I couldn't stand by and allow Junior to paw Irene and scare her that way," she said indignantly.

Junior?

"Since there were no gentlemen present to defend her, I took it upon myself to do so," she said haughtily, "and I would do so again."

He took another step toward her. "I wouldn't have let Junior hurt her," he said in defense of himself. "I don't think he would have."

"You don't know. . . ."

"You jumped the gun," he said accusingly.

Miss Winters was silent for a moment. Perhaps it was her way of agreeing with him. "Well," she said, her voice a bit softer, "what's done is done. I suggest we start walking so we can get to Rock Creek as soon as possible."

Jed looked over his shoulder, and his heart and spirits sank. What he had here was one slightly injured old man, a fat drunk, an old lady, two helpless young girls—he rotated his head to look at Miss Winters again—and *her.* There was no way they'd reach Rock Creek before dark. It was warm for December, but by nightfall it would turn plenty cold.

"This is what we're going to do," he said, tearing his eyes from the redhead. "We're going to head for those hills." He pointed to the southeast. "There's water there, and shelter from the wind, and that's where we'll spend the night. Tomorrow morning . . ."

"Absolutely not."

The unbending refusal came from behind him—which was no surprise. He rotated his head slowly to glare at Miss Winters. She leaned slightly forward, putting a little bit of weight on her cane. "We're going to walk down this road"—with a subtle and easy shifting of her body, she lifted the cane and pointed south—"straight for our destination. If we're lucky, someone will come along and assist us."

"No one's going to come along. . . ."

"Even if that's true, we'll be better off staying on the road."

He ignored the soft murmurs of the other passengers and stalked toward Miss Winters, no longer concerned about keeping his distance.

"It'll be dark in a couple of hours. Have you ever seen a coyote by moonlight, Miss Winters?" He was rewarded by the sudden paleness of her already fair face. "What about a bobcat?"

"If you're trying to frighten me . . ."

"I am," he said softly when he stood directly before her. She stared up at him, unflinching, with defiance and arrogance in her gray eyes. "I'm trying to scare some sense into you!" he shouted in frustration. "Why do I have the feeling I'm wasting my time?"

"You can bellow all you like," she said calmly. "And if you want to camp in the hills tonight, be my guest. But Bertie and I and anyone else who cares to join us are taking the road."

She spun on her heel and walked, back straight and head high, to the horseless stagecoach. "I do think I'll take a few of my belongings with me. The stage company will collect our baggage later, I'm sure, but I'll need a few things—"

Jed turned his back on her, tuning out the sound of her damned sensible voice. "Listen up," he said to the remaining passengers. "Get what you don't want to leave behind. God only knows what will still be here by the time the stage company gets around to collecting what's left. But, don't take more than you can comfortably carry." As the women moved obediently toward the stagecoach he added, "And if there's anything we can use as bedding, make it a priority. The air might feel comfortable now, but at night it gets damn cold."

As the ladies busied themselves going through the luggage that had been stored in the rear boot, Jed faced the gambler, Virgil Wyndham. Corpulent, drunk, and oily, he made no move to offer assistance.

"Hand it over," Jed said softly. Not even the driver, who was nursing his head just a few feet away, could hear him.

Wyndham raised his eyebrows in mock surprise. "Hand what over?"

Jed smiled coldly. "You've got a derringer up one sleeve, a knife in the boot, maybe"—he eyed Wyndham's massive and bright jacket—"maybe something more deadly tucked into an inside pocket of that coat."

"I assure you," Wyndham said indignantly, "I have nothing to hide."

"Don't make me search you," Jed whispered.

With a sigh, Wyndham began to divest himself of his weapons. There was indeed a derringer up the man's right sleeve, secreted in a neat little holster that fit to his forearm, and a wicked-looking knife was produced from the right boot. Further prodding was needed before he removed his jacket and produced another knife—this one with a short, sharp blade—and a pearl-handled six-shooter.

"I'm going to want that back," Wyndham insisted indignantly as Jed stuck the six-shooter into his waistband.

"You'll get it back," Jed assured the unctuous man. He snatched his coat from the ground and shook it out vigorously before slipping it on and letting the long folds fall into place.

When everyone was ready to go, he gave Miss Winters one last, long look. She'd retrieved her hat, a useless little bonnet with a gray feather that danced in the light wind, and had stuffed her tapestry bag until it positively bulged. "You're a fool," he said without hesitation. The witch smiled at him in answer.

Poor Bertie stood beside Miss Winters, her own bundle grasped tightly in two pale hands. "Are you sure we shouldn't stay with the others?" she asked meekly.

"Quite sure," Miss Winters answered, and then she turned about, her bundle in one hand and that blasted cane in the other as she started down the long, dusty road. She didn't look back. Bertie did.

Jed muttered a long string of curses, beginning and ending with "damnation," and then he thrust his saddlebags at the gambler and started down the road himself, taking long, impatient strides.

If Miss Winters heard him coming she gave no notice. Nose in the air, eyes unerringly forward, spine rigid, she was damned and determined to have her way.

Not this time.

He cut in front of her, and before she knew what was happening he picked her up and threw her over his shoulder.

After a short and peaceful moment of stunned silence, she screeched at him and whacked her cane against the back of his leg.

"Bertie," he said calmly, "take Miss Winters's cane before she manages to annoy me any more than she already has."

"Yes, sir," was the soft answer at his back.

"Bertie! How could you?" Miss Winters exclaimed in dismay, and Jed smiled.

He left the road and set his sights on the rock formation to the southeast. Even with this sad crew he should be there in no more than an hour and a half, well before dark. A quick glance over the shoulder that was not occupied by Miss Winters showed that everyone was following—at a distance.

"Cretin," Miss Winters hissed at his back.

Jed continued to smile. "Harridan," he answered softly.

She wasn't heavy at all; he could carry her all the way to the hills and never grow tired.

"Bully," she whispered.

"Battle-ax," he muttered.

She took a deep breath. "Mr. Rourke," she said in a breathless voice that still managed to sound intimidating, "I insist that you put me down this instant."

"Oh, you do?" he said without slowing his stride.

"Yes, I do, you . . . you buffoon!"

When he'd received Sylvia's pathetic plea for him to return to Rock Creek, he'd been glad of it. He'd grown tired of Pinkerton's, just as he'd grown tired of cowboying and mining and gambling, each in their turn. He'd counted on a bit of a vacation, time to ponder what came next, not a blasted ridiculous escapade.

Miss Winters slapped him lightly on the back, then again, harder. He ignored her. A moment later a sharp pain radiated from a point in the center of his back.

"Pinch me again," he said without slowing his step, "and I'll put you over my knee and give you the spanking you so richly deserve."

"You wouldn't dare," she mumbled, but she didn't pinch him again.

It had been a long time since he'd seen Sylvia.
When he visited Rock Creek he spent his time
with Eden and Sullivan and the rest of the guys,
if they were around. He had only seen Sylvia once
since she'd decided to take that slick preacher,
Maurice Clancy, as her second husband. Just as
well, he told himself. He got bored with everything else, sooner or later; he probably would
have found himself bored with Sylvia long ago.

"I hope you know I plan to press charges," Miss
Winters said calmly.

"For what?"

"Abduction," she snapped.

Abduction. He'd probably saved the ungrateful
woman's life, and here she was talking about having him thrown in jail. "Why is it," he muttered,
"that the prettier a woman is, the stupider she
turns out to be?"

"Perhaps," she said in a conversational voice
that was broken with every jarring step he took,
"because they've been spoiled from birth, relying
on a smile or a coy wink to gain for them what
a plain woman has to work for. If the brain isn't
used, Mr. Rourke . . ."

"You, Miss Winters," he said interrupting her
ridiculous monologue, "are a blithering idiot."

For a split second Hannah had the urge to say
"thank you." The urge passed quickly. She had
surely misunderstood his convoluted line of thinking.

When she lifted her head she saw a strand of
red hair that fell over one eye, and that traitor
Bertie following at a safe distance, carrying Hannah's cane and the tapestry bag she'd dropped,
the gray hat that had fallen from Hannah's head,

and her own bag. It was quite a load for someone as petite as Bertie.

"Put me down," she demanded once again, her voice lower than before.

"Nope," Rourke answered. "Where you go, Bertie goes, and I'd hate to see that sweet thing devoured by a coyote."

So he was enamored of Bertie. Why was she surprised?

"Now if it was just you . . ."

He really didn't need to continue.

"I'd be more worried about the coyote." There was a touch of humor in his grating voice.

"What if I promise to stay with the rest of you?" she said, surrendering. What choice did she have? She sighed. "Besides, I can't see the road any longer, so I'd likely get lost, and I'm getting a terrible headache."

The big man stopped. "Promise?" he asked.

She didn't like the teasing lilt in his voice, and one day . . . somehow . . . she was going to make him pay for this.

"Promise," she said softly.

He placed her on her feet so quickly her head spun. The entire world spun, for a moment. Once neatly contained strands of soft, dark red hair settled in disarray around her face as she took a deep breath and closed her eyes. Oh, yes, the man was going to pay.

"I'll take those," she heard him say, his humor bright.

When she opened her eyes he was gone, striding purposefully in the direction of the distant gathering of rocks that he seemed to think would be safe for the night. The tail of that buckskin coat danced around his long legs in a strangely entrancing sort of rhythm. His saddlebags were thrown casually and comfortably over his shoulder, there where she'd hung without dignity only a moment earlier. Bertie was there to offer low words of comfort, as the gambler and Irene silently followed Mr. Rourke.

Hannah took her cane and bag and ruined hat from Bertie, as Mrs. Reynolds laid a gentle hand on her shoulder. "It's for the best, dear," she said softly. "We really should stay together, and Mr. Rourke seems to know the area well."

"Yes, yes," Hannah muttered impatiently as she fell into step a short distance behind Irene, her eyes shooting daggers into Rourke's broad back. He'd humiliated her, treated her with disrespect, and taken advantage of the fact that he was physically superior. Cretin.

They hadn't gone far before she began to sweat. Her tapestry bag wasn't terribly heavy, but she was unaccustomed to walking long distances, and the skirt she wore was really too narrow for such an exercise. The jacket was much too warm and snug, and for a brief time she actually envied Rourke's open-necked shirt and Irene's inappropriate traveling dress.

An exasperated sigh from the rear made her turn her head. Mrs. Reynolds was having a terrible time with her baggage. Poor woman, she struggled with her two bags, and her face had turned quite red with the exertion.

"Let me help you," Hannah insisted, placing her bag on the ground and turning to face Mrs. Reynolds. "Goodness, why did you bring so much?" she asked as she took the largest bag.

Obviously relieved to hand over the burden, Mrs. Reynolds said breathlessly, "I couldn't leave behind the quilt I made for my granddaughter, and there are muffins and sweet breads and apples in this bag. I brought them for my son, but I thought we might need them this evening."

Hannah forced a smile. "How very thoughtful of you, Mrs. Reynolds." She slapped her useless hat on her head, giving her one less thing to carry, and handed over the cane. "If you'll carry this for me, I think I can manage your bags and mine."

"Oh, it's too much," Mrs. Reynolds protested.

"Nonsense," Hannah said sharply. "We can't have you falling behind." A glance over her shoulder showed her that they had already fallen behind. Jed Rourke strode forward purposefully, while Wyndham, the driver, and Irene struggled to stay close behind him. "Bertie, you go ahead," Hannah said, and the order was quickly obeyed. Bertie didn't want to get too far away from their self-appointed leader either, it seemed. "Mrs. Reynolds and I will bring up the rear."

With the hat on her head and the cane in Mrs. Reynolds's hand, Hannah was able to balance the three bags. She managed to hold the grips of the two smaller bags in her right hand and carried the larger bag in her left.

"There now," she said as she stepped forward, "isn't that better?"

"Oh, yes," Mrs. Reynolds said as she kept pace. "Those bags are quite heavy for an old woman like me. I was afraid I'd lag too far behind and get lost."

The bags were quite heavy for a younger woman

like herself, Hannah thought silently, her eyes on
Jed Rourke's back. With every long stride he
moved further and further away. If he insisted on
keeping them all together, why didn't he at least
look back to make sure everyone was keeping up?
If she could get to the road on her own . . . A
quick glance over her shoulder to the barren,
desolate landscape, showed no sign of the road.
Damnation.

"You're very kind," Mrs. Reynolds said softly.
"When I catch my breath I'll take back those
bags."

Kind? "You most certainly will not. We can't
have you hurting yourself, Mrs. Reynolds," Hannah said sharply. "I can carry the bags, but I'd
hardly be able to carry you." Her arms ached,
already, and there was still quite a long way to go.

If she thought about her predicament too
much, she'd stop right here and drop everything.
She did not carry her own baggage, she did not
trek through the wilderness like a lost porter, and
she most certainly did not follow cruel mountain
men into the wastelands.

But stopping was not an option; she knew that.
So she kept her eyes on Jed Rourke's back and
planned her revenge.

Hours with her father, and hours alone after
his death, had been spent reading. Hannah read
everything, novels, pamphlets, history. But her fa-
vorite reading material was tales of travel around
the world. She loved reading about distant cul-
tures she would never experience, enchanting
places she would never see. There was such diver-
sity on this planet!

Her eyes remained steadily fixed on Jed Rourke's

back. The Orientals, in particular, practiced inventive means of torture. Most common was the cangue, which was akin to a portable pillory. As long as the cangue is worn, the offending party cannot feed himself, and if not for kind passersby the criminal will starve. Then there's finger squeezing, and ankle squeezing, and the ever-popular whipping with bamboo. Of course, she doubted there was any bamboo growing in this part of Texas. . . .

"Miss Winters?" Mrs. Reynolds said softly, and Hannah was jerked from her reverie.

"Yes?"

"Is everything all right? Perhaps you should stop and rest for a few minutes."

If she stopped she'd never get started again. "I'm fine."

"But . . . why are you smiling?"

They were making good time. If he remembered correctly, and if the rains had been sufficient, there was a small lake in the hills ahead. That, together with the jerky he had in his saddlebags, would tide them over until they arrived in Rock Creek tomorrow.

Behind him he heard the strained huffing and puffing of his fellow travelers. He kept expecting to hear Miss Winters's strident voice rising above the grunting, perhaps as she called him cretin or barbarian or bully again. Jed smiled.

"Hey, mister," the driver said, his voice gruff and winded. "Maybe we ought to stop and wait for the others."

Jed's smile died. Someone had fallen behind,

and damnation he didn't have time to mollycoddle stragglers!

He turned around with a muttered curse and took a quick headcount. Wyndham and the driver were close behind him, and the two young girls stuck close together just a few paces behind them. It was a redhead and a gray one that bobbed in the distance.

Hell, he should've known. "Miss Winters!" he shouted, placing his hands on his hips. "If you don't mind!"

Instead of hurrying forward, she stopped in her tracks. Cantankerous woman. He was so intent on that untidy red hair, it took him a moment to realize that she carried three bags and Mrs. Reynolds carried only the cane.

Jed sighed tiredly and cursed beneath his breath as he tossed his saddlebags to the gambler. The portly man almost buckled under the weight, but Jed paid him no mind as he backtracked to the spot where Miss Winters and Mrs. Reynolds stood.

The little hat looked ridiculous, sitting cockeyed on her mussed hair. The feather danced in the wind, and so did the silky strands of hair that fell around Miss Winters's face. He half expected the women to start walking forward, to meet him halfway, but they stood their ground.

Hannah Winters had a pleasant, if ordinary, face, but at the moment there was something quite extraordinary about it; the color in her cheeks perhaps, or the angry flash of her eyes.

"Drop those bags," he said when he was close enough for conversation.

"I will not," she said breathlessly. "Mrs. Reynolds wants these . . ."

"Drop the bags!" he shouted, and she did.

"There's no need to bellow like a wounded animal, Mr. Rourke," Miss Winters said frostily. Her hair had fallen in disarray, her silly hat sat crooked, and she wore almost as much dust as he did. So how did she manage to maintain that annoying air of dignity?

He nodded to the cane Mrs. Reynolds leaned heavily on. "You don't need that?" he asked, his eyes steady on Miss Winters's flushed face. If he wasn't mistaken, she was a bit flustered by the question.

"Well, no, I don't actually require the cane anymore. When I sprained my ankle I found it quite useful, and I suppose I . . ."

She didn't have even a hint of a limp, no hitch in her step. "When was it, exactly, that you sprained your ankle?" he interrupted.

"I don't see what difference that makes," she answered, nose in the air.

"Just wondering if I might have to carry you awhile longer," he said in a low voice.

This time he was certain she blushed.

"You will keep your hands to yourself, Mr. Rourke."

"When was it, exactly?" he repeated.

"Two years ago," she admitted in a low voice.

Jed smiled widely. "Liked the feel of something solid in your hands, didn't you Miss Winters? Yep, I'd guess you liked having something handy to whack young bandits, impudent whippersnappers, and cretins with."

She pursed her lips. "Are we going to stand here

until dark, Mr. Rourke? I've enjoyed our little conversation, and I must admit I needed the break, but I suggest we keep moving." She bent to retrieve the bags.

"Drop them," Jed muttered before she could stand.

She straightened with fire in her eyes and more strength than he'd expected in her stance. She was ready for battle. "I will *not* abandon my things or Mrs. Reynolds's belongings in the middle of nowhere. If we move too slowly for you, if you don't care to wait for us stragglers, by all means leave us behind."

The fire in her eyes challenged him to do just that. He fought back a smile.

"Believe it or not, Miss Winters, I came to help." He stepped forward and she stepped back. With ease, he scooped the three bags off the ground. One small bag was tucked under his arm, and he grasped a leather grip in each hand.

Mrs. Reynolds, who had been quiet to this point, stepped forward. "Oh, how kind of you, Mr. Rourke." She turned to Miss Winters. "Isn't he just so gallant?"

Jed started walking toward the others.

"Well," Miss Winters said to his back, her voice clipped and cool, "There *might* have been a gentleman among his ancestors."

Since Jed was sure Miss Winters couldn't see his face, he smiled.

"But it's too early to be certain," she finished softly.

Three

Considering the circumstances, the place Rourke had chosen to set up camp for the night was adequate.

A large grouping of boulders sheltered their party from the wind that had grown cold the minute the sun set. A small pond of clear water was located not far from camp. And while the ground was rocky and hard, it was blessedly flat.Mr. Wyndham had, at Rourke's insistence, gathered wood for a fire. Mrs. Reynolds had passed around the sweets and fruit she'd packed for her son, and the six of them had shared a surprisingly pleasant meal of dried meat, muffins, apples, and water from a shared tin cup.

Hannah had been the only one to wipe the rim of that cup before putting it to her mouth, but then she'd had the misfortune to find herself seated next to Jed Rourke, and the cup she cleaned had come straight from his lips.

His response had been to laugh. Briefly and only once.

The rest of the party slept, curled up on and beneath clothing and blankets, all on a bed of hard, cold rock. Bertie and Irene lay side by side, warming each other with their closeness. The two girls had whispered for a few minutes after retiring, and then they'd fallen into a deep sleep. Mrs. Reynolds slept near the girls, there where a layer of cushioning clothing had been laid out for Hannah to sleep on. Hannah wasn't sleepy yet, not at all.

Virgil Wyndham, curled up like a small child, slept a good distance from the ladies, his back to the fire. The stagecoach driver snored alongside him.

Jed Rourke sat with his back to a boulder, his long legs stretched before him, his eyes on the dying fire. He had discarded his filthy hat shortly after sunset, revealing a longish, tangled mass of waving pale hair.

He was an irritating man, an unmannered bully, but Hannah had to admit, just to herself, that he was also a fine specimen of manhood unlike any she'd ever known. There was incredible strength in every inch of his tall body, unexpected grace in every move he made. Yes, he was uncivilized and brutish, but he was also an admirable example of the Western male.

"In case I forgot to mention it," he said in a soft voice. He didn't even turn his head to look at her. "You did good today."

"What?" she said, taking a single step toward him. "I believe you said I was a harridan and a troublemaker, and that if not for me we'd be in Rock Creek by now."

He turned his head and grinned at her. "Well, that's true, too. But in all the excitement you didn't panic and you didn't cry. You've got gumption, Hannah Winters. I like that in a woman."

She lifted her chin haughtily. "It was not my intention to impress you."

He shook his head. "Can't you just say thank you like a normal woman?"

There were a thousand suitable responses to that suggestion. How did a creature such as Jed Rourke know what was normal and what was not? Why on earth would she care what he, or anyone, thought of her? Instead she found herself uttering a quick, low, "Thank you."

He leaned his head back against the rock, closed his eyes, and grinned. "See? That didn't hurt at all, did it?"

Hannah turned her back on the infuriating man and continued to pace.

"If you're not going to go to sleep, then at least sit down," Rourke ordered in a low voice. "You're making me dizzy."

"I can't sit down," she whispered, not wanting to bother the others. "And I don't think I'll get any sleep tonight. I'm too . . . too . . ."

"Wound up," Rourke finished for her. "Everything that happened is flashing through your brain again and again until you're sure your mind will never be still."

"Yes," she said softly.

He patted the ground beside him. "Then come over here and tell me why a lady like you is headed to Rock Creek. I need to stay awake anyway. You can keep me company until your mind slows down." He turned his head to look at her. "It will, you know. Just takes some time."

Rourke sounded as if he knew what this turmoil was like, as if he'd felt just this way before. But he was so calm, so . . . complacent.

Moving from a standing position to a sitting one and maintaining any modesty was a task in her slim-skirted traveling outfit, but with Rourke's offered hand she managed the feat quite well. She sat beside him, and after only a moment's hesitation she rested her back against the cold stone of the boulder at her back.

"They call this place Wishing Rock," Rourke said, lifting a hand to point to the tall column that rose majestically to her right. "There are caves back in there," he added. "If it was raining or too cold, we could've taken shelter there, but . . ."

"But what, Mr. Rourke?"

"Ever been lost in a cave, Miss Winters?" he asked gruffly. "There's no telling how far back or how deep underground those caves go. I prefer to be out here, where I can see the stars overhead and feel the fresh air on my face."

"I don't think I'd like sleeping in a cave much, myself," she admitted. "I imagine it's quite dark."

"Quite," he agreed.

She studied the lifeless, cold rock formations that surrounded them. "Why Wishing Rock?"

He pointed past her, his arm coming close to her face. "See that tallest rock over there? The one shaped like a woman?"

She did.

"Touch the rock and make a wish, they say, and it will come true."

"How quaint."

"Not so quaint," he rumbled. "Legend has it the wish comes true, but with a twist. Wish for love and get obsession. Wish for revenge and the bullet that finds the heart of your enemy will also find the heart of your beloved. Wish for gold and you'll find it but never live to spend it."

"I don't believe in such nonsense," she said rationally.

"Neither do I," Rourke said lowly, "but I steer clear of that rock. Just in case."

Hannah looked at the rock shaped like a woman, Wishing Rock, and wondered what she would ask for if she were given the opportunity. And what would she be willing to give up to make that wish come true?

"So," Rourke rumbled lazily, "what takes you to Rock Creek?"

"My sister," she said. "She sent me a telegram asking me to come. I haven't seen her in more than twelve years." Hannah shivered. Twelve years was a lifetime. Would she even know Rose?

"Long time," he mumbled. "Why now?"

Just like a man: right to the point.

"I don't know," she confessed. "The tone of the telegram was rather urgent, but she didn't say what was wrong." She didn't want to tell Jed Rourke that the only reason her sister was likely to send for her was because she and her worthless husband needed money.

"What about you?" she asked, not wanting to talk about Rose anymore.

He shrugged slightly, lifting and dropping incredibly broad shoulders. "I got an urgent telegram myself. An old friend asked for my help. Seems her husband was murdered."

"Murdered?" Hannah sat up straight and looked directly into Jed Rourke's scruffy, hard face. "In Rock Creek?"

"Yep," he said nonchalantly. "Not that anyone's grieving the good reverend's demise."

"Your friend"—a *lady* friend, she realized—"was married to the minister? And he was murdered?"

"That's what she tells me."

Hannah leaned back. "Why would she send for you in these circumstances?"

"Like I said, we're old friends."

She sensed a hint of reluctance in his lowered voice.

"And I've been working for Pinkerton's for the past year or so. I guess she figured I could do something to help."

It was entirely possible that Jed Rourke would be a good man to have on one's side in times of trouble, Hannah conceded.

"Are you the seven-foot-tall, mean-as-a-snake Jedidiah Rourke the bandits had heard tell of?"

He grinned, and that wicked smile was all the answer she needed.

"Why were they afraid of you?"

"Oh, they weren't afraid of me. They were just curious."

She didn't believe that, not for a moment. They had been afraid, until they'd convinced themselves that this couldn't possibly be *the* Jedidiah Rourke.

"Why would they be curious?"

He gave the question some thought before he answered. "Because I have a number of very talented and dangerous friends," he said softly.

It was an insufficient answer, but already she knew Jed Rourke well enough to know he would not be bullied into telling more than he wanted to tell. "So

why were you on the stagecoach? They seemed surprised by your traveling arrangements."

He mumbled something obscene. "I get Sylvia's
telegram and I'm headed to Rock Creek. Since
I'm making good time, I stop in this little one-
horse town. I go to a nice-lookin' little saloon for
a drink and a game of cards before I settle down
for a night in a real bed." He shook his head. "I
shoulda known better. Not only did I lose my shirt
to a crooked gambler, my horse came up lame
the next morning. Bad luck," he muttered.
"There wasn't a bank in town to wire money from
my account, so I found myself in a sticky situation.
Had to get to Rock Creek somehow."

"I suppose your bad luck was fortunate for us,"
she conceded, realizing how frightening it would
have been to face the bandits without Jed Rourke.

"I suppose."

He was right. Her mind had finally begun to
slow down. Perhaps she'd sleep tonight after all.

"I could sure use a shot of whiskey right now,"
Rourke said lowly. "Wyndham had some, but he
drained his flask a while back. Ungrateful bastard," he grumbled.

"Turn your back, Mr. Rourke," Hannah said
primly.

Stubborn as usual, he turned his eyes to her
and pinned them on her face. "Why?"

She considered placing her hand on his hairy
cheek and forcing him to turn away, but she was
not so brave. She satisfied herself with a dismissive
wave of her hand and a softly spoken, "Trust me,
Mr. Rourke."

Moving slowly and reluctantly, he spun about
until his broad, buckskin-covered back was to her.

"Call me Jed," he said. "Nobody calls me Mr. Rourke."

Hannah kept her eyes on his back, in case he should decide to peek, and lifted her skirt slowly. She tried not to make any noise, but the rustle of fabric was loud in the dark, still night.

"Miss Winters," Jed said, mocking her prim tone, "what *are* you doing back there?"

"Patience," she said softly. "It's a virtue, you know."

"Not one of mine," he grumbled.

Hannah snatched the engraved flask from the garter at her thigh, and quickly righted her skirt. "You can turn around, now."

When Jed faced her again he eyed the flask, then clapped a large, long-fingered hand over his heart. "You're a magician," he teased.

"I carry the flask purely for emergency medicinal purposes," she said demurely. "But in these unusual circumstances I'll make an exception."

He took the offered flask and uncapped it. "Don't tell me, you had a cold a couple of years back."

If there wasn't something endearing about his grin she'd have snatched the flask away and drained it herself. She almost did just that, when Jed pinned his eyes to hers and wiped the rim of the neck with his thumb before lifting it to his mouth.

When he'd taken a healthy swig, he passed the flask to her. She wiped the rim with her sleeve before lifting it to her own mouth and taking a long, leisurely sip.

"So," Jed said when she returned the flask to him, "who is your sister? I know a bunch of people in Rock Creek. Maybe I know her."

"Rose Sutton," Hannah said softly.

"Rose Sutton?" It was clear by the tone of his voice and the way his eyebrows shot up that Jed knew her. "You're Rose's *sister*?"

Oh, not him, too! All her life she'd been reminded that Rose was the pretty one, that the two of them looked nothing alike. That the fact they were related was utterly *amazing*. "Yes, hard as it is to imagine," she snapped as she grabbed the flask from Jed and took another sip. The liquid burned her throat, but it did make her feel better.

He snatched the flask and took a long swallow of his own. Hannah found her eyes focusing on the workings of his throat, a long, muscular, utterly masculine throat. She blinked hard, dismissing her reaction as an effect of the liquor and her exhaustion.

"I never would've guessed," he muttered.

Hannah maintained her dignity. If rising to her feet in the slim skirt weren't such a chore, she would leap up this instant and walk away. Besides, the whiskey had already made her knees wobbly.

"You two don't look anything alike," Jed just *had* to say, "and as far as I can tell, Rose doesn't have an ounce of gumption."

It sounded like a compliment, but since she wasn't sure she didn't say thank you.

Hannah Winters swore she wasn't sleepy, took another sip of whiskey, then promptly fell asleep and slid to the side so her head rested against his arm. Jed grabbed the blanket Mrs. Reynolds had issued for his use, and draped it over Hannah's body.

Rose Sutton's sister. Damn, he never would've guessed it. Hannah had fire in her eyes, a fresh mouth, and a steely determination he would've respected in any man. Rose let Baxter and those brats of hers run all over her.

Okay, Hannah should've known when to back down and when to keep that pretty mouth of hers shut, but he couldn't fault her for defending Irene, or for sticking to her guns when she thought the road was the best route to Rock Creek. She was *wrong*, but hell . . . she didn't know that.

And she carried a flask under her skirt. Hot damn. He wondered if she kept the flask tucked against her thigh with a red garter. He could well imagine something racy and forbidden beneath that prim and plain skirt of hers.

Hannah mumbled something incoherent in her sleep and raked her cheek up and down against his arm as she tried to get cozy. She squirmed a little, then hugged his arm and settled into her deep sleep again.

Dying firelight danced on her face. Her lips parted slightly; her eyelashes fluttered. Resting, completely relaxed, she was a lot prettier than when she pursed her lips, and wrinkled her nose, and narrowed her eyes. And even then . . .

Her looks were different. Not exotic, not sweetly pretty, not ordinary in any way. When she relaxed like this her face had a charming quality he couldn't quite put his finger on. It was the lush mouth, he supposed, or the curve of her soft cheek, or the impish cant to her nose.

Ah, he'd like to get a good, long look at the garter on Hannah's thigh. He'd like to take her to bed for a week and discover what other kinds of interesting secrets she kept. Unfortunately, Hannah Winters wasn't the kind of woman a man bedded for a week and then walked away from, and that was the only kind of woman Jed had any use for.

Rock Creek was a definite disappointment. Hannah sighed tiredly as she finally caught sight of the small, dusty town. She was covered in dust herself, her arms ached from carrying the bags, and her feet and legs could certainly not go on much longer. She'd tried to twist her hair into a proper bun that morning, after awakening to discover herself clasping and resting against Jed's arm, but a number of strands fell soft and straight about her face. She exhaled and puffed away the hair that had fallen about her nose.

Fortunately for her, Jed had been sound asleep when she'd awakened just before dawn, and so had everyone else. No one had seen her sleeping in such an improper position. If Jed Rourke knew he'd certainly taunt her!

Tall and imposing and silent, Jed led them into town and directly down the center of the main thoroughfare. That weathered hat was perched on his head again, the worn brim sheltering his face from the sun and his startling blue eyes from her inspection.

The stagecoach driver broke away from the group and headed for the stage office, promising everyone that the company would collect their belongings from the abandoned stagecoach.

Without hesitating, Jed escorted the rest of them to the Paradise Hotel, which at three-stories high was the tallest structure in town but for the church bell tower.

Hannah struggled to catch up before Jed deposited them and went on his way. She should thank him, shouldn't she? He had been quite efficient in these trying circumstances.

But before she reached Jed, he dropped the bags he'd carried from Wishing Rock to Rock Creek on the floor of the hotel lobby, and a beautiful young woman who'd been dusting the front counter squealed and ran to him, throwing her arms around his neck. Jed lifted her off the ground and laughed as she kissed him on the cheek.

Unexpectedly, Hannah's heart fell. He'd never said he was married, but then she'd never asked. She should have at least suspected as much.

Not that it made one iota of difference to her if Jed Rourke was married or not.

Jed placed the beautiful woman on her feet and turned to face the haggard traveling party.

"Eden, honey, I brought you a whole passel of folks to be fed and fixed." Jed grinned warmly at the blond woman, and Hannah saw something that made her heart ache. He loved her.

"Mrs. Reynolds is here to visit her son. We'll have to send someone out to his ranch to let them know she's arrived." He winked at the older woman. "I imagine she'll want a nap and a bath while she's waiting."

"Bless you, Mr. Rourke," Mrs. Reynolds said as she fell onto a green sofa in the middle of the lobby.

"Irene here should have someone waiting for her," Jed continued. "Her pa's probably worried sick."

Irene leaned shyly forward. "No, I left school at the spur of the moment," she whispered. "No one is expecting me."

Jed's disapproval showed in his narrowed eyes. "Well, we'll get word to your folks, too, and let them know you're here."

"Thank you," she whispered.

Jed, his arm still draped casually around the blonde's shoulders, turned to the gambler next. "And this is . . ."

"Mr. Wyndham has been a guest here before," Eden said in a sweet voice that was only slightly distressed. "Your usual room?" she asked.

Wyndham nodded tiredly and trudged toward the desk to collect a key. Without a word of thanks he headed for the stairs.

When Jed's eyes landed on Hannah, the light in them faded, just a little. "And what about you, Miss Winters? Will you and Bertie be staying here or with your sister?"

"Here, I think," she said calmly. "From everything Rose has said about her home in previous letters, I don't think she'll have room for us." Besides, she'd be more comfortable with her own living quarters. Twelve years! Living with Rose would be like moving in on top of a complete stranger.

The blonde, Jed's Eden, left his side and approached Hannah with a smile. "Well, I'm dying to hear how all this came about, but I have a feeling the story will be better told on top of a bath, a nap, and a good meal."

Hannah wanted to hate Eden, for being so disgustingly sweet and considerate and beautiful, for throwing her arms around Jed's neck with such careless abandon.

"And you're Rose's sister?" Eden's blue eyes softened with what appeared to be sympathy. "My goodness, she must've written you about the . . ."

"Hold it," Jed snapped, his voice low. "Eden, turn around again. Slowly." There was a touch of menace in his voice.

Eden complied, turning slowly to face him.

"Son of a bitch," he muttered. "You're pregnant again, aren't you?"

"Just three months," Eden answered with a warm smile. "I'm surprised you can tell."

Jed grumbled something obscene.

"Watch your language, Jedidiah," Eden said in a low voice.

Amazingly enough, the vulgarity ceased.

Hannah had no desire to see the rest of this charming scene play out. "If you'll just tell me which rooms are available," she said, "I'd really like to . . . lie down a moment." Her head swam, just a little. The tiring events were catching up with her in a hurry. "Connecting rooms would be ideal, but adjoining will be sufficient."

Jed lifted his hand, pointing a stilling finger at her. "Just a minute," he snapped. "I'm not finished." He pinned cold, blue eyes on Eden. "I'm gonna kill him," he said. "That son of a bitch knocked you up again!"

Hannah was suddenly riveted by the conversation. She'd definitely missed something. . . .

Eden gave Hannah a long, warm smile. "Please forgive my brother. Jedidiah insists on treating me as if I were twelve, and since he has no qualms about voicing his strongest feelings on any given subject in front of anyone who happens to be present, well, it can be quite embarrassing."

Brother. Hannah barely withheld a sigh of relief, then silently chastised herself for that welcome comfort. Jed Rourke's life was none of her business. None at all. Still, he was a fascinating man. Any woman might find herself vaguely interested.

Eden turned to Jed with a serene smile. "The children will be so glad to see you, and you won't recognize Fiona. Your niece has grown a foot since you were here last."

Jed's face softened, just a little. "How's Teddy getting on with that rifle I gave him?"

Eden wrinkled her nose. "Very well, or so Sin tells me. I can't stand to watch when he goes out to target practice. Whatever possessed you to give a weapon to a child?"

Jed smiled, and when he did Hannah could see the resemblance she'd missed before. Fair hair, blue eyes, and that smile. Of course, Jed was well over a foot taller than his sister, and where she was tiny and delicate he was broad and rugged.

"He won't be a child much longer, Eden," Jed said softly. "The boy's growing up."

"Your rooms," Eden said, dismissing Jed's argument and stepping behind the long front desk to fetch two keys. "These are the nicest I have available. They don't connect, but are side by side on the second floor."

Hannah took the keys from Eden's hand, and their eyes met.

"You were going to say something about my sister?" Hannah reminded her. "Is something wrong?"

Eden's smile faded, and her eyes flicked over Hannah's shoulder to find Jed. "Oh dear, I guess you haven't heard," she said softly. "Rose's husband, Baxter, has been arrested for the murder of Reverend Clancy."

Four

Jed was waiting outside the schoolhouse when the students were dismissed. Standing in the school yard with his arms crossed, his legs spread, and his countenance stony, the students who ran from the building gave him wide berth.

All but Millie, who ran straight for him and leaped into his arms, knowing she would be well caught. And Teddy and Rafe, who grinned widely and greeted him with open joy.

He'd never liked kids much, but there was something about these three orphans Eden and Sullivan had taken in and made their own that got to him. They'd made him their Uncle Jed; they'd accepted him, after some initial contention, as family.

He kissed Millie on the cheek and marveled at how she'd grown. When he placed her back on her feet he ruffled Rafe's pale brown strands and told him, yet again, that when he was older he'd get his own rifle, and then he shook hands with Teddy, who at twelve years of age was already getting too old for publicly affectionate greetings from his uncle.

Damn, the boy had grown. Just a couple of years

ago he'd been skinny and short. And silent. Teddy would never be a chatterbox, but he did speak these days. He even occasionally smiled.

Millie took Jed's hand and tugged on it as she headed away from the school. "Let's go. No school until Monday! I want to hear all about where you've been and who you met and what kinds of adventures you had while you were away." She jumped up and down as she tried to pull him along.

Millie had always been an exuberant, loving child, and she adored hearing his stories when he landed in Rock Creek for a while. Rafe, who at ten was a year older than Millie, always listened intently, too, so to keep things interesting Jed usually embellished the stories. Just a little.

He'd never been able to fool Teddy, though.

"I need to have a word with your teacher first," he said. "You run along and I'll be right behind you."

Rafe and Millie left obediently, but Teddy lagged behind. "You just got here. Where are you going?" he asked in a low voice.

In spite of his surprise, Jed's expression didn't change. "What makes you think I'm going anywhere?"

Teddy didn't hesitate. "The twitch in your right eyelid. You only get it when you're ready to go. Ma calls it wanderlust. Pa calls it itchy feet."

His right eyelid did not twitch! He laid a casually raised finger there, just to see if it felt any different. "I may have to make a quick trip to Ranburne," he answered casually. "I'll just be gone a day or two. Thought I'd see if Reese might like to ride along."

Jed still had difficulty seeing Reese—his former

commander, a fine soldier, a fast gun who didn't take any shit from anybody—as a schoolteacher. A husband. A father. He shook his head as he turned his eyes to the schoolhouse door.

"You wouldn't ask Mr. Reese to join you unless you were expecting trouble," Teddy added, his voice much too grown up.

"I don't expect any trouble." After all, two on four were fair odds, when you figured that the two were himself and Reese and the four were bumbling bandits who couldn't find their own asses with both hands and a map.

"Then take me with you," Teddy suggested softly.

Jed looked into deep, dark eyes, a gift from Teddy's Mexican mother. "Nope," he said, without offering further explanation.

"I knew it," Teddy said with a shake of his dark head. "You are always looking for trouble, Uncle Jed." There was a touch of melancholy in his low voice.

Teddy headed for home, the Paradise Hotel, and Jed strode toward the schoolhouse. He reached the door as it swung open and Reese stepped into the sunlight, a small stack of books in his hands.

A schoolteacher!

Reese smiled widely. "Jed! I didn't know you were expected back."

"Neither did I," he said. "Sylvia wired me."

Reese's smile died. "Then you heard about Sutton."

"Yes." He still couldn't believe it. Baxter Sutton, the tenderfoot storekeeper. "I don't get it."

"There was talk about Rose and Clancy," Reese

said. "I didn't believe it, but the rumors were enough to get Sutton riled. Have you talked to Sylvia yet?"

Jed shook his head. "Nope. I'm not looking forward to that conversation, I have to tell you."

Reese nodded in commiseration.

"As a matter of fact, I was thinking of putting the chore off until, oh, maybe Sunday afternoon. After I get back from Ranburne." He had Reese's attention.

"What's in Ranburne?"

"The son of a bitch that stole my rifle." Jed smiled. "Wanna ride along?"

Reese might be a schoolteacher and a husband and a father, but a man didn't change that much in just a few years. He was still a good man to have beside you in a fight. Maybe the best.

He gave the request only a moment's consideration. "Why not?"

Jed leaned in and lowered his voice. "And I'm gonna need to borrow a horse."

Knowing the reason for the urgent telegram, Hannah couldn't possibly take time for a nap and a bath before searching out Rose. She left Bertie unpacking, and followed Eden's directions to the general store.

She stepped through an open door, and it took her eyes a moment to adjust from the bright sunlight to the dimness of the rustic shop.

Rose stood behind the counter. Twelve years had not been enough to destroy her beauty, but she did look haggard. Weary. As if some of the spirit that made her who she was had been drained out of her.

Rose lifted her head to see who had entered the shop, and when she saw Hannah she went stock-still. For a moment it was as if she didn't even breathe. Suddenly, she began to cry hysterically.

"You came," she said, rushing from behind the counter to greet Hannah with a tight hug and more tears. "Oh, you're here. I didn't know . . . I wasn't sure . . . It's been so long. . . . I didn't know where else to turn."

Hannah returned her sister's hug, then stepped back, steady, stilling hands on Rose's shoulders as she looked into pale, teary eyes. "I heard what happened. Baxter's been arrested?"

Rose nodded quickly. "He didn't do it, Hannah. I swear, he would never hurt a living soul!"

"I know," Hannah said softly. She'd never liked Baxter Sutton, not as a child and not as a cowardly adult who refused to fight in the war to which his neighbors marched. She'd never known exactly what her sister saw in the man she'd run off with, the man for whom she'd been willing to leave her home and family. But Baxter was not a murderer. If nothing else, he didn't have the backbone required for such an unpleasant task.

"But Baxter's in jail," Rose wailed, "and the trial starts in less than two weeks, when the judge comes through, and everyone thinks he did it!"

Hannah took a deep breath. Well, obviously the people of Rock Creek didn't know Baxter Sutton well. The coward was incapable of murder.

"Let me have a talk with the sheriff," she said sensibly. "I'm sure we can straighten this out."

After all, she made a profit running a planta-

tion, while those around her, men who considered
themselves superior, sold their land a piece at a
time to keep their heads above water. She sent
men who mistakenly thought they could woo their
way into her bed and her bank account packing,
and if any tears were shed they were *theirs*, not
hers. She could surely handle a backwater sheriff
who had arrested the wrong man.

"But first, tell me what happened."

Rose held on to Hannah's arm as they walked to
the back of the store and a pair of ladder-back chairs
there by the stove. They sat down, facing each other.
Hannah couldn't help but notice that Rose's hands
trembled as she clasped them in her lap.

"It all started with senseless, vicious, untrue gossip," she said, her voice lowered even though they
were alone in the store.

"What kind of gossip?" Hannah asked calmly,
when it seemed Rose would go no further.

"About me and the Reverend Clancy," she whispered, lifting her pleading eyes. "They weren't
true, I swear. Reverend Clancy had made a . . .
an improper suggestion a few weeks earlier, but I
let him know plain and simple that I was a married woman and that I was not interested in his
offered *counseling* sessions." She shook her head.

"This is the *Reverend* Clancy?" Hannah asked,
amazed.

Rose nodded and sniffled. "Yes."

"But you refused his advances."

Rose nodded, vigorously this time. "I did, but
he kept asking and coming into the store when
Baxter was chopping wood or collecting a ship-
ment and no one was here but me. Sometimes
I'd turn the corner and there he'd be, a smile on

his face and his hands . . ." She shuddered. "I didn't tell Baxter, not for a while. I didn't want to upset him."

"Heaven forbid," Hannah muttered.

"But eventually I did have to tell him, when I heard the whispered rumors, when people started to look at me differently." Her eyes teared up again. "I didn't want Baxter to hear that nonsense and wonder . . ."

"So you told him about the reverend's behavior," Hannah said, interrupting before Rose could start crying all over again.

"Yes. The next morning Baxter went to see Reverend Clancy, just to tell him to leave me alone. When he burst into the rectory he found the preacher already dead. He didn't know Clancy was dead at first, just that he was bleeding, so he tried to help. He got blood on his hands, and when he saw the knife laying there on the floor he picked it up."

Hannah groaned aloud. Baxter's intelligence had not grown in the past twelve years!

"And then Sylvia, the preacher's wife, walked into the room and saw Baxter standing there with the knife and the blood . . . and she screamed and the sheriff came and they put Baxter in jail."

They got no further before two loud, rambunctious youngsters barreled through the front door.

Rose leaped to her feet and quickly dried her tears. "Boys, come meet your Aunt Hannah."

The two straw-haired, identical twins approached her with skeptical expressions on their young faces. They would be eleven now, she remembered.

"Is this the brilliant Aunt Hannah who's going to get Pa out of jail?" one of them asked.

Hannah raised her eyebrows at his insolent tone.

"Jackson," Rose reprimanded, "remember your manners."

"What's for dinner?" Jackson asked. "And if it's chicken again, I'm not eating. I'm sick and tired of chicken." He looked Hannah up and down. "And I'm not giving her my bed just because she's your sister."

"Now, boys, when we have a guest . . ." Rose began calmly.

The other child, Franklin, turned his back and walked away. "I'm going to the river," he said.

"You have homework . . ." Rose began.

"I'll do it later," Franklin shouted as he left the store. Jackson followed his brother.

Rose just sighed and reclaimed her seat.

Rose had given birth to the twins within a year of marriage, but according to her letters the delivery had been difficult, and there would be no more children. Perhaps that was the reason, Hannah surmised, the boys were such spoiled brats. It appeared to her that what they needed was a good spanking and a night or two without supper.

"I'll go talk to the sheriff immediately," Hannah said, rising from her seat.

"And you'll stay with us?" Rose said. "We have a large living area upstairs. Don't pay any mind to what Jackson said. This . . . situation has been very difficult for them."

Having met the twins, Hannah was doubly glad she'd decided to stay at the hotel. "That's very sweet of you," she said. "But I have a companion with me and we're already checked into the hotel. I don't want to be underfoot." This situation was

difficult for Rose, too. Didn't the children understand that?

Rose nodded as if she understood. Perhaps she
was even a little relieved.

Hannah gave her sister a smile. "Now, let me
see what I can do with your simpleton sheriff."

Jed was headed for the hotel when he saw her
crossing the street. No one walked quite like Hannah Winters, he thought with a grin. Cane in
hand, head high, dark red hair bouncing, he
would recognize her anywhere. Anytime.

She was headed straight for the jail and Sullivan's office. He changed direction and followed
her.

No doubt Hannah was going to confront Baxter
about what he'd done. She'd poke that cane of
hers through the iron bars and call him a cretin
and a bully, and then she'd most likely pack up
her sister and the Sutton twins and take them
back to Alabama.

She threw open the door to the sheriff's office
and marched inside, Jed several steps behind her.

"You imbecile," she was saying as he opened
the door. "Baxter Sutton is a coward who doesn't
have the spine for murder."

Sullivan looked silently down at Hannah, a dis-
concerted expression on his face.

"I insist that you release him immediately."

Jed closed the door quietly behind him, catching Sullivan's eye as his brother-in-law replied,
"Ma'am, I can't do that."

"Of course you can," Hannah insisted. "You're
the sheriff, isn't that correct?"

"Yes, ma'am."

"Then I'm going to *assume* you have some authority here? Is that also correct? Or are you a simpleton sitting at this desk as some kind of joke?" She rapped the top of his desk with her cane.

"Jed," Sullivan said, stepping around Hannah, looking relieved to have the excuse to leave her behind. "Good to see you. When did you get back?"

Jed grinned. "Don't let me interrupt. You finish up your business." He leaned casually against the closed door. "I can wait."

Hannah turned slowly and placed wide, intelligent eyes on him. "Are you here to report the robbery?"

"Among other things."

She took a deep breath. Ah, she was still tired, exhausted from the excitement and the long walk and the news that her brother-in-law had been charged with murder. He wanted to pick her up and carry her to bed, cover her with a soft quilt, and make her stay in that bed for at least three days. He wanted to crawl into that soft bed with her. Silly thoughts.

He nodded at her. "You go ahead and finish what you were saying."

Sullivan narrowed his eyes in disgust and turned to face Hannah again.

But Hannah kept her gaze riveted on Jed. "Baxter didn't kill anyone. He is incapable of violence. Your incompetent excuse for a sheriff has jailed the wrong man and a murderer is loose on the streets of Rock Creek." Her eyes pleaded with him to agree.

"Doesn't seem like Sutton at all," Jed allowed.

Sullivan shook his head. "I know, but he was

caught red-handed. He had the knife in his hand, and he was covered with Clancy's blood."

"I can explain that . . ." Hannah began.

Sullivan lifted a silencing hand. "I've heard the story a thousand times."

Hannah cast a cutting glare in Sullivan's direction. "Incompetent *and* rude. How charming."

"You'll have to forgive him," Jed said, trying to save Hannah from digging herself a hole she couldn't climb out of. "It's his heathen blood that makes him so damn rude."

Sullivan shot a glare at Jed.

"That," Jed continued, "and living with my sister and four . . . make that four and a *half*," he added darkly, "kids. Hannah Winters, I'd like to introduce you to Sheriff Sinclair Sullivan, my no-good half-breed brother-in-law and father to the most beautiful little girl in all of Texas, my niece Fiona."

Hannah went paler than before, which was a small miracle.

Sullivan sighed despairingly. "You two know each other, I take it."

Jed winked at the pale woman standing before the desk. "We spent the night together."

The color returned quickly to her face. "We did not spend the night together. At least, not in the way you're making it sound. Oh, how ill-mannered you are!" She turned to Sullivan. "Obviously my sister and her family do not belong in this godforsaken town. If you will release Baxter to me, I will take him and his family with me, and I promise you they will never return."

"Sounds like a good deal to me," Jed muttered.

Sullivan shook his head. "Miss Winters, I'm sorry. Baxter is here to stay until the judge comes

through town and he has a right and proper trial.
I'm just doing my job."

Hannah looked like she wanted to smack Sullivan with her cane. Jed wondered what would happen if she did. If Sullivan raised a hand to her . . .
Jed stilled the odd surge of unnecessary protec-
tiveness. Sullivan would never raise his hand to a
woman, and if he did . . . this one could take care
of herself.

"May I see my brother-in-law?" she asked, just
a touch of defeat in her voice.

"Sure." Sullivan opened the door at the back
of the room and led Hannah down the hallway
to one of the two cells in the Rock Creek jailhouse. He left her there, standing before the bars.

From the outer office they couldn't hear what was
said, but Jed noted that Hannah kept a distance
between her and the bars as she spoke in a low voice.
She didn't raise her voice and she didn't poke her
cane through the cell bars. She spoke softly and
nodded her head when Sutton replied.

"What happened?" Sullivan asked simply.

Jed told him about the stagecoach robbery, leaving out the details of Hannah's interference and
her stubbornness when it came time to walk to
their destination.

"I recognized one of the bandits, young fella
from Ranburne," Jed confessed. "Reese is going
to ride with me over that way this afternoon. We'll
take care of it." He looked down the hallway to
a whispering Hannah. "Do you think he did it?"

"Hell, I don't know," Sullivan grumbled.
"Doesn't look good for him."

The door flew open and Sylvia, dressed in black
and weeping openly, threw herself at Jed. "I heard

you were here," she sobbed. "Oh, thank you for coming. Thank you. Thank you." She draped her arms around his neck and held on tight.

Sullivan excused himself, leaving the main office to supervise Hannah's visit with her brother-in-law.

Jed gave Sylvia the hug she was begging for, then set her on her feet. She looked good, as always. In spite of the tears, her face was lovely and unlined and creamy smooth, and her figure was as fine as ever. Marriage to the reverend had agreed with her.

"I've heard all about what happened to Clancy," he said. "I'm real sorry."

Her tears didn't completely dry, but her eyes hardened. "Maurice wasn't a perfect man, but he deserved better than a knife through the heart," she said lowly. "That . . . That vixen Rose seduced him, and then in a jealous rage Baxter murdered my husband. I want him to hang," she whispered. "Promise me you'll make sure Baxter Sutton hangs."

He placed a comforting hand on her shoulder but made no promises. The last thing he needed was to get tangled up with Sylvia again. She'd been a good lover, for a while. Until she'd started talking marriage. Until she'd given him that ultimatum. *Marry me or I'll find someone who will.* He'd stepped aside and let her commence her husband hunting, which was what she'd been up to all along. Which was what she'd be up to again, soon.

No, Maurice hadn't been a perfect husband, but then it was unlikely Sylvia had been the perfect wife. When she'd propositioned Jed a couple years back and he'd turned her down, hadn't she promised to find someone who would be willing to sleep with a married woman? Sylvia always kept her promises.

She attempted a smile. It was weak and watery. "You're the only man I could ever depend on," she cooed. "When Maurice was killed, all I could think was *Jed will know what to do. Jed will take care of this.*" She lifted a hand and placed it on his cheek. "And now you're here, and everything's going to be all right." She laid her head against his chest and breathed deep. "I've missed you so much."

Her arms snaked around his waist. "Promise me," she whispered. "Promise me you'll see Sutton hang for what he's done."

Jed lifted his head as he tried to come up with a response that would appease Sylvia and get him off the hook at the same time. And his eyes met Hannah's.

She glared up boldly, with pale gray eyes that cut right through him. There were no tears, no anger, no reproach readable in those eyes.

"Go ahead, Mr. Rourke," she said coldly. "Promise your friend that you'll see an innocent man hang to appease her need for vengeance."

Sylvia lifted her head but didn't release her hold on Jed. "Who is this woman?" she snapped.

Hannah gave Sylvia a tight little smile. "I'm the woman who's going to find out who really killed Reverend Clancy." She lifted her chin and shot a cutting glance to Jed, fearless and determined. "Get in my way and you'll be sorry you ever met me."

Jed was stunned. No one . . . *No one* spoke to him that way. *He* was the one who did the intimidating around here. "What makes you think I'm not already sorry?" He gently but firmly set Sylvia aside and glared down at Hannah. His best glare, and she didn't back down!

"No sorrier than I am that I had the misfortune to be riding on the same stage with you. And would it kill you to take a bath now and again?"

"Jed," Sylvia crooned, reaching out to touch his arm. He shook her off.

"Would it kill you to act like a real woman, just once?" he countered.

She glared up without flinching. "Ruffian."

"Highfalutin' old maid."

"Ill-bred ne'er-do-well."

He raised his eyebrows. "Shrew."

She turned about quickly. "Sheriff, you haven't seen the last of me."

Sullivan said nothing as Hannah flung open the door and exited the building. Sylvia pouted and wept silent tears. And Jed stared at the open door.

"Why do I have the feeling I just missed something?" Sullivan muttered.

"What an awful, *awful* woman," Sylvia cried.

"I'm almost tempted to hand Baxter over just to get her out of town," Sullivan said with a half smile.

Jed laid his eyes on his brother-in-law. "I have a feeling that's the only way you're going to get rid of her," he said, feeling oddly exhilarated and disappointed at the same time. He gave in to a smile. "And you'll be seeing a lot of our Hannah. She's staying at your place."

Five

Hannah's estimation of Rock Creek did not rise in the hours following her confrontation with the sheriff. The bathing facilities in the Paradise Hotel were located on the ground floor, just off the lobby, rather than near or even more preferably *within* her second-floor room. Her attempt at a short nap after her bath was dismal, as an incredible number of children ran up and down the stairs and past her door, laughing and talking in high-pitched voices.

Her room was clean and *did* have some of the extra touches that make a hotel room special. An extra blanket and pillow, lovely lace curtains, a small stack of books on the dresser. Still, the room was much smaller than her bedchamber at home.

She dressed in a dark blue gown and twisted her hair back and up before descending the stairs for dinner. Fully prepared, considering the disappointments of her trip thus far, for a tin plate of beans and a jar of dirty water, she was pleasantly surprised by the delightful aroma that wafted from the dining room as she approached.

The long room was deserted, but for a crowd around one table at the opposite end.

Jed's pretty sister, Eden, greeted Hannah with a wide smile. If she understood correctly, this poor woman was married to the ignorant sheriff who had jailed Baxter. The sight of the sheriff, surrounded by three older children who all talked at once while he bounced a younger child on his knee, confirmed that fact.

"Miss Winters," Eden said as she took Hannah's arm, "you must meet the family."

Hannah started to protest. No, she really *musn't* meet the family. But Eden was so cheerfully insistent, Hannah found herself looking down at a seated sheriff and four small faces.

The sheriff stood, the fat-faced toddler snug in his arms. "Miss Winters, Jed said you were staying with us."

Eden's eyes widened. "You two have already met?"

"Yes," Hannah said softly, biting her tongue before she finished with, *I'm afraid so.*

"Wonderful," Eden said, and Hannah couldn't bring herself to argue with the woman. "This little girl," Eden said brushing the child's cheek with a soft, fond finger, "is Fiona."

The most beautiful girl in Texas, according to Jed, Hannah remembered. Fiona was indeed beautiful, with big hazel eyes like her father, and curling dark hair that framed chubby cheeks.

Eden introduced the other children, Millie, Teddy, and Rafe, and they all greeted her politely. Well, she'd give the sheriff this: his children were much more well-behaved than her own nephews!

Sheriff Sullivan was, she conceded, a rather handsome man. He had the same rough and informal manner Westerners seemed to prefer, in his cotton shirt, worn denims, and scuffed boots. If only he weren't a complete idiot!

"Sin," Eden said with a smile, "let's invite Miss Winters to join us for supper. Everyone else has already eaten, and I would so hate for her to dine alone."

The expression on the sheriff's face told it all. He was every bit as terrified by the prospect as Hannah herself was.

"That's very nice of you," Hannah said, "but..."

"We can't allow you to eat alone."

I eat alone every night. "Bertie will be down soon."

"Oh, Bertie ate supper with Irene, just before Irene's father arrived to collect her." With that, Eden breezed into the kitchen.

The sheriff, *Sin,* Eden called him, pulled out a chair for Hannah while he balanced his daughter in one arm. Having no choice, Hannah sat.

She half expected Jed to come waltzing into the dining room at any moment. Her eyes drifted to the doorway, and once, when she thought she heard a sound from the lobby, she held her breath. Oh, she was so silly! He was probably comforting the widow, his old *friend,* who had made him promise to see that Baxter hanged.

The children, who had already eaten, took their leave. One after another they said good night to the sheriff. The little girl kissed him on the cheek and whispered something in his ear. The smallest boy kissed him on the cheek, too, and smiled when he said good night. The taller boy, Teddy, embraced the sheriff and the toddler in one all-encompassing hug, then took little Fiona and headed for the lobby. The sheriff watched them leave the room.

A man who looked at his children like that, with such undisguised love in his eyes, couldn't be all bad, Hannah decided reluctantly.

The eyes the sheriff laid on her, after the children had gone, were entirely different.

Hannah lifted her chin. "When I prove that Baxter is innocent, you're going to look like a fool," she said in a lowered voice.

"In this instance, I wouldn't mind looking like a fool," he said tersely. "I don't want to see Baxter hang any more than you do."

"Then why . . ."

"I'm just doing my job," he said softly.

Their brief conversation ended as Eden came to the table bearing a tray laden with three full plates. She placed the chicken and dumplings, on very nice china plates Hannah noted, around the table. A young girl bearing another tray, with three drinking glasses, an ewer of water, and a bottle of wine, scurried from the kitchen. Once they were all deposited on the table, she took both trays and returned to the kitchen.

Eden took her place and smiled at her husband and then at Hannah. "I wish Jed had stayed awhile longer," she said as she poured water into the sheriff's glass and then into her own. When she offered the jug to Hannah, Hannah declined and reached for the wine. After a day like today . . .

Why did her heart feel so heavy? "Where did he go?" she asked.

Eden rolled her eyes. "He took Reese and went to Ranburne to get back his rifle."

"The rifle that was stolen in the stagecoach robbery?"

Eden nodded.

"How did he know to go to Ranburne?" She remembered too well stopping in the town that was so much like Rock Creek. They'd had a bite to eat and stretched their legs. Mrs. Reynolds had joined them there. Had the bandits targeted them at that time?

"He recognized one of the outlaws," the sheriff said lowly.

A surge of anger welled up inside Hannah. Jed was going to get himself killed, going after bandits like this! Riding off without so much as a good night's sleep. Riding off with her insults still burning his ears.

"Well, Sheriff, isn't that your job?" she snapped.

A sudden hush fell over the table. Even Eden's smile faded, for a moment. "Jedidiah often acts as an unofficial deputy when he's in town," she said.

"I see," Hannah muttered.

"And in this room, there's no need to be so formal," Eden continued. "This is Sin, or Sullivan if you prefer, and I'm Eden."

Ah, the casualness of the Westerner. "I'm Hannah," she said, almost reluctantly. The sheriff was her enemy, right? She did not want to be on friendly terms with him! Still, it seemed Eden was determined.

They ate without discussing Jed or Baxter. While she picked at the delicious chicken and dumplings, Hannah's head spun dizzily. Why had Jed gone after that bandit over a rifle! Stupid, stupid

man. He would get himself killed over something
so inconsequential as a weapon.

She couldn't help but wonder when he'd return. Or if he would come back at all. Suddenly
she wished her last words to him had not been
so harsh, but she hadn't known they would be the
last words he'd hear from her, and she'd been so
angry. That woman had been hanging all over
him!

Not that she was jealous. Not that she had any
right to be jealous.

She ate as much of the meal as she could handle, then stood to bid Sin and Eden good night.
She was at the doorway when she turned, planning to ask when they expected Jed to return, but
she didn't say a word.

Eden stood at her husband's side, his hand in
hers, and as Hannah watched Eden lowered herself onto his knee. Neither of them saw her; they
had eyes only for each other.

Now, this was something to be truly jealous of.
Hannah knew she would never have the kind of
closeness Eden and Sin and their family had. No
one would love her that way, and she would never
be able to love anyone so completely. She guarded
her heart too closely, these days.

Without interrupting, she turned about and silently left the dining room.

Jed stood in shadow on one side of the saloon's
bat-wing doors. Reese was positioned on the other
side, in shadows so dark even Jed couldn't tell
exactly where he stood.

When the kid walked out, half drunk and completely happy, Jed reached out, grabbed his collar, and reeled him in.

"Hello, Junior," he whispered.

By the time the kid had recovered from the shock and opened his mouth to scream for help, Jed had the barrel of a borrowed six-shooter pressed to Junior's cheek. "Now, we can do this easy, or we can do it hard. I want my rifle and my six-shooter back, and I want everything else you took from the passengers on the stage. You hand it over and I'll ride away peacefully. You don't, and there's gonna be war."

The kid trembled, but answered bravely, "One man against four. You don't have a chance. I don't care if you are *that* Rourke."

Jed whispered in the kid's ear, "If you know anything at all about me, you know I don't go to war alone."

The snick of Reese's trigger being cocked was loud in the night, louder even than the dulled din that wafted from the saloon. The kid went cold.

The darkness was deep. Junior didn't know if he was up against two or all six. If he were smart, he knew it didn't matter.

"All right," he said. "I'll get what I can. But some of it's gone. Rance gave some of that jewelry to a saloon gal, and Tom paid off his bill at the hotel with some of his cut. I'll get together what I can, I swear."

"Rance and Tom, you say. Who was the fourth?" Jed asked softly.

"Called himself Newton," Junior said, suddenly very cooperative. "He rode in a couple weeks ago and asked the rest of us if we'd like to make some easy money. He's been watching the stages come through, waiting for someone who looked like they had money."

Hannah.

"He left town this morning with his cut."

Jed swore beneath his breath. That man was the one in the black bandanna, no doubt. "Well, that's too bad." He tightened his grip on Junior. "Now, where can we find Rance and Tom?"

"I don't want nobody to get hurt," Junior said. "I'll get you everything I can, but there's no reason for anyone to get hurt."

"You seem to be a lot more concerned about there being no bloodshed when the gun is pointed at you. Why is that, exactly? You don't mind scaring women and little girls, but when it's you who's scared . . . That's a different matter, is it?"

"I . . . I'll be good from here on out, I swear it. I'm a new man."

Jed wanted, more than anything, to beat Junior to a pulp before hunting down Rance and Tom. But since they'd have to hand the outlaws over to Sheriff Tilton when all was said and done, he controlled his urge.

After a surprisingly good night's sleep, Hannah dressed in a blue serge skirt and white blouse, and donned her most comfortable walking boots. A fashionable hat decorated with a blue and red ribbon completed the outfit.

Today she would begin her investigation. The answers she needed to free Baxter were out there. All she had to do was ask the right questions.

After a filling breakfast, Hannah and Bertie headed to the general store. Bertie was a gentle creature, and the very idea of searching for a murderer made her turn pale and begin to shake. Hannah didn't mind. She had other plans for Bertie.

"Good morning," she said as she walked through the open doors and caught Rose's eye. Rose was already hard at work, stocking shelves. Her boys, the annoying Jackson and Franklin, sat in the back of the store playing checkers.

Rose returned the smile. "Good morning."

Hannah's eyes swept the small, rustic store. This was the life her sister had chosen. Who was to say her choice had been a bad one? "I'm going to do a little exploring on my own today," she said.

"Exploring?" Rose asked, her smile fading.

If Rose knew Hannah intended to investigate the murder herself, she'd no doubt object. So there was no need to tell her. "I thought perhaps you could use Bertie's help in the store, as she has no desire to examine the town as I do." Hannah cut her meek companion a glance that demanded, very clearly, that she keep what she knew to herself.

"If she doesn't mind," Rose said hopefully.

"I'll just have a word with my nephews," Hannah said as she made her way to the back of the store. "Then I'll be on my way."

The boys did not even have the courtesy to look up from their game and greet her.

Hannah raised her cane and forcefully thwacked it on the middle of the board. Checkers bounced and scattered.

"Hey!" one of them, she could not be sure which, protested.

She had their attention. "Do you know who I am?" she asked as they looked up with insolent eyes.

"You're our mother's sister," one of them answered. "So what?"

Hannah leaned down and placed her face close to theirs. "I am your very rich Aunt Hannah," she said softly. "Annoy me, and I will cut you out of my will without so much as a penny."

"So . . ." one began.

The other raised his hand to silence his twin. "How rich?"

Hannah smiled. "And you are?" she asked.

"Jack."

"Well, Jackson, I could buy this little town ten times over and still have money in my bank account." She pinned her eyes to his and saw a spark of intelligence there. Good. "I have enough money for you and your brother to live quite well on for the rest of your lives. You'll never have to do a hard day's work. You'll never have to worry about going hungry." She gave him a tight smile. "But you mustn't annoy me."

"What do we have to do?" Franklin asked.

Hannah looked at them both, in turn. "I expect better manners from my blood kin than I've seen from you two. You're no better than heathens, but I imagine that can be remedied."

"So, we have to start being polite all the time?" Jack asked, incredulous.

"Yes," Hannah said tersely. "Most especially, I expect you to treat your mother with the respect she deserves. If you distress her, I will not only cut you two out of my will, I'll take my cane to your backsides and whale the tar out of you."

"You wouldn't dare," Frank muttered.

Hannah glared at him. "Would you care to test me?"

Apparently he did not.

"Now," Hannah said as she straightened her spine, "put away your game and go help your mother. You boys are certainly old enough to assist in the operations of this establishment."

Franklin started to protest, but Jackson shushed him and began to gather the scattered pieces of their game.

She was halfway to the front of the store before she heard one of them whisper, "How long will we have to wait before she dies?"

She smiled as she stepped onto the boardwalk.

"Sorry this trip wasn't more exciting," Jed said as they rode toward Rock Creek.

"I don't go out of my way searching for *exciting* these days," Reese answered. "I'm not disappointed."

He had his rifle, his six-shooter, most of the jewelry that had been taken, and some of the cash. Junior, Rance, and Tom were locked up in the Ranburne jail. The leader, who had worn the black bandanna and called himself Newton, was likely long gone.

"Heard from Nate and Cash lately?" he asked as Wishing Rock came into view.

"No," Reese said, his voice low and tinged with disquiet. Once they'd all been Reese's to command. Maybe he still felt responsible for them, their lives. Their mistakes.

"From what I hear, Cash is really making a name for himself," Jed rumbled.

"And Nate is doing his damnedest to keep Cash alive. Watching his back, cooling him down when he can. When he's sober," Reese added softly.

Cash had always been quick with his gun and his mouth, and his reputation as a gunslinger had only grown in the past couple of years. It was only a matter of time before that reputation got him killed.

And Nate . . . Hell, Nate was more of a lost soul than Cash had ever been.

"I still can't believe the kid is married," Jed grumbled. Rico had always been such a charmer, such a ladies' man. *Married!* It was almost as inconceivable as his sister married to that half-breed Sullivan.

"Eden's going to have another baby," Jed grumbled. "Like she needs another mouth to feed! Another kid to chase after and take care of and . . . and . . . Damn that Sullivan."

"She seems happy about it," Reese said calmly. "You knew?"

"She told Mary a couple of weeks ago."

Jed sighed tiredly. If Eden didn't so obviously adore Sullivan, if she weren't so happy, if Sullivan weren't one of his closest *compadres* . . . he really would have to kill the man.

"So," he said, just trying to make conversation, "tell me what happened with Clancy."

"Not much to tell," Reese said, his eyes trained ahead as if he couldn't wait to get home. "There was some nasty gossip about Rose and Reverend Clancy. I don't know if it was true or not, but you know what kind of man he was."

"Yep." A womanizer, a charmer . . . a lecher.

"Anyway, one morning Sylvia steps into the parlor and finds Baxter standing over Clancy's body with a knife in his hand and blood all over his clothes. She screamed, people came running. . . ." He shrugged. "I never would've thought it of Baxter."

"Hannah thinks he's innocent," Jed said thoughtfully. "But the evidence is pretty condemning."

Reese turned his head and squinted against the sun. "Who's Hannah?"

Unconsciously, Jed grinned. "She's Rose's sister. I met her on the stage." He rattled the vest pocket where the jewelry he'd recovered rested. "Most of this is hers."

Reese smiled. "Is that why you were so damned and determined to recover everything, and not just the rifle and six-shooter?"

Jed's grin disappeared. "Of course not. I did my best to recover everything because it was the honorable thing to do."

"I see," Reese murmured.

"Quit looking at me like that," Jed grumbled.

"Like what?"

"Like I just sprouted another goddamn head!"

Reese turned his gaze to the road ahead, once again. "So, what's she like, this Hannah?"

Jed took a deep breath. "Meanest woman I ever did meet," he said fondly. "She's also fearless, spunky, and right pretty."

"Fearless?" Reese glanced briefly to the side. "Odd attribute for a right pretty woman."

Jed's smile crept back. "When I yell at her she looks me right in the eye and calls me names. She doesn't so much as flinch when I glower at her and return the favor." He shook his head in wonder. "She went after those bandits with nothing but a cane and her smart mouth." The smile didn't last. "If I hadn't been there she probably would've gotten herself killed."

"Sounds like this Hannah's a handful," Reese said in his wisest voice.

"You might be right about that."

When Rock Creek came into view, they spurred their horses to a gallop. Reese was anxious to get back to his wife and kid, Jed imagined, and he . . . Well, he was just along for the ride. He was in no hurry to get back to Rock Creek for any reason at all.

The town was always crowded on a Saturday, as ranchers from the surrounding area came to shop and visit. People filled the street and the boardwalk as they took care of the weekend chores. Kids ran and shouted.

Through it all he saw her. Hannah, in a white blouse, dark skirt, and a silly little hat, stood outside Three Queens . . . practically nose-to-nose with a rough cowboy who had to lean forward and down to meet her. As Jed watched and approached on his borrowed horse, Hannah said something that made the cowboy mad. The young man responded hotly and Hannah whacked him on the side of his leg with her cane. His response this time was to smoothly draw his gun and point it at her belly.

Jed groaned out loud and spurred the horse forward.

Six

Rock Creek was populated by the most uncivilized, crudest forms of humanity imaginable, as evidenced by the young man, one Oliver Jennings, who pointed a revolver at her midsection. All she'd done was ask him a few questions, then reprimand him when he'd been uncooperative. For that he drew his weapon.

"You hit me," Oliver said, incredulity in his eyes as he jabbed the six-shooter's muzzle against her. Again.

Surely he would not shoot her here, in the middle of a crowded street! "You were insolent," she defended herself. "If you would simply answer my question . . ."

"What's going on here?"

The sound of that voice, as Jed sneaked up behind her, sent chills dancing down her spine.

"This danged woman *hit* me with her cane," Oliver said, his eyes following Jed as the larger man placed himself beside Hannah.

"It's a bad habit she has," Jed said, apparently supremely unconcerned about the dire situation before him. "One of these days I'm going to take that cane away from her and break it over my knee."

"You will not," Hannah protested.

Oliver grinned as if he liked the idea just fine. While he smiled and nodded in agreement, Jed's hand shot out and he smoothly snatched the weapon from Oliver's grasp.

"But if anyone's going to *threaten* her," Jed finished as he expertly spun the confiscated six-shooter, "it's gonna be me."

The young, hotheaded Oliver was no match for Jed Rourke, Hannah thought proudly. Oliver was not much taller than she was, and he was downright skinny—a scarecrow of a man next to Jed. He backed down sheepishly, taking the six-shooter after Jed spun open the cylinder and emptied the bullets onto the street, mumbling in a boyish voice the apology Jed demanded.

She was just about to thank Jed for his assistance when she noticed the expression of fury on his face.

"What the hell do you think you're doing?"

"I'm investigating Reverend Clancy's murder," she said sensibly, "since no one else in this horrid town has seen fit to do so."

He took her arm and steered her toward the hotel, which was directly across the street from the entertainment house where she'd found Oliver. Walking a bit too quickly, he all but dragged her along. Dignity was impossible.

He stopped in the lobby and glanced around, frowning at the folks who milled about, socializing on this mild December Saturday. The grip on her arm did not loosen. He peered into the dining room and saw the few patrons who were enjoying

a late luncheon. With a curse, he dragged her
toward a door at the rear of the lobby.

Beyond the door an enclosed garden awaited.
No December bloom added color to the day, but
the plants were well cared for and laid out in neat
rows, and there were several benches, one against
the hotel's outer wall, others scattered through
the garden. Jed dragged her to the bench situated
farthest away from the door.

"Sit," he commanded, all but shoving her onto
the bench.

"I will not," Hannah said as she burst to her
feet to face him.

He laid two big hands on her shoulders and
gently forced her to sit. When she had complied,
since she had no other choice, he continued to
lean forward, placing his face close to hers.

"Hannah Winters, I want you to tell me exactly
what you've been up to."

"I told you, I've been . . ."

"Investigating," he interrupted. "Yes, I got that.
Exactly *how* have you been *investigating*?" His blue
eyes narrowed threateningly, and a muscle in his
beard-roughened jaw twitched.

And still Hannah was not afraid. "I've been talking to people, asking questions. Your Reverend
Clancy was a horrible man," she said. "There are
any number of people in Rock Creek, and no
doubt beyond, who might have wanted him
dead."

"But only one who was found standing over his
body with a knife in his hand."

"Clancy seduced Oliver's sister. Were you aware
of that fact? He offered to counsel her after her
husband died, and while she was mourning and

looking for support, he took advantage of her. From what I've heard, I doubt she was the only one."

"I didn't say Clancy was a nice man or a good preacher. I just said they found Baxter standing over his body with blood on his clothes and a knife in his hands."

She lifted her chin. "Purely circumstantial," she argued. "And I know Baxter Sutton would never commit murder, just as I know Rose is too smart to be taken in by a philanderer like Reverend Clancy."

Jed sighed tiredly and sat beside her. Close. Too close. She scooted away, just a few inches.

"Hannah, you don't know Baxter and Rose anymore. Twelve years is a long time," he argued sensibly. "And people change."

She pursed her lips and turned her head to study the garden. Jed Rourke's face was too disconcerting. How was she supposed to argue with him! "Maybe," she said softly. "But people don't change that much. Inside, where it counts, they stay the same."

"I could argue with you about that one," Jed said tiredly. "But I won't. Not now, anyway." He reached into his vest pocket and drew out a handful of gold and sparkling gems. "I believe these belong to you."

She held out her hands and he dropped the jumbled fistful of jewelry onto her waiting palms. "However did you manage to retrieve this, and so quickly?"

"I recognized Junior," he said calmly.

"Why didn't you say something while we were being robbed?"

Jed set cold, blue eyes on her face. "Because I didn't want everyone there to end up dead."

He was right, of course. Not that she would tell him so. "Well, thank you," she said softly. "I am particularly pleased to see my mother's brooch here. Everything else can be replaced, but that . . ." She choked back the tears that threatened. She was not normally so sentimental! "Well, thank you."

Hannah wondered if a kiss on the cheek was in order, simply as a thank-you. She leaned slowly and hesitantly toward Jed, her eyes on that hairy cheek of his. She stopped long before her lips came near his cheek.

"You're welcome," he said gruffly, and then he squirmed. Had no one ever thanked him before?

"I wish I could convince you," she said softly. "I know with all my heart that Baxter is innocent."

Jed rotated his head slowly to look at her. His eyes narrowed suspiciously. "Don't try that old trick on me," he grumbled.

"What old trick?"

"A pretty girl batting her eyelashes at me isn't going to make me change my mind," he said with a shake of his head. "You can pout and quiver all you want, but I'm too damn old to fall for that one."

Hannah shot to her feet. If her hands weren't filled with the jewelry Jed had retrieved, she'd slap his face. "I am not pouting or quivering," she said indignantly, "and I never bat my lashes. I am not a *girl*. I'm a fully grown woman."

She turned to stalk away, then realized that she'd left her cane leaning against the bench. She'd leave it and return later, if she weren't afraid Jed really would break it over his knee as he'd threatened to do earlier.

Sheepishly, she turned to face him. "Would you slip the cane through my arm?" she asked.

He smiled, as if he could see right through her, as if he knew she was shaky on the inside no matter how calm and unyielding she appeared to be. "Of course, Miss Winters," he said as he stood, retrieved the cane, and slipped it between her elbow and body.

Cane securely caught in her arm, she turned about and stalked away. She had almost made it to the hotel door when she realized that in addition to all the insults, Jed had also called her *pretty*.

"Miss Winters," Jed called.

Her heart skipped a beat just before she turned to face him, the hotel door at her back, the garden between them. "Yes, Mr. Rourke?"

"Join me for dinner?"

With great effort, she withheld a smile. "I'd be delighted."

Jed didn't know what had possessed him to ask Hannah to join him for dinner. She was the most infuriating woman he'd ever met. Most men probably ran away from her in terror when faced with the prospect of sharing a meal with her.

He'd also been possessed by the need for a long, hot bath, and he'd dragged some of his best clothes from the bottom dresser drawer of his room on the third floor. Nothing fancy, just a pair of brown twill trousers and a clean shirt.

Maybe Hannah was the most infuriating woman he'd ever met, but he liked her anyway. She stirred his blood; she made him laugh. She surprised him. It had been a long time since anyone had truly surprised him.

He walked into the dining room at precisely the arranged time. Since it was Saturday, the dining room was crowded. The hotel guests, as well as some of the folks from outside Rock Creek who had come to town for the day, ate and visited over roast beef, boiled potatoes, and dried apple pie. Eden had set aside the best table, the one in the far corner, for him.

And Hannah was nowhere to be seen.

Jed paced in the dining room for about five minutes before Eden shooed him out. Ejected from the dining room, he paced in the lobby for another ten minutes.

She wasn't coming. She'd changed her mind, or . . . He came to a halt as he realized what she'd done. She'd accepted his invitation just so she could make him squirm when she didn't show! Just like a woman!

A rustle on the stairway made him turn his head. The emotion that shot through him felt oddly like relief. Maybe relief tinged with pleasure. Hannah, in a fancy dark green silk gown, descended the stairs slowly. She was as bundled up as ever, with silk and lace to her chin and long sleeves covering her arms. The gown showed off her shape though, and a fine shape it was. Her hair had been twisted up with more curls than usual, and at her throat she wore the brooch he'd recovered. Damn, she was gorgeous.

And she had left her cane behind.

"I hope I didn't keep you waiting," she said, her voice soft.

Suddenly his collar seemed too tight. "No," he answered. "Not at all."

He offered her his arm and she took it, and together they headed for the dining room.

"You look good," he said softly as he held out her chair and she sat down. The full skirt of her fancy dress rustled. She blushed.

"Thank you," she said. "So do you." Impossibly, she blushed a deeper shade of rose.

He'd never met a woman who had the uncanny ability to look right through him the way Hannah did. Even when she blushed, her eyes remained steady and strong.

"That's your mother's brooch?" he asked, nodding to the cameo she wore at her throat.

She touched the brooch with pale, easy fingers. "Yes. She passed away when I was six and Rose was nine. I don't remember her well, but when I hold her things sometimes she seems . . . closer, as if I can smell her perfume or remember the sound of her laughter." Her fingers fell away and she lowered her hand to her lap. "I'm sorry. I guess that sounds silly."

"No," he said. "That doesn't sound silly at all." And he was doubly glad he'd been able to recover the cameo.

Eden brought two plates to the table, and that girl she'd hired was right behind her with wine and two glasses. If his little sister didn't wipe that smug grin off her face, he was going to . . . Hell, he wasn't going to do anything. Let her enjoy watching her big brother make a fool of himself. After all, it didn't happen often.

Dinner was good, as always, and the wine was tasty and not too sweet. Hannah was agreeable, as she talked about her home and her mother. When she relaxed and talked about her yearning to someday travel the world and her dreams of seeing the places she read about, her face lit up and her eyes sparkled.

"Why don't you just do it?" Jed asked as Eden placed two slices of apple pie and two cups of coffee before them. "Just pack up and go."

The question seemed to put Hannah off. She straightened her spine and her lips thinned. "I can't just run away from my responsibilities," she said primly. "People depend on me."

"You're here," he argued.

"I had no choice. My sister sent for me, so I made arrangements for the foreman and the housekeeper to see to the running of the plantation in my absence. This is not a very busy time of the year for us, in any case."

He didn't quite buy it. Hannah hadn't seen Rose in twelve years, but she'd come running when her sister asked. "Why can't they run things while you go to Egypt or Spain or one of those other places you want to see?"

She shook her head in a crisp denial. "It's just a silly dream," she said. "I can't actually pack up and . . . and take off on a whim."

Jed pushed his pie aside and leaned forward. "Why not?"

Hannah's gray eyes went <u>wide</u>. "For one thing, it's irresponsible."

"I do it all the time," he argued. "When the spirit moves me, when I get bored with one place or curious about another, I just go."

She smiled. "As I said. Irresponsible."

He smiled back. "Face it, Hannah. That's the

reason you're really here. You were sitting at
home in that big ol' lonely house, and here comes
Rose's telegram, an excuse to get out. You don't
care if Baxter is found guilty or not. You're just
out here looking for a little adventure. So you . . .
you antagonize bandits and cowboys and all but
dare them to shoot you, all for a little fun.''

Hannah bristled. "If you think being threatened
at gunpoint is my idea of fun, Jedidiah Rourke, you
don't know me at all." Her eyes snapped and crack-
led. The color rose in her cheeks. "And if you think
I don't care if my sister's husband is falsely con-
victed of murder, that I would come here for my
own entertainment with no regard for the only family I have, then I have no desire to see that you get
to know me any better than you already do.''

"Don't get your hackles up," he said calmly.

Hannah pushed back her chair and stood
slowly. "Barbarian," she said as she looked down
at him.

Jed rose to his feet and glared across the table
and down at her. "Tyrant."

"Ape."

"Prissy fussbudget."

Her eyebrows rose elegantly, just before she
spun around and walked from the dining room
like a queen leaving her audience behind. She
didn't hasten her step, and she didn't look back.
Not once.

Hannah paced her small room by the light of
a single lamp for half an hour before she even
began to calm down. Jed Rourke was the most
maddening man she had ever met! How dare he

insinuate that she was here in Rock Creek not out of familial obligation, but seeking a thrill for herself. Insinuate? No, he'd bluntly accused her of being nothing more than a selfish adventuress.

She opened the window and looked down on the garden where she and Jed had sat that afternoon. Why did every conversation with that man turn into an argument? No matter how hard she tried to be civil, they always ended up having harsh words.

Ah, she thought as a cool breeze washed over her face. At home, no one ever argued with her. They agreed with whatever she said because their jobs depended on it. Her social acquaintances didn't challenge her, either, but then all the women her age were married and had children, and their conversations always veered in that direction. Children and husbands. Which was why Hannah never remained long at the few social functions she attended. She was not a wife and mother and never would be, and she was not a twittering female on a quest for a man. Since all the women in the county near her age fit solidly into one category or the other, that left her isolated.

Over the years she had become the rich, eccentric spinster Hannah Winters, who talked about traveling but never did, who spent more time with her books than with living, breathing people. Why bother to argue with her? It didn't matter what she said or thought, anyway.

The December air turned cold with a shift of the wind, and she slammed shut the window. The people of Rock Creek argued with her, didn't they? Not only Jed, who was the most aggravating offender, but everyone. The bandits, the hotheaded cowboy, the sheriff, the women she had tried to interrogate in her murder investigation. None of them minded telling her she was wrong.

She had never been wrong. Well once, eight years ago, she'd made a colossal mistake, but since then . . . Since then she'd become more cautious.

Hannah recognized Bertie's cautious knock on the door.

"Come in."

Bertie opened and closed the door quickly. "Would you like me to help you get ready for bed?"

"No," Hannah said, her eyes remaining on the garden and the night below. "I can manage."

She could, with little difficulty, dress and undress herself and arrange her own hair. There had always been someone handy to assist her in her personal matters, but suddenly she wanted, more than anything, to be left alone. She didn't want anyone hovering over her. Not Bertie, not Jed Rourke. No one.

"How is Rose managing?" she asked, turning her back on the view from her window. "She seems so tired."

Bertie nodded. "She is tired, I think. And worried, of course." Her eyes lit up. "But the boys were a great help this afternoon. They wanted me to be sure to tell you how well behaved they were."

Of course the twins had been well behaved, Hannah thought with a sinking heart. She had bought them, the same way she bought loyalty and friendship and obedience from everyone around her.

Hannah laid her eyes on Bertie. "Tomorrow

morning I want you to move in with Rose," she said, the idea striking her as being quite brilliant. "She needs your help more than I do."

Bertie nodded obediently.

"Is that all right with you?" Hannah asked softly.

Bertie looked at her with obvious surprise. "Yes, ma'am. Whatever you want. And I do like Miz Rose very much. But will you be all right here by yourself?"

"Yes," Hannah said confidently. "I'll be fine. Thank you for asking."

"In the morning, you said." Bertie backed toward the door.

"Yes. Get a good night's sleep."

When Bertie had retired to her own room next door, Hannah closed the curtains across the window that overlooked the garden. She removed the brooch from her throat and held it in her hand. Her mother had talked about traveling. It was one of the few things she remembered of her mother, those whispered conversations as together they leafed through books in her father's library, reading about places around the world.

Just get up and go, Jed said. He made it sound so easy.

She smiled as she placed the brooch on the dresser and began to unfasten her buttons. He had looked magnificent tonight, hadn't he? Without that filthy hat he favored covering his head, his hair was quite attractive. Golden blond and wavy and soft, freshly washed and just a little wild. Such long hair was not in fashion, but it suited him somehow. It must be the way the strands touched his broad shoulders, or the way they framed his sharply delineated, if shaggy, jaw.

If only she could convince him that Baxter was innocent.

Her pleasant thoughts disappeared swiftly. As long as the grieving widow wept and pleaded and laid her hands all over him, what chance did she have?

Jed stared in dismay at the entertainment house, Three Queens, before him. This used to be a perfectly good saloon, before Rico's woman had moved in and ruined it. Now there was music all the goddamned time, and the place had been cleaned up and cursed with a woman's touch. . . . And there wasn't a single whore working in Rock Creek. Lily and Eden had converted them all, one at a time.

But he could still get a drink here.

He spotted Rico right away, standing behind the bar, grinning, while some cowpoke in town for the weekend drank up a week's pay.

Rico handed his chore over to the regular bartender, Yvonne, when he saw Jed.

"I heard you were back," Rico said as he approached. "You never come into town without making a scene, do you?"

"It wasn't my fault this time."

"It is never your fault," Rico said with a grin.

Jed looked in dismay at the crowd. The place was jumping. Noisy. Bustling with customers. "I need a drink," he grumbled. "And a quiet corner."

"This way."

Rico led him past customers, who greeted them both enthusiastically, to the storage room at the back of the place, a cubicle that was little more than a glorified closet. When the door was closed and the noise dulled, Jed closed his eyes in relief.

"You know, I miss this place the way it was when Cash ran it," Jed grumbled. "Liquor. Women. A couple of chairs. Nothing fancy. I'm goddamn tired of fancy."

Rico reached for a bottle on the back shelf and grabbed a couple of glasses from another. He poured them each a healthy shot.

Jed finished his off in one swallow, then took a deep breath while Rico refilled the glass. Already he felt a little better.

"How's Lily?" Jed asked as he stared at the amber liquid in his glass.

"Very well," Rico said with a wicked grin.

"And the little girl? Carrie?"

"She is doing fine, as well."

Jed listened for a moment to the muted sounds of the piano on the other side of the door. "And I can hear for myself that Johnny plays as impressively as ever. Is he doing okay here?"

"*Si,*" Rico said softly.

Jed nodded his head, then took another drink. A sip, this time. "Tell me something," he said casually. "When you first met Lily, did you know she was the one?"

"*Si.*"

"How? I mean, you always had women hanging all over you, kid. It's not like you couldn't have settled down with one of them years ago. How did you know *she* was the right one?"

Rico nodded, looking oddly like a wise man. Ha! He was still just a kid, no wiser than Jed or any other man in Rock Creek. "I looked at her and I knew."

Jed glared at the kid. "You can do better than that," he grumbled.

Rico searched for a better answer but couldn't come up with one. "No, it is as simple as that." He leaned in close, even though they were all alone in the storeroom. "Have you met a woman?"

"No," Jed protested. "Well, yes, I have *met* a woman, but not like you're thinking."

"You did not look at her and know your world had changed?"

"I took one look at Hannah and I knew she was trouble," Jed muttered. "Big trouble. And so far I've been right." He cursed beneath his breath. "If I were smart, I'd ride out of here in the morning and never look back."

"But I have a suspicion you will not," Rico said wisely.

Wise*ass* was more like it.

"No," he whispered.

"And why not?"

He sighed, then groaned, then tossed back his drink. "Because if I do, that mouth of Hannah's is gonna get her killed."

Rico lifted his own glass in a silent toast.

Seven

A definite chill had moved in overnight, so Hannah wore her gray wool suit and matching hat as she set out on Monday morning. Bertie had moved in with Rose and her boys, and they all seemed to like the arrangement. Even the twins liked Bertie, and Rose could certainly use the help.

Living in the hotel without her companion was surely not proper, but Hannah found she didn't much care. Continuing with her investigation in spite of the opposition she met at every turn was unladylike, as well, but then she had long ago give up any aspirations to become a *lady*. The expectations involved were much too harsh.

As she walked down the main street of Rock Creek, heading unerringly toward the church, a gust of wind tried to blow her back. A sign from above? A warning? Surely not. She leaned into the wind and continued on.

Interviewing Sylvia Clancy was not a chore she looked forward to, but in order for the investigation to be complete it was necessary. Mrs. Clancy had been the one to walk in and find Baxter standing over her husband's body. Her testimony could convict an innocent man.

She was also, in Hannah's estimation, the prime suspect. After what she'd learned about Reverend Clancy, the woman certainly had motive for murder!

Of course, there were any number of men in the area who also had motive, if half of what she'd heard were true. Still, Mrs. Clancy, Jed's old friend Sylvia, had been right there in the house. She could have very easily stabbed her husband and then retired to the kitchen to wait for someone to come by and become her patsy, or else for an opportunity to make a tragic and emotional discovery . . . perhaps as someone was passing by outside the rectory and could hear her shrill screams.

Sylvia Clancy had shifty eyes, Hannah remembered from their one meeting in the sheriff's office. Narrowed and dark and furtive, they were the eyes of a woman who had something to hide. Or so she convinced herself as she arrived at the rectory and rapped on the door with the head of her cane.

After a sharp "just a minute" and the following delay that bordered on rudeness, Sylvia Clancy answered the door. Hannah kept her chin high and her spine straight, but her heart sank. Sylvia was straight from the bed, at this late morning hour, with her hair disheveled and her eyelids drooping with sleep. And still she was striking in a way Hannah knew she would never be. No wonder she and Jed were *old friends*.

"I can see I've come at a bad time," Hannah said, taking a step back. "I'll drop by later."

"No," Sylvia said, pulling her wrapper tighter around her shapely body as she threw the door open wide. "Come on in. I should've been up hours ago, but I'm afraid I didn't sleep well last night."

Hannah tried to feel sympathy for the woman,
who had lost her husband in such a tragic and
violent way. Unless, of course, Sylvia was the one
who had murdered Clancy. If that was the case,
she deserved no sympathy.

She stepped directly into the main room, a parlor that was furnished in mismatched odds and
ends that looked comfortable but a little shabby.

Sylvia sat on the sofa and motioned to a nearby
chair for Hannah. She wondered if it was the very
chair Reverend Clancy had been murdered in, and
almost declined. Still, it would be best if this inter-
view were as informal as possible. Sylvia probably
wouldn't open up if Hannah paced the room and
glared down at her as she asked her questions.

She perched on the very edge of the chair. "I
won't take much of your time," she said. "I'd like
to ask you about the morning you discovered Baxter standing over your husband's body."

Sylvia's face hardened; it seemed her entire body
tensed. "I suspected that was the reason for your
visit. You've been asking a lot of questions about my
husband since your arrival in Rock Creek."

"I only want to prove that Baxter is innocent,"
Hannah explained. "Surely you want the real
murderer caught." Unless, of course *she* was the
real murderer.

"Baxter Sutton stabbed my husband in the
heart," Sylvia said, her posture relaxed, her eyes
hard. Where were the tears she had shed for Jed's
benefit? Where was the weeping widow? "I'll see
him hang for it."

"Did you hear anything unusual that morning,
at some time before Baxter arrived?" Hannah
pressed.

"No," Sylvia snapped.

"Can you think of anyone in particular who might've wanted your husband dead?" Hannah had compiled her own long list, but perhaps Sylvia had one of her own.

"No."

Hannah was about to ask yet another question when a muffled sound stopped her. Someone had dropped something. A man's deep voice mumbled a soft curse. The sounds came from behind a closed door to her left. The bedroom door, no doubt.

When she laid her eyes on Sylvia, the woman smiled contentedly. "Did Jed tell you about us?"

Her heart sank; then it rose into her throat and threatened to choke her. "He did say you were old friends."

"That's one way of putting it," Sylvia said softly as her eyes cut to the bedroom door. All was silent there, now. "I suppose you've already discovered that Jed is a remarkable man."

Hannah lifted her chin. She would not be intimidated by this woman! "I've discovered that he's an ill-mannered barbarian with a foul mouth and a disturbing propensity for making demands."

Sylvia only smiled. "Those can be admirable traits, in the right circumstances. I'll take a foul-mouthed barbarian over a prissy gentleman in the bedroom any day."

The woman was not only a possible murderer, she was vulgar, as well. Hannah cut a quick glance at the bedroom door, *willing* the door down, *willing* daggers at the man behind that door. Of course, the door remained closed and the man behind it remained unharmed. Jed Rourke, that libertine!

"Well," Hannah said as she rose quickly, "I've taken enough of your time."

Sylvia did not rise to see her to the door. Just as well. But the widow did call out, as Hannah laid her hand on the doorknob.

"If you try to make Jed choose between us, you'll lose," she said, her voice soft and confident.

"I know," Hannah whispered as she closed the door behind her.

The last thing she wanted to do was socialize with Jed's sister and her friends, but Eden's invitation was so warm, so heartfelt, that Hannah found she could not refuse. The entire day had been a waste of time. She'd discovered nothing new, except that Jed Rourke's taste in women was sadly lacking.

A bit of afternoon tea would be nice, she decided, as Eden took her arm and led her into the dining room.

Fiona and another little girl, who appeared to be a tad older, played together on the floor. They each had two rag dolls, one for each hand. Two other women sat nearby, at one of the largest round tables in the room, talking over tea.

"Hannah Winters," Eden said. The women at the table turned their attention to Jed's sister. "This is Mary Reese"—a wave of her hand indicated an attractive, plainly dressed woman with pale brown hair—"and Lily Salvatore."

Lily Salvatore was a stunning woman, dark-haired and black-eyed. The cut of her gown was, well, not outrageous, but not prim, either.

"Hannah was on the stage with Jedidiah," Eden

JED 101

said as she pulled out a chair for Hannah and
then for herself. "They were robbed on the road
between Ranburne and Rock Creek, but no one
was hurt and most of their belongings were recovered." She smiled. "Hannah is Rose's sister."

The knowledge of the upcoming trial damp-
ened their enthusiasm at that bit of news, but they
both smiled and greeted her warmly.

"And this is Georgie," Eden finished, indicating
the other little girl playing at their feet. "Mary's
daughter and Fiona's very best friend."

They talked the way good friends often did, fin-
ishing one another's sentences, subjects overlap-
ping, all talking at once, on occasion, and still they
didn't miss a beat. In a matter of minutes Hannah
felt like she knew these women. Mary was warm and
caring, a woman not easily flustered. Lily was the
owner and a performer in Three Queens, the establishment across the street, and she had not been
married long. Eden was cheerfully enthusiastic and
unfailingly optimistic.

When talk turned to the upcoming trial, the
mood sobered. "I still haven't heard from Jo,"
Mary said with a shake of her head. "I don't even
know if she's received my letters, if she knows
what happened to her father."

"Do you think she'll come back to Rock Creek,
now that he's dead?" Eden asked.

Mary shrugged her shoulders. "I don't know."

Hannah listened intently. It seemed even
Clancy's own daughter wouldn't have anything to
do with him! Not that she blamed this Jo.

She had been silent through most of the get-
together, but she felt compelled to add, during a
lull in the conversation, "Baxter didn't do it."

All eyes turned to her, and she saw sympathy and regret in every pair.

"Please don't think that I'm defending Baxter because he's married to my sister and I feel some kind of . . . of obligation to defend him." She took a deep breath and steeled herself, bravely lifting her chin. "The fact of the matter is, he's a spineless coward who doesn't have the guts to commit a murder."

Mary seemed to consider her argument, and Eden nodded and spoke up. "Well, you have to admit, Baxter never has been of much use in a crisis. He always preferred hiding to confrontation."

"This is very true," Mary said softly. "But the evidence is rather condemning."

Hannah explained, again, how Baxter had found the body and foolishly picked up the knife. The ladies were skeptical, but she could see that they at least considered the possibility.

Their gathering was interrupted when Jed entered the dining room, booted footsteps heavy on the plank floor.

On short, chubby legs, Fiona ran to her uncle, who cradled his head with one large hand and frowned mightily at the floor.

Hannah glared at him, hoping he could feel the daggers she put in her mightiest glare.

Eden jumped to her feet. "Headache?" she asked.

"Yes," Jed grumbled. "You got any of that medicine?"

In spite of the headache he smiled and lifted Fiona into his arms.

"Of course," Eden said as she stepped into the kitchen.

Fiona giggled with delight and grabbed Jed's nose. Holding the toddler, he looked bigger than ever, imposing and rough and . . . somehow sweet. Oh, after this morning she *knew* he was not sweet!

"Here you go," Eden said, exiting the kitchen with a brown bottle in her hand.

Mary and Lily rose and said good-bye, and Mary collected little Georgie and two of the rag dolls. They made plans to meet again on Thursday afternoon, and even said they hoped to see Hannah there. She was quite touched by their warmth and genuine hospitality.

Eden took Fiona from Jed's grasp and handed him the dark brown bottle. He uncapped it as if he planned to take a swig directly from the bottle.

"Hold it," Hannah snapped as she shot to her feet and stepped toward the big man. "Exactly what is that?"

He lifted his eyebrows and held the bottle, label out, for her perusal.

She took the bottle from him and set it aside. "You shouldn't be taking this," she said, leaving no room for argument. "It can be addictive, you know."

"I only take it when I get one of these headaches," he said.

She could see the pain in his eyes, in the set of the muscles in his jaw and his neck. "Sit down," she ordered.

He glared at her and stubbornly planted his feet.

Eden exited the dining room, declaring that it was past time for Fiona's nap. She left the room with the brisk walk of a woman making her escape.

"Please," Hannah said softly, when it appeared that Jed had no intention of doing as she asked.

It was the *please* that got him. He pulled out the nearest chair and sat down.

Hannah moved behind him and laid her hands on his shoulders. If anything, the tension in them increased. "Relax," she said lowly.

"If you hit me I'll put you over my knee and . . ."

"I have no intention of hitting you," she said. *Not yet.* "Look down."

He obeyed, and she moved her hands from his shoulders to his neck, her fingers slipping beneath honey blond strands of hair that were surprisingly soft to the touch. "You really shouldn't take that medicine," she said as she began to massage his neck. "It's not good for you."

"It works," he grumbled.

"So does this," she said, pressing her fingers into his neck and kneading the tight muscles there. "Goodness, no wonder you have a headache. You're much too tense."

"It's been a rough week." Ah, his voice already sounded better, less strained.

"I know." His muscles yielded to her touch, as she kneaded the small circles on the muscles in the side of his neck. "You need to relax."

His neck was warm, strong, and well shaped. As her fingers began a rhythm of massage on his tensest muscles, she closed her eyes and relaxed herself. She wished, with all her heart, that she had not gone to Sylvia Clancy's house that morning, that she didn't know the odious woman and Jed were lovers.

"Lift your head," she ordered tersely. While she should allow him to suffer, or to take that dreadful medicine, she still felt she owed him. Her fingers

JED 105

moved to his temples, where they massaged gently. A satisfied moan escaped from his lips.

"Breathe deeply," she said, and he obeyed without question. The pressure at his temples was softer than what she'd applied to his neck, not much more than a gentle stroking. "Now tilt your head back and look at me," she ordered in a low voice.

He did, tilting his head back slowly. She moved her fingers to his forehead, stroked deeply from the center outward. Eyes closed, face relaxed, Jed Rourke was oddly beautiful. Oh, he was rough and hairy and craggy, but there was a symmetry in his face, a distinct blend of perfection and ruggedness.

He opened his eyes and pinned his gaze on her. And then there were the eyes, she was reminded, blue and penetrating.

"It's gone," he said, wonder in his voice.

"Of course." She dropped her hands and stepped back.

Jed stood slowly and faced her. "Where did you learn to do that?"

"I read about it. The Orientals use massage frequently in their medical treatments."

"You *read* about it?"

Hannah nodded.

"You've never done it before?"

"No." Perhaps she had done something wrong. The way he *looked* at her . . ." Well, I did try it on myself a few times," she admitted, "just to see if it would work." She sounded like a blithering idiot! Why had she been compelled to try this on Jed? She should've let him suffer, or else sat back silently and allowed him to take that addictive medicine. He was going to laugh at her. There could be nothing worse, nothing more humiliating . . .

"You're a wonder, Hannah Winters," he said with a smile.

A wave of relief washed through her, followed by a rush of anger at herself for feeling that relief. A proper woman would simply thank him and walk away, and she would definitely not speak her mind about the man's personal life. But Hannah hadn't ever been quite proper.

"So your headache is gone?"

"Completely."

She lifted her chin and looked him in the eye. "Since you're feeling better, I feel free to tell you that you are a complete moron whose poor taste in women is only exceeded by his complete lack of fashion sense and good hygiene."

His smile faded. "My poor taste in women?"

"Surely Mrs. Clancy told you I was her caller this morning? Really, Jed, her husband's barely cold and you're . . . you're . . ."

"I'm not doing a goddamn thing," he said, lifting his hands in supplication, "but following you all over town to make sure you don't go and get yourself killed."

She forgot all about his indiscretions. *"Following* me?"

Smug and self-satisfied, he grinned at her. The headache was obviously gone. "Following you. From the hotel to the rectory to the general store to the livery to the barber shop to the general store again and finally back here. You did good today, Hannah. No one tried to shoot you."

"You didn't follow me to the rectory," she said. "You were already there."

"I was not." He didn't *look* as if he felt guilty, as if he'd been caught red-handed.

"Sylvia told me herself. . . ."

Jed leaned in close, bending down to place his face close to hers. "I don't care what anybody told you. I wasn't there."

"I . . ."

He lifted a finger to silence her. "Let me tell you something, Hannah," he said quietly. "I've done a lot of things in my life that I'm not proud of, but I've never lied about any of them. Ask me," he challenged. "Ask me anything."

"Are you and Sylvia . . . Did you . . . Are you . . ." Oh, it wasn't like her to stammer and stumble over her words!

"Let me help you out here, darlin'," Jed said with a wink. "Not anymore."

Darlin'. No one had ever called her darlin' before. "So you weren't the man who was hiding in her bedroom this morning?" she pressed.

"Nope." Not only did Jed deny being that man, he didn't seem at all concerned that another man had been there.

Hannah took too much comfort from that realization. If he still cared for Sylvia, wouldn't he be jealous? "Why on earth are you trailing after me all day?"

"To keep you from getting killed," he answered without hesitation.

"Why?"

His blue eyes bored into her. A muscle in his jaw twitched. "I don't rightly know."

Hannah only had one more question. She was fairly sure she knew what the answer would be, but she needed to hear it from his own lips. "Do you think Baxter is guilty?"

This time there was no hesitation. "Yes, I do."

Standing in the lobby, Jed greeted the kids when they came in from school, lifting Millie off her feet and swinging her around before setting her on the ground to hear Rafe brag about the good grade he'd gotten in English. Teddy asked Jed if he'd like to engage in a little shooting competition down by the river, after he'd finished with his homework. *That impudent whippersnapper,* Jed thought proudly as he accepted the challenge.

When Eden and Fiona walked into the lobby, Eden put the toddler down and tried to shush the children, who were all talking at once.

"Uncle Jed has a headache," she said in a lowered voice.

"No, I don't," he said with a smile.

"You took the medicine?" she asked, frowning. "It usually puts you to sleep."

He shook his head. "No. Hannah fixed my headache."

Eden narrowed her eyes suspiciously. "She *fixed* it?"

Jed grinned widely. "Yes ma'am, she did." The woman never ceased to amaze him.

Fiona ran straight to Teddy, who handed his books to Rafe and picked up the child. She patted his cheeks and said "Teddy, Teddy, Teddy," in quick babylike talk that sounded nothing like the boy's name yet was still recognizable.

"There's milk and apples and biscuits in the

kitchen," Eden said. "You three get a snack and then do your homework."

The children obeyed, talking as they walked into the dining room. Teddy continued to carry Fiona, leaving Jed and Eden alone.

"Have a seat," Eden said as she sat on the couch and patted the space beside her.

Jed almost groaned aloud. Eden was wearing her sweetest, most insistent "we-need-to-talk" face.

But he sat obediently.

"You know," she said thoughtfully, "I always imagined that one day you would show up at my door with a sweet, young bride. Someone who would tame that vulgar mouth of yours and make you stay in one place for longer than a month or two."

"Sounds like hell to me," Jed grumbled.

She chastised him with a glance. "It's what you need Jedidiah."

"No," he said gently. "It's what *you* need. The fact of the matter is, I'll never get married. You know how I am. I get bored with any place or any person after a time. There's always a better place out there to see, a better woman to . . . well, a better woman. Would you really want to do that to some sweet, young gal?"

Eden pursed her lips. "It's just not natural."

Jed grinned.

"And now you seem to be courting Hannah Winters, and while she is a . . ."

"Whoa," Jed snapped, his grin fading. "I am not *courting* anyone, and if I were, it wouldn't be that . . . that woman. She's nosy and sharp-tongued and bossy as hell."

"Well, you did have dinner with her Saturday night," Eden said with wide eyes.

"As *friends,*" Jed added.

"You've never had a woman friend before."

I've never met a woman like Hannah. He bit that response back, kept it to himself. Eden would read too much into such a simple statement. "There's a first time for everything."

"Just as well," Eden said, patting his cheek affectionately. "One day I'll find that sweet young girl for you and you'll settle down right here in Rock Creek and have a dozen children."

"Heaven forbid," he grumbled. "Christ, Eden, I thought you *liked* me."

"I adore you," she said with a smile. "And I know what's best for you."

He narrowed his eyes, feeling strangely defensive. "Are you trying to tell me that Hannah is not what's best for me?"

"As long as you're just friends . . ."

"Well, what if I changed my mind?" he challenged. "What if I decided I did want to court her?"

"It's just that she's . . . I do like her, but she's not . . ." Eden bit her lower lip.

"You have no say in my love life, Eden Sullivan," he snapped. "What makes you think you know better than I do what I need in a woman?"

"Well, if this isn't the pot calling the kettle black," she countered with a soft smile. "If I remember correctly, you forbade me to marry Sin."

His nose twitched, his shoulders tensed. "That was different."

"How so?"

How so? He should have a quick answer for that

one, a *hundred* quick answers. Nothing came to mind.

He glanced nervously toward the dining room entrance. "Do you think Teddy's finished with his homework, yet? I promised him we'd have target practice this afternoon. He's still pulling a bit to the right."

"Teddy hasn't even had time to finish his after-school snack, much less his homework."

Jed fidgeted on the sofa.

"I only want you to be happy," Eden said softly.

Jed laid eyes on his sister. All his life he'd protected and sheltered her. Handing her over to Sullivan had been hard. Letting her go completely had been damn near impossible. Eden often accused him of treating her like she was still twelve, and maybe she was right.

"I am happy," he assured her. "I like my life the way it is. No ties, no obligations. When my feet get to itching, I move on. I'll wander to the day I die. *That's* what makes me happy."

"I don't believe you," Eden said simply and decisively.

Eight

Hannah's investigation was maddeningly unsat-isfying. Days of interviews revealed nothing new. Reverend Clancy had been a fire-and-brimstone preacher on Sunday and a libertine the other six days of the week. A large number of people in Rock Creek had reason to want him dead. Most were satisfied to pin the crime on Baxter and be done with it.

Jed continued to follow her, trailing behind at a distance. She didn't want to prove him right in his assessment of her inadequate social skills and the inevitable result, so she behaved with uncom-mon decorum. She hit no one with her cane, and no matter how difficult it was, she kept her tem-per under control. She would not give Jed Rourke the satisfaction of coming to her rescue again!

As the date of the trial approached, Rose looked worse and worse. It was evident she wasn't sleeping well, if at all, and Bertie confirmed that to be the truth. Most of Friday was already gone, wasted, and the judge would be here to try Baxter on Monday morning!

In Hannah's estimation, Baxter Sutton was a poor excuse for a man. He'd declined to serve in the war, opting instead to move West. To run from conflict. The man had no spine, and no apparent charm to make up for that lack.

But Rose must love him to suffer so. Hannah began to suspect that if Baxter hung, Rose would die shortly thereafter.

And for all his faults, Baxter did have one redeeming quality. He might not be courageous, but at least once in his life he had made a stand. When Elliot Winters had refused to give Baxter Sutton his eldest daughter's hand in marriage, Baxter and Rose had eloped. True, Baxter had not actually stood up to the irascible Elliot Winters, but he had come for Rose in the night and taken her. He had refused to be denied his love.

For that alone, Hannah felt compelled to save him. It appeared that the only way she could do that would be to act as his attorney. While she had no formal training, she felt certain she was as qualified as any man in Rock Creek to take on the chore.

The trial would take place in two days. Two days!

Head high, dejection pushed down as far as possible, she headed for the jail. Perhaps today Baxter would remember seeing something or someone unusual that morning. It was inconceivable that the wrong man would hang and a murderer would go free.

She found Sheriff Sullivan seated at his desk. Judging by the expression on his face as he rose to his feet, he was *not* happy to see her.

"I'd like to see my brother-in-law," she said crisply.

"Sure." Sullivan opened the door that separated the office from the hallway and the two plain cells that completed Rock Creek's jailhouse. It was always gloomy, as if the light that broke through the two small windows was dimmed not only by winter, but by the very atmosphere of the jail.

Sitting on the cot at the rear wall of his cell, head down, Baxter was pale and thinner than she remembered. He'd lost weight in the week she'd been here.

"Any luck?" he asked, no hope in his voice.

"No," she said, refusing to lie to him about the situation. "Did you remember seeing anything that morning, anything that might be of help?"

He shook his head. "I was so angry when I marched over there to see Clancy, I didn't notice anything or anybody."

Exactly what she'd been afraid of. "I'll serve as your attorney," she said crisply. "You're going to need someone to stand up there with you and try to make sense of this."

"Thank you," he said softly, not arguing as she'd expected him to. Baxter lifted his head and laid weary eyes on her. "I want you to promise me something," he said softly. "If they find me guilty, I want you to take Rose and the boys and get out of Rock Creek as quick as you can."

"I don't know if Rose will agree. . . ."

"I won't have her or the boys watch me hang," he interrupted. "Promise me."

"I'll do what I can."

"Promise."

She nodded once. "All right. You have my word."

Baxter laid back on the narrow cot and covered his eyes with his arm. He had already given up.

"But there's still a chance that you'll be found innocent," she said, trying to inject some hope into her own voice.

"I don't think so," he said in an expressionless voice. "I appreciate you trying, Hannah, I really do, but all you can do for me now is get Rose and the twins out of town when it's over."

She wanted to reason with him, but in truth she had no argument. "If you remember anything, send the sheriff to me with a message. I'll come right away."

"Thanks, Hannah," he said, never lifting that concealing arm from his face.

She was not surprised to find Jed in the sheriff's outer office, sitting on the edge of Sullivan's desk and talking in a low voice.

All her frustration, all her anger, coalesced into a white hot ball of pain that centered in her midsection. "As you can see, no one's killed me yet."

"Good for you," he said plainly.

She turned her attention to the sheriff. "Don't you feed your prisoners? Baxter looks like a scarecrow!"

"I take him food three times a day. I can't make him eat," Sullivan said sensibly.

She'd started with such good intentions, but all her plans had fallen apart. It pained her to know she wasn't going to be able to find the real killer. Damnation, she was not equipped for such a task. Jed and Sullivan, their friends Reese and Rico . . . If they set their minds to finding the real killer they could no doubt do so. Once again she had fallen short.

If she could make anyone understand, it would be Jed. She turned her eyes to him, trying to smother her frustration. "He's innocent. I swear it."

Jed shook his head. "I know you believe that. . . ."

"I believe it because it's true," she interrupted.

"Hannah . . ." he began.

She could hear the censure in his voice. She needed to hear no more.

"Your *old friend* cries on your shoulder and bats her lashes at you and just like a man you fall for her artifice without a second thought. She . . . She begs you to see that a man hangs for a crime he did not commit, and you pat her on the head and say 'Of course, sugarplum.'" Hannah reached out and smacked Jed on his chest with the flat of her hand. "If I cried and batted my lashes and told you Baxter was innocent, would you believe me then? What exactly does it take, Jedidiah Rourke, to get through that thick skull of yours?"

He was not at all moved by her impassioned plea. "I don't believe what Sylvia said because she cried and batted her damned lashes. You're the one who's looking at everything all cockeyed." He pointed an accusing finger in her face.

"Don't shake that finger at me," she demanded.

"I'll do whatever I damn well please," he seethed.

"Keep shaking that finger at me and I'll break it off."

"Try and you'll be picking your ass up off the floor before you know what happened."

Sullivan cleared his throat. "Am I going to have to lock both of you up?"

Jed dropped his hand and Hannah took a step back. "I just can't believe," she said softly, "that I'm going to have to watch the wrong man hang."

With that, she spun about and left the sheriff's office. Jed was right behind her.

Keeping Hannah at a distance for the past several days had been a good idea. She took care of her little investigation, and he watched. So far she'd minded her manners, and he hadn't been called upon to step in on her behalf.

She was in a huff now, stalking toward the hotel with her nose in the air and her spine straight . . . and just a little wiggle in her hips. He smiled at her back. If she knew how good she looked stalking away in a huff, she'd likely change her style.

Eden thought he needed a sweet, young girl. Jed knew better. If he ever decided to settle down, he'd take a saucy woman like Hannah over a piece of fluff any day.

Of course, he had no intention of settling down, so it didn't make much sense to ponder the possibilities. Still, as Hannah stalked away he pondered. He most definitely pondered.

Movement to the right caught his eye. Oliver Jennings, the cowboy who'd drawn his gun on Hannah last week, was walking down the boardwalk. Their paths, if Jed calculated correctly, would bring them face-to-face right about the hotel entrance.

The mood Hannah was in, she was unlikely to yield way to the cowboy. Jennings was a hothead, but he was basically a good enough kid. Jed really, really didn't want to have to shoot the boy.

"Hannah," he called.

She stopped in the street. Hesitated. Then turned slowly. "Yes?"

She stood there, cane in hand and chin high, as he approached. "You need to cool off. Let's take a walk."

"I do not need to cool off, and the wind has picked up. It's too cold for a . . ." She stopped midsentence, and it seemed her face fell, just a little. God in heaven, she looked lost. "All right," she conceded. "Maybe a leisurely stroll wouldn't be a bad idea."

This time, instead of following, he walked beside her. Jennings passed safely by, casting a sharp glance in their direction, and then Jed led Hannah through the hotel lobby and out the back door. They walked down the garden path, then through the gate at the back of the garden.

Leisurely stroll? Hannah's step was purposeful and determined as she strode away from the heart of town. There was nothing *leisurely* about her pace or her demeanor. She remained silent. It just wasn't natural.

Finally, a decent distance from the hotel, she stopped. The tip of the cane tapped nervously at her feet, and a gust of wind whipped a strand of red hair loose and lashed it across her pale face.

"When Baxter first began to call on Rose," she began, her voice soft but strong, "there was talk of war. Most of the men were quite . . . tireless about the subject, but Baxter never had much to say. I thought it was simply because he didn't want to distress Rose. My sister has always been delicate," she explained. "From the beginning, the talk of war disturbed her."

Smart woman, Jed thought, but he kept his mouth closed. He didn't want to interrupt Hannah, not now.

If she weren't a lady, he'd be planning ways to
get past that door tonight.

"No," she said softly. "I'm not hungry."

As she pulled away from him and went through
the garden gate he considered arguing with her.
He didn't.

She had managed to avoid almost everyone for
a full day. Hannah Winters, who never gave up,
who never backed down, didn't know what to do
next. She was, for the first time in her life, completely and totally lost.

And to make matters worse, Eden Sullivan had
decided to hold a gathering of friends in the
lobby of the hotel. Hannah had tried to gently
decline the offer, but Eden was insistent.

Hannah got the feeling that no one refused
Eden Sullivan.

She'd make an appearance, do her best to be
polite, and then retire early. Claiming exhaustion
would not be a lie. Still, she took the time to don
her best blue silk and to fix her hair. There was
no reason to become shabby just because she happened to be residing, for the moment, in a shabby
little town.

By the time she descended the stairs, the party
was well underway. Eden had laid refreshments
on the long front counter, and the friends in the
room talked and laughed softly, with the kind of
camaraderie one found among close friends and
the kind of family Hannah herself had never
known. The sheriff stood behind his wife, his
arms wrapped loosely but protectively around her.
Mary Reese and her husband, who was the most

unlikely looking schoolteacher Hannah had ever seen, sat side by side on the green sofa, and Lily Salvatore, dressed for the performance she would give later in the evening at her entertainment house, sat in a fat green chair with her handsome husband, Rico, standing behind her, his hands placed proprietarily on her shoulders.

Jed sat in a matching chair, his long legs thrust before him casually as he laughed at something Rico had said. He still wore his buckskin duster, as if he were prepared to stand up and depart at any moment.

When he lifted his head and saw her standing on the stairway, his laughter died.

Oh, she was a fool for not insisting that she did not want to attend this gathering! Turning and running now would make her look like a ninny, though, so she continued down the stairs with all the grace she could muster.

Everyone was paired up, everyone but her and Jed. How mortifying.

She had met everyone present, and out of the entire crowd she had only managed to annoy Sheriff Sullivan. And Jed, of course.

The mood sombered a little as she walked into the midst of them all. They were all thinking of Baxter, she imagined. Well, she wouldn't stay long. Once she was gone they could resume their merriment unimpeded.

Jed stood and offered her his chair, a gallant move that, for some reason, made Rico and Reese grin wickedly. Hannah ignored them. She didn't know them well, but they were probably ill-mannered cretins like their friend Jed.

Eden poured a cup of punch and handed it to

Hannah, but Hannah declined the offered sweets. She hadn't been able to eat much in the past three days. Her stomach was tied in knots.

Hannah sipped her punch and sat back to listen. Rico and Lily talked about their business. Apparently Lily had made significant changes in Three Queens since coming to Rock Creek.

Mary and Reese talked about the school and the children there and their own Georgie, and Reese even commented that the Sutton boys seemed to be maturing, at last. Hannah withheld a despairing sigh. Her blackmail had worked so well.

Eden and Sullivan talked with great affection about the baby that would be born early in the summer. Goodness, they already had four children, but they seemed truly ecstatic about this one. The way they looked at each other and touched so easily and familiarly was strikingly tender. They would probably reproduce until the hotel was filled, Hannah thought with a touch of rancor and more than a touch of envy.

She listened until the room started to swim and her heart pounded. The voices surrounding her became harsh and meaningless. Her skin felt suddenly hot, her cheeks flushed. She didn't know why she suddenly felt trapped and nervous and downright ill; she only knew she had to get out of there. Now.

Standing slowly, she used her cane for real support. "If you'll excuse me," she said when all eyes turned to her. "I think I need a breath of fresh air."

Without looking at any one of the curious people surrounding her, she headed for the back door and the fresh garden air that would surely bring her to her senses.

She heard the hum of lowered voices behind her as she stepped outside and closed the door, and with her eyes closed she took a deep breath of cold air. When the door opened, a moment later, she knew without looking that it was Jed who had followed her.

"Are you all right?" he asked softly.

She started to say "Yes, of course," but couldn't make herself lie to him. Everyone else, maybe, but not Jed. "Have you ever failed miserably?"

"Yep," he answered without hesitation.

"I haven't," she whispered. "Until now. I don't know what to do."

"You've done everything you can." His voice was low and soothing. "It's time to sit back and let the chips fall where they will."

She shook her head but remained silent. How could she?

"It's cold out here," Jed said. She expected him to try to herd her back inside, but he didn't. He took off his buckskin coat and draped it over her shoulders. The coat was heavy, and on her short frame the hem hung to the ground. It enveloped her, cocooned her. The warmth, from the coat and the man who had been wearing it, seeped into her with a gratifying rush of heat.

"Thank you," she whispered.

"You look like you have a headache," he said, and before she could protest, he lifted his big hand and laid it on her, cupping her neck. With gentle fingers he began to massage her neck the way she'd massaged his, when he'd had a headache himself.

She knew she should protest, tell him to take his hand off of her this instant, but like the buckskin jacket, that hand was intensely comforting. She closed her eyes and savored the sensations. His touch was so warm, strong and yet gentle, familiar and soothing.

When her headache began to fade, she whispered, "Christmas is coming in less than two weeks, and my nephews might have to watch their father hang before the holiday arrives." The very idea made her heart lurch in her chest. "All my life I've bought what I wanted and needed, but I can't buy justice for my family."

Jed moved his hand from her neck to her shoulder, and forced her to turn around and face him. She didn't falter, but tilted her head back to look him in the eye without fear. Even in soft moonlight he was craggy and rough, all bristles and granite. How could such a man possess such a tender touch?

"Let it go, Hannah," he whispered.

"I can't."

"You've done everything possible, more than anyone else would have."

"It wasn't enough."

Jed took a deep breath and exhaled slowly. "Even if Baxter is found guilty, he might not hang. The sentence is up to the judge. If I say a few words in his behalf, maybe the judge will go easy on him."

"Easy how?"

"Prison," Jed whispered.

Baxter wouldn't last long in prison, and they both knew it. Still, it was kind of him to offer.

"Thank you," she said.

For a long, very still moment, Jed stared down at her. She didn't look away; she didn't play coy. Not with Jed. Finally his head began to move, almost imperceptibly, toward hers. Dipping and slanting, bending until his face was lost in shadow. Hannah held her breath. He was going to kiss her.

Oh, she wanted him to kiss her. There was no reason for her desire, no logical explanation for the yearning that filled her. No matter how she tried to reason it away, that yearning remained, strong and steady.

She allowed her eyes to drift shut. She held her breath. Heavens, she could feel him moving slowly, inexorably closer.

The door opened before his lips met hers, and they each took a quick step back. Hannah's eyes flew open.

Of all the people in the world . . .

"Jed," Sylvia crooned, "Eden said you were out here."

"Nice of her," Jed grumbled.

"I have to talk to you," the widow said softly, casting a murderous glance at Hannah.

Suddenly the air was cold again. "Your coat," Hannah said succinctly, whipping off the buckskin and handing it to Jed.

If he had anything to say in response, she didn't hear it. She shut out everything and entered the hotel lobby, said a quick good night to the folks who were still gathered around the green sofa, and climbed the stairs.

Nine

No matter how she tried to calm herself, Hannah was wracked by a nervousness she didn't normally experience. Baxter's trial would get underway tomorrow morning. Tomorrow! She'd been so sure that she would be able to find the real killer, but she had nothing, not even a viable alternative to offer. All she had was the lame argument that no one had actually seen Baxter thrust that knife into Reverend Clancy's heart.

Church services that morning were conducted by a traveling preacher who had taken over for the departed Reverend Clancy until a permanent replacement could be found. The sermon had been dull and lifeless, and half the men in the church had been snoring in their pews before it was done.

Hannah herself hadn't slept well in three nights. How could they doze off so easily when an innocent man was about to hang?

Ah, but only she and Rose believed Baxter to be innocent. She'd been able to convince no one else.

Entering the hotel lobby, she felt a wave of complete and utter desolation wash through her. Hopeless. This endeavor she'd taken so to heart was absolutely hopeless! Seeing Virgil Wyndham, obviously just from his bed and making his way to the dining room, did not cheer her mood.

"Miss Winters," the gambler said with a half smile and a tip of his small-brimmed hat. "How lovely to see you." He followed this polite greeting with a small belch he almost managed to stifle with a raised hand.

"Mr. Wyndham." She nodded politely with every intention of continuing on without so much as slowing down.

Wyndham managed to ruin her plan by stepping deftly into her path. "I heard about your family's bad fortune," he said, raising his eyebrows in what he might have intended to be a sympathetic expression. "How dreadful for you."

"Thank you for your concern," she said, taking a step to the side so she could make her way around him.

His step mirrored hers. "If there's anything I can do," he offered. "Anything at all . . ."

Well, she hadn't spoken to Wyndham, since he was a visitor and not a resident. But he did have a regular room here at the hotel. He was her last hope. How dreadful.

"Were you acquainted with Reverend Clancy?" she asked.

Wyndham smiled. "I'm afraid I'm not a church-going man, Miss Winters."

"Of course not." She sighed.

"But if I hear anything," he added with a wink, "you'll be the first to know."

"Thank you."

Thank goodness, the gambler finally nodded

his farewell and sauntered off toward the dining room.

Hannah was heading up to her room to freshen up before the noon meal and he was heading downstairs when she ran, almost literally, into Jed Rourke. For some reason, she found it easiest to take her frustrations out on him. Simply looking at him fired her anger.

She could manage a moment of politeness even with that weasel of a gambler, but Jed brought every emotion to the surface. There was no way she could nod and smile and offer a meaningless greeting.

"I didn't see you in church this morning," she said, glancing up sharply. She always had to tilt her head back to look him in the eye, and with him standing a couple of steps above her, the distance was exaggerated. Dressed entirely in buckskins and leather, with that battered wide-brimmed hat that shaded his eyes on his head, he looked as rough and tumble as ever.

"I wasn't there."

The widow Clancy hadn't been there, either, Hannah thought bitterly. Jed denied being involved with Sylvia, and Hannah wanted to believe him; she truly did. And yet when she thought of the two of them together it made her blood boil. What man could resist a woman like Sylvia Clancy when she all but threw herself at him?

"Are you going down to lunch? Or breakfast?" she asked sharply.

He grinned. "Neither. Rico is riding with me out to the Benedict ranch to look over a couple of horses. I need a new one." He winked at her insolently. "Try to stay out of trouble while I'm gone."

"I've managed quite well without you for the past twenty-nine years," she said coolly. "I think I can make it though one day without your supervision."

"I'm glad to hear it," he said, stepping down and around her, his arm brushing against her casually as he passed. Big and warm and solid, his nearness, his easiest touch, was nearly overpowering. Oh, that blasé collision was no accident at all!

"Animal," she mumbled as she resumed her trek up the stairs.

"Vixen," he said just as softly, and with what might have been a touch of affection.

She didn't look back, but opened the door to her room and stepped inside, gratefully closing it behind her. "Brute," she whispered, satisfied in some small way that she had, this once, gotten in the last word.

She almost stepped past the folded piece of paper on the floor. Someone had apparently slipped it under her door. Considering the run-ins she'd had with the residents of Rock Creek in the past week, she fully expected a threat of some kind.

But when she unfolded the paper she got a surprise. The letters were written in a firm, even hand.

I know who killed Reverend Clancy. Meet me at Wishing Rock. Sundown. Tell no one. If you do you'll never know the truth.

Trembling with excitement, she refolded the paper. She'd known all along that someone in Rock Creek had to know the truth. Obviously this person was afraid of being seen talking to her, but had decided to reveal what they knew before the trial got underway. Not everyone wanted to see an innocent man hang.

Had the person who wrote the note slipped it beneath the door while she'd been in church? Or was he, or she, still lurking in the hotel somewhere?

Or had she passed him on the stairs moments after he'd slipped the note under her door?

If that were true, if Jed had written this note, what did he really want? To discuss the trial? Of course not. If that was the case, he would have asked her to join him in the dining room after the lunch crowd left. Instead he'd left town with the excuse of purchasing a horse, so she'd have no opportunity to ask him outright if he'd written the note. His wink on the stairway took on a whole different meaning, with this note in hand.

Why did she feel like this was a test of some kind?

If Jed had, indeed, written the note, the request might have nothing at all to do with Baxter's trial. The very idea made her heart skip a beat. She was not completely ignorant where men and their ways of thinking were concerned. There were times, brief moments, when Jed liked her more than was natural. When he looked at her and an unexpected sparkle touched his eyes, when he grinned and she saw something there she couldn't quite decipher. Last night he'd almost kissed her, under the cover of darkness, in a moment of weakness. But of course he wouldn't want anyone to know that he felt anything for someone like her.

Tell no one.

It would serve him right if she tore his note into a hundred small pieces and forgot his enigmatic request. Let him wait. It would serve him right for being so confident that she'd do as he commanded.

But she had to consider the possibility that Jed had not written the note, that someone really was ready to tell her what had happened to Reverend Clancy. Either way, it would be foolish of her to do as the note commanded and ride out to Wishing Rock alone.

She freshened up at the basin and redressed her hair. Her church dress was too fancy for a noon meal in the Paradise Hotel, so she removed it, hung it up neatly, and laid out a warm, sensible gray skirt and matching jacket, and a blouse with a touch of lace at the collar. She also chose her most comfortable boots. As she studied the ensemble, she realized the skirt was cut wide enough for riding, and the jacket was lined and would protect her against the wind. She dressed in the outfit, then collected her velvet cloak from the wardrobe.

She was not afraid of Jed Rourke or any other man who might be waiting for her at Wishing Rock. After dinner, she'd see the man at the livery about renting a gentle horse and a sidesaddle.

"Hellcat," Jed muttered to himself as he and Rico rode south.

"What?" Rico asked, glancing to the side.

"Nothing," Jed said with a wide smile, adjusting the brim of his hat so it shaded his eyes.

The trip out to the Benedict ranch was a quick

one, on a mild, cool day like this one. Away from town the sun seemed warmer, the air sweeter and calmer. It was surely that fresh, cool air that made his insides feel lighter. Damn near buoyant, in fact.

"You are scaring me, *amigo,*" Rico said as the Benedict place drew near.

"Why's that?"

"I have never seen you smile so much. I fear you are losing your mind."

"May be," Jed said without anger. "May be."

"It is a woman," Rico said wisely.

"May be," Jed said, his grin fading slowly. It wasn't like him to allow another person to affect his mood this way. And a woman! *That* woman, in particular! It made no sense at all. Hannah was meddlesome and cantankerous, and had a fresh mouth on her.

For some reason, those qualities endeared her to him. Too bad she had a plantation waiting for her in Alabama, responsibilities and roots. Too bad Hannah Winters was everything he'd spent a lifetime running away from.

But sometimes he took one look at her and wanted to run to her, not away. He wanted to toss her over his shoulder one more time and carry her off. To where, he didn't know. He never did.

"So, you are going to get back together when her mourning is past?"

"Mourning?" Jed cast Rico a surprised glance. Would Hannah go into mourning for Baxter?

Wait a minute. Back together? The kid was obviously talking about Sylvia, not Hannah.

Jed grinned. "You're not so all-fired wise after all, kid," he said. When Rico tried to question him further, Jed spurred his borrowed horse toward the Benedict ranch.

The miles between Wishing Rock and Rock Creek went by more quickly on horseback than they had on foot. Fortunately, getting lost was not a possibility, since the rising mound of stone was visible from just north of town.

"Wishing Rock," Hannah whispered, her eyes on her destination. Jed had told her, the night of the robbery, about the legends surrounding the tall rock. As she rode toward the place where she and the other stagecoach passengers had spent that night, she asked herself what she really wanted, and what she would be willing to pay to have her most heartfelt wishes come true. The legends were nonsense, of course, but still . . . she wondered.

First of all, she wanted Baxter to be freed, but that was not a personal desire. It was a craving for justice, a desire for what was right and fair. She also wanted Rose to be happy, to be reunited with her husband and to put this nightmare behind them. Could they do that in Rock Creek? Likely not. There would be too many bad memories for them there, too many averted glances from those who had been so quick to condemn Baxter.

A cold wind whipped her hair, and she grabbed even tighter to the saddle horn as the stiff breeze pushed the hood of her velvet cloak back and tore her hair loose from its once-neat knot.

Wishing for justice and her sister's happiness was one thing. What did she want for herself?

It was not a question she asked herself often, but the answer came to her immediately. She wanted someone to love her the way Baxter loved Rose. That was an impossible wish, of course, magical rock or no magical rock. What else did she wish most dearly for? Her heart sped up and her blood went cold. Ah, she knew the answer to that question too well. She wanted to close her eyes and go back in time and . . . Well, she thought, shaking off her melancholy as she always did, that wish was as impossible as the foolish whim that she might inspire great love in a worthy man.

A more practical approach was called for. What did she *want*?

She wanted . . . She wanted to know what it was like to kiss a man like Jed Rourke. A man who was, for all his faults, a real man in every sense of the word. She wanted to surrender all her reservations, to dismiss her nagging doubts and fall into his arms. Just once. That was not an impossible wish, was it? No, it was very, very real.

Wishing Rock grew closer with every step of her rented horse. She would arrive just before sundown. Was the informant already there, waiting? Or would he arrive behind her?

And would it be Jed who arrived?

Benedict had offered a good selection of horses, and Jed had picked a sorrel gelding that was sturdy and tall. And fast. Hellfire, he could race this damn horse, if he had a mind to.

Back in Rock Creek, Rico said good-bye and headed off to Three Queens, the establishment that had once been a perfectly good saloon, and Jed went into the hotel hungry and anxious to see Hannah.

Eden and all the younguns greeted him enthusiastically, and he promised the boys a shooting lesson later in the day. Eden fed him, and all the while he ate he kept glancing toward the dining room entrance, waiting for Hannah to appear and give him hell for one reason or another. She never did show.

Once his late lunch was finished and the kids were settled down, he called Eden over to the table. "Where's Hannah?" he asked, trying to sound completely indifferent.

"I don't know," Eden said with a small frown. "I haven't seen her since dinnertime. Rose came by a while back looking for her, and we couldn't find her. I imagine she's out questioning people about the murder. She's quite upset about the ordeal, you know," Eden added in a lowered voice.

"Yes," Jed said absently. But even when Hannah was questioning everyone in town, she'd made a point of checking in with her sister often. She made her way from one place to another, asking questions and getting herself worked up and stopping by the general store on occasion. She hadn't just . . . disappeared.

He felt an unpleasant tingle down his spine. A tingle of warning. "I'll run over to Rose's and see if she's shown up there."

The town was quiet on a Sunday afternoon, the streets all but deserted. There was no sign of a cantankerous hellion who liked to stir up trouble wherever she went. Rose and Bertie hadn't seen Hannah since church let out. No one he passed and questioned on the street had seen her. By the time he got back to the hotel he was troubled. What had the fool woman gotten herself into this time?

"Maybe she's sick," he mumbled as he entered the hotel lobby. No one was there to hear him. He bounded up the stairs and pounded on her door. "Hannah! If you're in there you'd better speak up before I bust down this door!"

He expected Eden to come rushing up the stairs to chastise him at any moment, but no one appeared. The hallway remained deserted and too damn quiet as he waited for an answer.

"Hannah!" he shouted, giving the door one last thump with his fist before laying his hand on the knob and finding the door unlocked.

Jed shoved the door in so hard it banged against the wall. It was clear from the doorway that Hannah was not here, sick in her bed. Nothing was amiss, in fact, he noted as he stepped inside. Her clothes hung neatly in the wardrobe. Perfume, a brush and comb, and a fancy container of powder sat on the dresser.

Fool woman. What the hell has she gotten into today? Jed thought as he turned back toward the door. As he did, he saw the slip of paper lying in the center of the neatly made bed. He scooped up the paper and unfolded it. As he read the note he began to curse, low and foul.

He crumpled the note in his fist and tried to still the return of that warning tingle.

"She wouldn't have," he muttered to himself as he ran out of her room and down the stairs, stuffing the note in his pocket as he went. "Surely she wouldn't have."

But he knew in his heart that if Hannah thought there was even a small chance she could clear Baxter, she'd ride out to Wishing Rock and whatever danger waited there without a single second thought.

Ten

Hannah grasped the reins of her rented mare as she paced by the tall rock with the decidedly feminine shape and began her wait. Sundown was coming. The sun hung low in the Western winter sky, its brilliance fading already. Sheltered from the wind by the grouping of rocks, it was not so cold here, and still she was chilled to the bone. The rocks apparently hadn't soaked up even a little bit of the winter warmth that shone down on her. Instead, they seemed to retain last night's cold.

She saw the rising dust of a rider headed her way and stopped pacing to watch the cloud make its way toward her. Her heart thudded much too hard, and she couldn't quite manage to take the deep breath she felt she needed. What if she found herself out here, far away from town, in the company of the killer? Maybe he had lured her out here in order to do away with her the way he'd done away with Reverend Clancy.

That was a risk she was willing to take.

In a matter of a very few minutes she made out the horse in that cloud of dust, and the figure of a man on its back. The horse itself was not familiar, but before too much time had passed the rider was more than clear. No one else in town was quite so tall, in buckskin and leather that almost blended into the brown and gray backdrop of this desolate landscape. The tail of Jed's long buckskin coat whipped around him, and he leaned low over the horse's neck. He rode full out, as if racing to get here.

She didn't know whether to be elated or disappointed. If Jed actually had any information about the murder, he'd share it with her openly. He wasn't afraid of anyone. He wouldn't care who knew that he was helping her.

Her heart fell. Except Sylvia. He had promised the widow he would see Baxter hang, hadn't he? He wouldn't want his *old friend* to know, if he had secrets about the murder to reveal.

Then again, this assignation might have nothing at all to do with the murder or tomorrow's trial.

She prepared herself to do battle with Jed, if need be, steeling her heart and her spine as he came closer and closer. Even when he was near enough to see her waiting, he didn't slow his pace.

Suddenly his head jerked to the side. He reached over his head to draw a rifle from the scabbard that hung at his back. He drew the weapon smoothly, expertly, guiding the horse with his legs and quickly taking aim at a smaller cropping of rocks across the way. Hannah turned her eyes in that direction and saw what had no doubt caught Jed's eye. The glint of a rifle barrel.

She ducked behind a rock as the rifle fired. Not at Jed, but at *her*. The bullet pinged off the rock above her head, and a few shards of chipped shale came raining down. Her rented horse immediately bucked and shied, jerking the reins from her hand and bolting for town, flying past Jed and his finer steed.

From his saddle, still riding at a breakneck pace toward her, Jed returned fire. Hannah covered her head and cowered behind Wishing Rock.

It was a setup. Someone had lured her out in order to shoot her! That was, no doubt, the real killer out there. She came up on her knees and peeked through a crack in the rocks, hoping for a glimpse of the shooter. Jed's return fire kept him low, so she could see nothing.

This was proof that Baxter was innocent! Why else would someone try to stop her from defending him?

Jed's horse climbed the small incline to her sheltered position, and he smoothly dismounted. "Are you all right?"

She nodded as he knelt beside her and took aim through the crack in the rock.

"Fool woman," he muttered as he fired at the man who had ambushed her.

She ignored his insult. How could she argue with him now? Later, though . . .

"How did you know where I was?"

"I read the note," he said as he quickly and smoothly lowered the lever, brought it up with a snap, and fired again.

The working of the weapon was expertly carried out by gifted hands, every move crisp and precise.

Hannah admired the process, for a very short moment, and then dismissed her inappropriate admiration. "You went into my room?" she asked, incensed at the invasion of her privacy.

A bullet bounced off the rock behind her, sending shards of rocks and pebbles pinging to the ground. Jed cursed, low but quite succinctly.

"Come on." He grabbed her arm and dragged her back and around a corner. "Wait here," he said, shoving her through a small opening into a very dark cave.

She remembered what he'd said the night they'd spent out here, about the deep darkness and the possibility of getting lost. And hadn't he mentioned bobcats and coyotes that day? She couldn't possibly go in there. Another bullet pinging off the rock wall changed her mind.

Jed sheltered her from the front. Behind her there was only darkness.

He cursed beneath his breath as he reloaded. There are two shooters," he said gruffly. "And one of them's moving to the side."

A bullet hit the wall of rock above their heads, and pebbles came raining down. Jed pushed her a bit further into the cave. More bullets, a barrage of them, found the same target, and before she knew what was happening larger rocks began to fall from above, too. A few at first, then a waterfall of rocks, small and large.

When the big boulder rolled down, Jed shoved her back. The mouth of the cave fell inward, crumbling and filling the opening, cutting off the soft rays of sundown. Rocks fell all around them, and Jed pulled her roughly back and away from the avalanche. In a matter of seconds it was over, but for the ping of the occasional small rock falling into place. And she and Jed were left in complete darkness.

* * *

"Are you all right?" Jed asked as he laid his hand against the place on his head where a falling rock had glanced off. He could already feel a small lump, but there was no bleeding.

"I'm fine," Hannah said, sounding absurdly calm. "What about you?"

"Fine," he grumbled.

The cave was inky black, so dark he couldn't see his own hand in front of his face, much less Hannah.

"How do we get out of here?" she asked.

He shook his head and closed his eyes. "I don't know that we do."

"What?" she asked, her voice crisp and cool as the air in the cave. "You pulled me into this hole in the rock and you don't know a way *out*?"

He took a deep, calming breath. Arguing with her now wouldn't accomplish anything. Except maybe to make him feel better. "There probably is a way out, but I don't know that we can find it until the sun comes up. We can make our way back, and wait for light."

"Probably," she said softly.

"Probably."

He heard Hannah breathing slowly, deeply, as if trying to calm herself. "Well, your friends will come to check on us if you're not back soon, right?" she asked. "They'll see what happened and dig us out."

Jed groaned out loud. "I didn't tell anyone where I was going."

"Why not?" she snapped.

"Because I was in a hurry to save your ungrateful ass," he shouted. His voice was too loud in the darkness. A few pebbles were dislodged and rained around them.

"There's no need to bellow," she said softly. "And I am not ungrateful."

These caves were intricate, he'd heard. Some routes would lead them down, deeper into the ground. Others would lead them back and up, perhaps to an opening higher in the rock formation. The problem was, he couldn't see a damn thing.

He carefully lifted his rifle and placed it into the leather harness that hung at his back. Hands free, he reached into his pocket for the tin he always carried there. "I'm going to strike a match," he warned, "so we can get a feel for where we are."

He opened the tin and pulled out one match, feeling with the tips of his fingers to determine just how many he had. Not many. He struck the match against the wall of the cave and it flared to life.

Before checking out the cave, he looked Hannah over, just to prove to himself that she was all right. She looked disheveled and dusty, but unhurt.

Her eyes met his bravely.

"We'll be all right," he assured her.

Behind Hannah, the cave grew wider and taller. In the dim light of the single match, he saw three tunnels off the back of the underground chamber. Three tunnels, three choices. He had no idea if any one of them would lead to another exit.

The match burned down to his fingers and he shook it out.

"This is what we're going to do," he said, his voice calm but stern, leaving no room for argument. As if that would make a difference to Hannah. "You will hold on to my coat, and we'll move deeper into the cave. No matter what happens, don't let go of me. Got it?"

"Yes," she said.

"There's no exit here, so waiting would be foolish. We want to move back and up. When the sun rises, if we're in the vicinity of an opening we'll see some light."

"That makes perfect sense," she said, no sign of panic in her voice.

He pocketed the tin of matches and patted the tin to make sure it was deeply seated. They couldn't afford to lose their only source of light. He'd already decided to take the tunnel to the far left, so he placed the palm of his left hand against the cave wall to get his bearings. Without being told, Hannah closed the distance between them and, after reaching out blindly and finding his shoulder, raked her hand down and grabbed his coat, there near the waist. Her hold was secure, but she didn't tug against him.

Taking small, careful steps, he made his way around the cave to the tunnel opening. Hannah was right behind him, holding on and breathing against his back. The only noise was the sound of their breathing and their footsteps on the stone floor.

Finally, his hand slipped around the corner of the tunnel he had chosen. He hated to use another match so soon, but they couldn't walk into this tunnel without knowing what awaited them.

He took a match from his pocket and struck it on the stone wall. It flared and illuminated the tunnel he had chosen. The path led slightly up, then narrowed into a space too small for Fiona to crawl through.

"Shit," he muttered, moving quickly to the next tunnel before the match burned down. This one widened, but led unerringly downward. The third and last tunnel, which they reached as the match was about to die out, was wide and even, and seemed to slope upward. Just a little. The flame burned his fingertips before he shook it out.

"This is it," he said, trying to sound confident.

"Are you sure this route will lead us out?" Hannah asked.

"Nope," he answered as he stepped into the tunnel. He'd taken several steps, one hand against the wall to guide him, when he spoke again. "Didn't I specifically tell you to stay out of trouble today?"

Hannah tugged gently on his coat. "I didn't know someone was going to send me a note and ask that I meet them, now did I?"

"That's a woman's reasoning for you," Jed muttered. It was hard to tell, but it seemed the trail was heading up.

"That was the real murderer shooting at us, you know," she said reasonably. "Do you believe me now? That Baxter is innocent?"

"I figure that could've been anyone you've met and badgered since your arrival," he countered sourly.

"You just can't admit that you're wrong," she said in a despairingly weary voice. "How like a man," she added softly.

They'd walked in silence for a short distance before Jed stopped. He had to know where he was going, and he couldn't see a damn thing. He took another match from his pocket and struck it. The path before them moved fairly straight ahead, meaning they were moving deeper and deeper into the rock and no closer to the surface.

He glanced over his shoulder to Hannah, who was, for all her serenity, pale and a little shaky. With her cane in one hand and the other hand clutching at his jacket, her red hair falling in disarray around her face, her fancy cloak covered in dust, she still looked like a lady. A lady with a quick temper and a mouth to match maybe, but . . . he lowered his gaze.

"Hannah, darlin', do you have your flask with you today?"

She turned up her nose, just before the match burned to his fingers and he had to shake it out. "I don't think it will do either of us any good to get tipsy while we're lost in this cave. We need our wits about us."

He ignored her prim censure. "Are you wearing anything made of linen?"

She was silent.

"Linen, Hannah. A petticoat?"

"My petticoat is made of silk," she said frostily.

"What about your drawers?"

He heard her disgusted sigh. "This is a new low, even for you, Mr. Rourke."

"Hannah," he said softly, "take off your drawers and give them to me."

"I will not," she said sternly.

"And hand over the flask and the cane."

"Have you lost your mind?" she snapped.

"May be," Jed muttered. "May be."

* * *

His voice came out of the darkness. "I hate to ask, but I'm not wearing anything that will burn."

Burn. He was beginning to make sense. Hannah tapped the cane lightly against the wall, to orient herself and Jed. Without being prodded, he gently took the cane from her grasp. With care, she lifted her skirt and removed the flask. Using the same method, she tapped it against the wall. Jed took it, his fingers barely brushing over hers.

"You wouldn't leave me here, would you?" she asked as she lifted her skirt and untied the tapes at her waist. In this complete darkness, she didn't have to worry about Jed seeing anything, unless he decided to waste one of his matches to get a view of her with her skirt bunched around her waist. She worked quickly, just in case. Tapes untied, her drawers dropped easily to the ground.

"Of course not," Jed answered.

It was too dark in here, so dark she was dizzyingly disoriented when she didn't have Jed to hold on to. Cold air whipped around her legs before she dropped her skirt and retrieved her undergarment.

"All right," she said, moving cautiously forward. "Here it is." She held out the linen drawers. "Would you care to tell me exactly what you're doing?"

"I think I can make a torch."

Her cane, linen drawers, and some high-quality whiskey. Of course!

He moved closer. She heard his breath and his booted feet on the ground before her. Cautiously, feeling his way around, he took the offered item from her.

Hannah stood very still, one hand on the wall to

steady herself, while Jed went to work. She heard the tearing of fabric as he began to fashion the torch. She knew he was pouring the whiskey, totally by feel in the complete darkness, when he muttered, "What a waste." He waited a moment longer, for the liquor to seep into the fabric, she assumed, and then a match flared to life. He set the match to a bundle of what looked like damp rags at the top of her cane, and the flame took hold.

As dreary as the cavern was, the view was preferable to the complete darkness they'd battled through thus far.

Jed wasted no time. He turned and held up the torch to illuminate the tunnel before him. "Let's go," he said, glancing over his shoulder to flash a rather bleak grin in her direction.

The trail went briefly downward, which caused Jed's heart to drop, but a few minutes later the path turned up again. The torch he'd fashioned lit their way, flickering on the walls that regularly widened and then threatened to close in on them.

They couldn't go much farther tonight. Besides, unless a breeze ruffled the flame of the torch, he had no way of knowing if they were near an opening in the rock. Best to wait until morning, when hopefully a ray of light would lead them out of the cave.

Hannah kept up without a word of complaint, and when the tunnel forked and he picked one on instinct alone, she didn't argue. Still, she had to be tired.

As soon as he found a good place to stop, they'd settle in for the night.

"What color is it?" he asked, glancing over his shoulder.

"What color is what?" Hannah asked peevishly.

"The garter," he said with a grin.

There was not enough light for him to tell if her pale face blushed pink or not, but she was definitely mortified by his personal question.

"I was kinda hoping it was red," he added.

Her eyebrows lifted. "I do not own a red garter, Mr. Rourke," she said primly. "Not that it's any of your business."

"Too bad," he said as he trained his eyes on the tunnel ahead.

They walked a while longer before stepping into a clearing where the floor was relatively flat and the ceiling was high.

"This will do," he said, searching the floor for a crevice. Finding one, he jammed the end of Hannah's cane into it. The torch, securely in place, lit the chamber dimly.

"This will do for what?" Hannah asked, wiping the back of her hand across her face and pushing away the unruly strands of red hair that had fallen over her eyes.

"We'll spend the night here," he said, removing the rifle and harness from his back, taking off his long coat, and laying it on the ground, over what appeared to be the smoothest part of the cavern floor.

Hannah stared longingly at the makeshift bed.

"Sit down," he ordered. "You look tired."

Again she didn't argue with him, but lowered herself to sit on the buckskin overcoat. The torch flickered ominously, threatening to go out. It wouldn't last much longer, he knew, and he only had two matches left. He'd seen no sign that this cave was home to any predators, but that didn't mean one wasn't waiting around the next corner. He saw no reason to share that concern with Hannah.

Someone had gone to an awful lot of trouble to lure her out here, and if he hadn't found that note on her bed . . . she'd be dead now. Hannah's tongue was no match for a couple of well-aimed rifles. The thought made his blood boil. When he got out of here, someone was going to pay for this.

The torch flickered weakly, the light threatening to die and then flaring up again.

"Sit with me before it goes out," Hannah said softly.

He didn't argue, but sat beside her, the rifle close at his other side. Once the torch light died they'd be lost in complete darkness again. She didn't want him too far away when that happened, and he couldn't blame her.

"Are you afraid?" she asked, staring straight at him with those fearless eyes of hers.

"No."

"What if we don't find a way out tomorrow?"

"We will."

She didn't look down or away, wouldn't accept his assurance at face value and take comfort in it. "You don't know that," she whispered. "We might never find our way out of here."

He should've known better than to try to comfort Hannah with false hope.

"Well, everybody goes sooner or later. It's not the first time I've faced the possibility of death."

"It doesn't frighten you?"

"Of course it does. I'm not stupid. But I can take comfort in the fact that I've got no regrets about the way I've lived my life." It was the truth. He'd come close to death too many times during the war, and had begun to live each day as if it might be his last. "I'm not leaving anything undone. I don't wish I'd lived a single day differently. I've had a good life."

"No regrets," she repeated softly.

He smiled at her. "I imagine you're the same way. By God, Hannah, I've never met a woman like you before. You say what you think and you back down from nobody."

She pinned her eyes on his face and remained silent.

"What about you?" he asked softly, his smile fading. "Are you scared?"

"Terrified," she whispered.

The torch flickered and went out.

Eleven

Hannah held her breath for a long moment after the torch light extinguished. The plunge into darkness was complete, and somehow more frightening than anything that had happened to this point. If, come morning, they didn't see a hint of light, this inky blackness was the last thing she'd know.

"It must be nice to live with no regrets," she whispered. "You're wrong about me living that way, too. I have more regrets than I can list in a single night." She was suddenly certain they were going to die here, and she would never get the opportunity to live even a single day of her life the way Jed did.

"What kinds of regrets?" he asked, his voice low and gruff.

Only his presence kept her from succumbing to complete panic. His warmth and his voice were so near, and they comforted her. In truth, they were a tether to her sanity.

She shook her head slowly. "There are too many," she whispered.

"Pick a few."

Did she want to spend her last night reminiscing about her regrets? She hadn't been exaggerating when she'd said there were too many to list. But she didn't want to sit here in silence, either. In complete darkness she could see nothing. She could just feel, and smell, and hear. She didn't want silence to go with the darkness.

"I wish I'd spent more time with Rose, instead of waiting until this calamity brought me here," she said. "I should have stood up to my father when he insisted that she was no longer my sister, and after he died . . . After he died I should have asked Rose to come home and bring her family with her."

"Why didn't you?"

How like Jed Rourke. Right to the point. "I don't know." The stone was cold beneath her backside, even with Jed's coat spread across the floor. Now that they were no longer moving at a steady pace, the air seemed colder, almost icy. "Father was not an easy man to defy, and after he passed away . . . I don't know. Maybe I was afraid she'd say no. Maybe I was afraid she'd say yes, and come home, and then turn out to be like everyone else." Like the *friends* who came to her when they needed money, like the men who courted her with one eye on her and the other on her bank account.

"What else," Jed asked, not pressing for explanations. "What else do you regret?"

It didn't matter that she might die here. She was not about to reveal her deepest regrets to Jed Rourke. "I regret that I never went to Paris."

"Paris, Texas?" he asked, puzzled. "Ain't nothing special. I can tell you that."

"Paris, France," she said with a smile in the dark. "And Egypt and Italy and the Orient. I've read so many books about those places, in the comfort and safety of my library, but until I came here I'd never stepped foot out of Alabama."

"Rock Creek is a harsh place to start your world travels," Jed said with a touch of humor.

"Yes, I realize that."

She didn't want to sit here and agonize over all her mistakes! The prospect was much too depressing.

"What about you, Jed? Do you truly have no regrets? Not a single one?"

He breathed long and slow. The sound was comforting in the dark. Real and honest. "Well, maybe one."

"I knew it. I told you my deepest regrets, the least you can do is share your one."

He shifted his big body beside her, sighed once. "Ever since I met you, I've wanted to do something."

Her smile faded. Whatever he wanted, it would likely not be pleasant. She remembered when they'd first met, on the stage to Rock Creek. They'd argued constantly, and he'd had to forcibly carry her away from the road. She'd called him something terrible, hadn't she? On more than one occasion.

His hand on her shoulder startled her, and as that hand moved slowly and cautiously to her cheek she knew what Jed wanted, what he regretted not doing. He was going to hit her. Well, it was only fair. She'd slapped him soundly, once, and had whacked him with her cane on more than one occasion.

And now it was her fault he was trapped in a cold, dark cave. He'd come here to rescue her, after she'd stupidly followed the instructions she'd received in the anonymous note.

She closed her eyes and steeled herself for the blow that was sure to come. Jed was a gentleman, in his own way, so she expected the blow would be tempered, somewhat.

When he laid her lips over hers she was so shocked she jerked slightly away. But when she realized what it was that Jed regretted, that he had no intention of *hitting* her, she leaned forward and into the kiss.

His lips were firm and tender, and when he placed his hand at the back of her head she felt completely and totally encompassed in warmth and affection. Oh, you wouldn't think it to look at the man, but he had a gentle way about him, when it was appropriate.

Jed moved his mouth over and against hers, tasting and raking, nibbling and sucking. Hannah tasted back. They shifted their bodies gradually and drifted close to each other, an arm lifting here, a shoulder dropping here. When Jed tilted his head and pressed his face to hers, his mustache hairs tickled her nose and the roughness of his beard rubbed roughly against her chin. She liked it. She liked it all.

And all the while they kissed, her insides leaped and her heart constricted. She couldn't breathe properly. Her knees began to wobble.

Jed broke the kiss, suddenly and with a muttered curse. For a moment she wondered if she'd done something wrong. Good heavens, she didn't want him to *stop*.

"Hannah Winters," he finally whispered, "you take my breath away."

Hannah decided that was, perhaps, the nicest compliment she'd ever received. Still, *thank you* seemed inappropriate at the moment. "That was . . . nice." Oh, she was never at a loss for words! Jed would think she was a stammering idiot. "And I'm not quite so cold anymore, except for my backside," she added quickly, trying to salvage her pride. "I swear, I feel like I'm sitting on a block of ice."

Before she knew what he intended, Jed scooped her up and dragged her onto his lap, facing him. Strong arms locked around her waist, and he held her there.

"Better?" he asked gruffly.

Hannah wound her arms around his neck, to steady herself and for additional warmth. "Yes, thank you. Much better." She'd never sat in a man's lap before, so she held herself stiffly away from him, trying for a proper position. Not that it mattered. No one could see her here, not even Jed.

"Relax," he said, tugging slightly against her waist so that she fell against his chest.

She did, allowing herself to melt into his broad chest and lay her head on his shoulder. He held her close and tight, his arms securely around her. It just made sense, she reasoned, for them to share body heat in these dire circumstances.

"Nice," he mumbled, his mouth close to her ear.

"Well, it was," she whispered. "Forgive me if my response wasn't eloquent enough for you."

He muttered something that was surely obscene.

"Scoundrel," she whispered.

"Hussy," he countered.

"Shaggy beast," she said softly, and not without affection, her fingers finding and ever so softly caressing the ends of his long hair.

"Virgin," Jed sighed. "I swear to God, Hannah, if you weren't a . . . a damned *lady*, I'd have you here and now. You make me crazy, and I want, more than anything"—he took a deep, stilling breath—"never mind."

For the first time, she was glad of the darkness. She didn't want Jed to see her face at the moment.

"I'm not, you know," she whispered.

"A hussy?" Jed asked, shifting his weight and readjusting her on his lap. "Hell, I know . . ."

"A virgin," she interrupted.

No regrets. She didn't know what it was like to live that way, to take what you wanted and everyone else be damned. Oh, she could be difficult, she knew that, and she was accustomed to having her way. But that didn't mean she always got what she wanted.

She lifted her head and laid her hand over Jed's beard-roughened cheek. Her thumb brushed his mouth, and as she leaned forward to kiss him she had no regrets. Not a single one.

The information sank into Jed's muddled brain as Hannah, amazingly enough, kissed him. She came to him hesitantly, the muscles in the shapely back he caressed taunt and her kiss uncertain. He was pretty sure she held her breath.

She took her mouth from his, dragging her lips slowly away and hesitating so that at the last second their mouths barely touched. "Do you mind?" she whispered, and he heard the uncertainty in her lowered voice.

He threaded his fingers through the hair at the back of her head and held her close. "That you're not a virgin?"

She nodded. He couldn't see her, but he felt the uncertain dip of her head.

He kissed her quickly and softly, his mouth barely touching hers. "Not if you don't mind that I'm not a virgin, either," he teased. He couldn't deny that he was curious, but the questions he had could wait. The way he felt right now, those questions could wait all night. Maybe even forever.

Since the moment he'd met Hannah he'd alternately wanted and cursed her. Now that he had her in his lap, cuddly and willing and with no avenue of escape, he didn't know where to start. Damnation, he'd never not known where to start before!

He wanted their coming together to be perfect, for her and for him. He didn't want her to regret this, whether they found their way out tomorrow morning or not.

While he kissed her, he brushed his hand up her side and over the swell of her breast. She filled his hand, soft, warm, and full, and inhaled sharply when he brushed his palm over her nipple. But she didn't draw away or stop kissing him.

Hannah kissed like she did everything else, no holds barred. There was innocence in the way she came to him, as if she'd never kissed before, but there was no shyness in the way she tasted and sucked, or in the way she answered when he slipped his tongue into her mouth.

If this really was the end, if tonight was his last night on this earth . . . Hell, he couldn't think of anyone he'd rather spend it with.

He snaked his hand beneath Hannah's skirt, feeling his way up her leg. Again she tensed, her entire body stiffening in his arms. But she relaxed slowly, unfolding in his arms and accepting the presence of his hand on her calf, her knee, her thigh. His palm skimmed over the garter, and he stopped his upward progress to trail his fingers over it. He felt silk and lace, a satin ribbon.

"Black," she whispered, taking her mouth from his just long enough to breathe the single word.

"What?" he muttered.

"The garter," she said, raking her mouth over his. "It's black, with a small, pink satin rose on the side."

He found the rose with his fingers. Damnation, black was *almost* as sexy as red. Impossibly, he got harder, more impatient to be inside her. What was wrong with him? He wasn't a kid about to get his first lay!

And neither was she.

He left his examination of her garter behind and trailed his hand up her leg, his fingers teasing as they crossed from stockinged leg to silky bare thigh. The skin he caressed was soft and yielding, warm and sensitive. Hannah quivered as he rocked his fingers there. He felt the quiver in her lips as well as in her thigh, just as he felt his own growing urgency in the thud of his heart and the growing ache in his body.

When he touched her intimately she inhaled sharply and stiffened, but only for a moment. After her initial reaction she melted against him, and as he began to stroke with his fingers she parted her legs a little wider and deepened the kiss that continued uninterrupted.

He had long ago stopped feeling the cold air that filled the cave. Right now all he felt was Hannah, her willingness and her desire, and his own need to have her. It drowned out everything else.

With his arms supporting her as if she might break, he laid her down on his buckskin coat and pushed her skirt high. She kissed him while he hovered above her, anxiously working the buttons that held his trousers closed, freeing himself to sink inside her at last.

She spread her legs wide, wrapped them around him as he guided himself inside her wet, tight body.

Her body yielded to him, but the acceptance was gradual, almost prudent. She wasn't afraid, he knew she wasn't afraid, but she was cautious. Uncertain, still. He pushed deeper with care, taking his time, mindful that he didn't want to hurt her, not even a little. Taking his time at this moment was the hardest thing he'd ever done, but it was right, and it was worth it. With every moment that passed, every heartbeat, every sigh, she gave more of herself to him.

And then he was inside her, completely, fully. He hated the darkness, because he wanted to see her face. He wanted to watch her shatter beneath him. He wanted to see her lips as they parted and cried out.

He stroked gently, withdrawing and thrusting to fill her again. Soon she began to rock with him, to meet each thrust with one of her own.

They were so in tune he felt every change in Hannah: the way she rose to him, the catch in her breath, the increasingly insistent beat of her heart. She held him tight and swayed against him, and when she climaxed, her inner muscles squeezed and milked him. She inhaled sharply, and exhaled with his name on her tongue.

One last time he buried himself inside her, thrusting deep and hard as he pumped his seed and gave in to the most intense pleasure he'd ever known.

Ah, he could die happy here. He could lay his head down on Hannah and expire in the dark a very happy man.

"Oh, my," she said breathlessly as she draped her arms around his neck, "that was extraordinary."

"Extraordinary. That's a lot better than *nice*," he teased.

"Yes, but . . . but it was so . . . so . . ."

He laid his forehead against hers. Maybe she wasn't a virgin, but what had happened between them had been a new experience for her. He had felt it in her response and he heard it now, in her voice. "You want to tell me about it?" he whispered.

"No," she said softly. "Not . . . not like this."

He kissed her, sensing that Hannah needed to be kissed every bit as much as he'd needed to be inside her.

Clothes righted, hearts beating slower, Hannah and Jed snuggled between his buckskin coat and her velvet cloak. She still glowed from the inside out, with a warmth that didn't fade now that the lovemaking was over.

She had never known there was such pleasure to be had from being with a man.

"Do you want to tell me now?" Jed whispered.

She sighed and nestled up against him, for comfort more than warmth. "I hardly think you would find the story interesting."

"Is he one of your regrets?" His low-pitched voice rumbled within his chest, against her ear.

"The big one," she whispered.

"When we get out of here, do you want me to kill him for you?"

In spite of the apparent seriousness of his offer, she smiled widely. "Thank you, but that won't be necessary."

She was lost inside a huge rock formation, deep within the earth, and might not find her way out. Wishing Rock might be her gravestone, and yet . . . at the moment she felt no panic. How could she? Jed held her fast, and her body still thrummed with the memory of what they'd shared.

"His name," she said softly, "was Richard." Handsome, sweet, refined Richard. "I'd known him all my life. I told you what had happened with Rose, how she and Baxter ran off not long after the war began. Well, for the next few years, there was no talk of suitors or marriage or anything other than war and survival.

"When the war was finally over, my father found himself in better financial shape than his neighbors. He'd buried most of his money, and when the war was over he became close to those he needed to befriend in order to keep what he had. Many times, when we were alone, he said that while he was loyal to the Confederacy he was not stupid." Goodness, she had never known a more stupid man than her father! Why hadn't she realized it then?

The air in the cave was cold, but she was not. Jed's chest was hard but comfortable to rest against. She felt sheltered here. For the first time in her life, someone protected her. Against the cold, against loneliness.

"It wasn't long after the war that Richard came calling," she said lowly. "He was attentive and gracious, and completely relentless."

Jed stiffened. "Did he force himself on you? If he did, I swear, I'll . . ."

"No," she interrupted.

Jed's entire, wonderful body, the length and breadth of it, eased in her arms.

"After several months of arduous courting, Richard took me aside and told me he loved me. He asked me to marry him, and in the heat of the moment, we . . . we . . ."

"I don't need the details of this part," Jed said roughly. "I don't think I'd like it."

She would spare him the details of the way Richard had taken her virginity, quickly and painfully, against a stable wall. She would spare him, as well, the mortifying detail that she hadn't cared that it had been painful, that she had thought herself in love and willing to do anything and everything to keep that love alive.

"We went to my father to tell him the good news, and for Richard to formally ask for my hand in marriage." She felt the cold again. No matter how warm Jed was, no matter how tightly he held her, the chill would not abate. "My father refused," she whispered. "He told Richard that if he took me as his wife I was all he'd get. That if I married him I'd go with nothing but the clothes on my back." She swallowed hard. "I was ready to go, to run away with the man who loved me, the way Rose had. To escape from that house and my father."

Jed ran his hands up and down her back, comforting her as if he knew what was coming.

"Richard didn't even look at me as he left," she whispered. "He just turned and walked away. I could still feel him inside me. I burned and bled, and even worse, I could hear his words, *I love you,* echoing in my ears, knowing as he closed the door behind him that it had been a lie."

"Maybe I will kill him," Jed whispered.

Hannah ignored him. She had never spoken about this to anyone. Not ever. She tried so hard not to even think about that night. "After Richard left, my father told me that if I was going to be foolish enough to spread my legs for every man who told me he loved me, that I'd damn well better learn to be careful about it, because if I shamed him with rumors or a bastard child he'd kick me out without a dime. He told me, in no uncertain terms, that I wasn't the kind of woman who would inspire a great love. Such honors were reserved for beauties like Rose."

"Your father sounds like a real son of a bitch."

"He was a lonely, bitter man."

Jed kissed the top of her head. "He was also wrong. You're the most remarkable woman I've ever met. If that Richard had found himself momentarily with even *half* a brain, he would've carried you out of there that night and told your father to go to hell."

Hannah closed her eyes and brushed her cheek against Jed's chest.

"But I'm glad he didn't," Jed said softly, his

voice a bit calmer. "If he had, you wouldn't be here now."

He liked her. She knew it was true, as he held her and told her he was glad she was here, trapped inside the rock with him.

"I can't believe I told you all that," she said. "I've never told anyone what happened that night."

"I guess I'm just an easy man to talk to."

"You are," she agreed, making herself more comfortable against his chest. "And right now that night seems like . . . like such a long time ago." An age ago, not worth secret tears or a lifetime of regret.

Hannah was about to doze off when Jed's voice intruded on her half sleep. "If we get out of here, is tonight going to be one of your regrets?"

"No," she answered without hesitation and with a soft smile on her face.

Twelve

Hannah woke slowly, remembering as she came awake where she was, how dire the circumstances were. She didn't feel at all frantic. Her nose was buried in Jed's warm chest, his arms encircled her, and her legs were entwined with his. The ground was hard, the air cold, and her muscles ached from walking through the sloping tunnels and sleeping on a bed of rock.

And she felt oddly wonderful.

"You're awake," Jed whispered.

"Yes," she murmured. "Did you sleep at all?"

"A little."

She had no idea if it was day or night; she couldn't begin to decipher how much time had passed since she'd fallen asleep in Jed's arms.

Soon they would have to get up and resume their trek through the caverns, waiting for a speck of light or a hint of wind to reveal another exit. If there was one.

But for now . . . For now she was content to lie here, warm in the cold cave, Jed's arms protecting her from the hard, harsh rock.

His hands rubbed up and down her back, the movement slow and comforting. She closed her

eyes and savored the caress of those big hands as
they dipped lower to cup her backside and pull
her tighter against him.

So close against Jed's body, chest-to-chest and
thigh-to-thigh, she felt almost a part of him, as if
she could dissolve and seep into him. His arms
were strong and held her close. The length of his
manhood pressed against her, hard and insistent.

He wanted her. There was no ulterior motive
to his desire, no secrets behind the need. He
wanted *her.* It was a simple emotion, an uncomplicated passion.

She wanted him, too, more than she'd ever
thought possible.

When he tilted her head back and kissed her,
she met his ardor without restraint. Lips parted,
tongue searching, she gave herself over to the intense physical need that coursed through her
quickly and easily.

Perhaps she should be shy, demure and coy, but
that had never been her way. And what she felt
demanded boldness. A hungry parting of her lips,
a raw exploration of Jed's mouth with her tongue.

Without reserve, she laid her hand over the evidence of his desire, the long, hard length beneath
his buckskin trousers, and as he kissed her deeply,
she trailed her fingers up the length and back
down again. He shuddered, faintly, from the lips
that captured hers to the long leg that draped
possessively over hers.

Jed pushed up her skirt and laid his hand on
her thigh, trailing his palm up to caress her bare
backside and pull her even closer. Impossibly
closer. Her body tingled in anticipation; she quivered from the inside out.

Working entirely from feel, she began to unfasten the buttons that restrained him. It was a slow process, but one by one she managed, her fingers working deftly and without hurry.

Jed lifted her leg and moved it so her thigh draped over his hip, bringing them even closer together. Her body throbbed, her heart increased its pace and pounded hard as she pressed her chest to his and crooked her thigh higher, raking it up his side.

His hand grazed up her leg, from her knee to the bare flesh of her inner thigh. A large, rough palm rested there for a moment as they kissed, and then he touched her intimately. He found the sensitive nub near her damp entrance and stroked it until she trembled with the need to have him inside her. Her body quaked at its core, in anticipation and in urgency.

She couldn't tell Jed that she loved him, though she was beginning to suspect it was the truth. He had stirred her blood in one way or another since the moment they'd met. What they had was more than physical. He made her angry, and happy, and he brightened her whole world with a word or a grin. Jed brought her alive for the first time in her life. She had certainly never felt this way about any man before.

No, she couldn't tell him that she loved him, but she could return last night's compliment without giving away too much. "Jed Rourke," she whispered, "you take my breath away."

He entered her then, pushing himself inside her slowly, stretching her impossibly. The sensation erased all thoughts of love and dire circumstances, until there was only this.

He stroked her languidly, rocking against and into her without the impatience she herself felt. Heavens, he really did take her breath away. She rocked into him, trying to urge him deeper, threading her fingers through his hair and holding on tight as if that would somehow help. His pace increased in time with the urgency she felt growing with every thrust.

With a growl, he smoothly rolled her onto her back, thrusting deep to fill her completely. She cried out as almost immediately an intense pleasure billowed through her. She felt Jed's fulfillment as she cried out, delighted in the shudder and the release deep inside her body the way she delighted in every other sensation he'd introduced her to. She arched her back, determined to savor every tremor, every lingering quiver of their shared pleasure.

He drifted down to cover her heavily, to breathe deeply in her ear and kiss her neck, there just beneath the earlobe. All was heavenly, until she suddenly realized that it was much *colder* than it had been a few moments ago.

"Oh," she muttered, then louder. "Oh!"

"What's wrong?" Jed asked, lifting his weight from her body.

"I rolled off your coat," she said quickly.

He remedied the situation immediately, whirling onto his back and carrying her with him. When they came to a stop she rested atop him, her head on his chest, her legs straddling him.

"Well, this is a rather interesting position," she whispered as Jed grabbed her cloak and covered them both with it.

"Hannah Winters," he said softly, "you are a wicked woman."

"Complaining?" she asked.

"No," he whispered.

For a few moments they lay there, together and warm and satisfied. Soon it would be time to move on; she knew that. She also knew that if anyone could find a way out of here, it was Jed Rourke.

He tensed beneath her. "Did you hear that?"

"No."

Moving quickly, he set her aside and rose to his feet. "Listen," he whispered.

As she righted her clothes she did listen, straining. "I don't hear anything."

"Give me your hand," Jed ordered, and she obeyed, lifting her arm, knowing he would find it in the dark. He did, grasping her hand firmly and assisting her to her feet. "Time to move on."

"I know," she whispered.

By feel alone they found and donned their outer garments, her velvet cloak and his buckskin coat, the rifle and leather scabbard. They never drifted far apart. Wandering too far apart in this darkness could be disastrous. She could not imagine being lost in this inky enclosure without Jed.

He found her face with his fingers and kissed her quickly. Trailing those fingers over her shoulder and down her arm, he found and clasped her hand.

"Let's get out of here, darlin'."

He struck a match to get his bearings. Without a hint of light, he and Hannah might wander around in this chamber without ever finding their way out.

Going by the position of the torch that he'd jammed into a crevice, he noted the tunnel they'd emerged from. At the opposite end of the cavern there were two other tunnel entrances.

He glanced down at Hannah just before the flame reached his fingers. Her hair was in tangles, she was covered with dust and dirt, and her clothes were ripped and in disarray.

And she was so beautiful his heart damn near stopped.

Holding Hannah's hand, he picked a tunnel. There was nothing to do but forge forward, putting one foot in front of the other and hoping for the best. They hadn't gone far when the tunnel narrowed, and he and Hannah could no longer proceed side by side.

"Grab on to my coat, like you did yesterday," he said, resting one hand against the wall and reluctantly releasing his hold on Hannah. His fingers drifted over her palm as she took her hand from his.

She obeyed without question, grabbing on to his coat, and they proceeded with caution. She stayed closer today than she had yesterday, her body so near to his he could feel the brush of her breasts against his back. There were no tears, no weepy questions about whether or not they'd ever get out of here. . . . She just held on and followed silently. Damn, what a woman.

The path they were on definitely led up. He took careful steps, to keep from tripping over some unseen obstacle as he made his way up the dark pathway.

They'd been walking for at least a quarter of an hour before he heard it again. A noise. A voice. His name.

"Did you hear that?" he asked, his voice low.

"Yes," Hannah whispered.

He struck the last match and held it before him. The path led straight ahead and slightly upward. Before he could move forward or shake out the match, a faint gust of wind drifting through the tunnel blew out the flame. In the renewed darkness, he grinned widely.

"We're going to make it out of here, Hannah," he said as he stepped confidently forward.

"I know." She sounded not at all surprised.

It wasn't long before a hint of light made the darkness not quite complete. Shadows took the place of inky black. He could see the shape of his hand against the wall.

And someone called his name again.

"We're here!" he shouted.

There was no place to go but straight ahead. The light increased as they went, and so did the breeze. The medley of gruff voices, prettier than any music he'd ever heard, grew louder.

They could see the tunnel ahead, now, and still Hannah didn't release her hold on him. He didn't want her to. They stepped up and into a wide chamber much like the one they'd spent the night in. Sunlight spilled in from a crevice fifty feet above and laid its bright, beautiful mark on the cavern floor. Jed looked up and saw a couple of familiar faces looking down.

Rico grinned, and Sullivan swore softly.

"I knew if anyone could find us, it would be you two," Jed said gratefully.

"Miss Winters is with you?" Sullivan asked.

In answer, Hannah peeked around Jed's side. She continued to hold on tight. "I'm here."

Rico tossed down one end of a rope, and Jed set about tying it around Hannah's waist. He double-checked each knot, and tied the rope around twice, just to be safe. When he was satisfied that she was securely and safely hitched, he laid his hands on her shoulders and looked her in the eye. "You ready?"

"For anything," she whispered, grabbing on to the rope with both hands.

He grinned and gave the order to pull her up. Immediately, she was jerked off her feet and hauled up. He held his breath as he watched her dangling in the air, and breathed again only when he saw that Reese was there to help her once she'd reached the gap in the rock above.

Moments later the rope dropped again, and Sullivan stuck his head through the aperture.

"Tie yourself up good, Jed. It's going to take all of us to lift you out of there."

He quickly cinched himself up tight, and then lifted one hand and gave the okay.

His skyward movement was considerably slower than Hannah's had been, but then he weighed almost twice as much as she did. When he was close to the top he began to climb, hand over hand, toward the bright sunlight.

The light hurt his eyes, but the sun on his face was warmer, more wonderful than he could've imagined. When he reached the top and hauled himself onto the rock, Reese and Hannah were there to help him the rest of the way out.

By the light of day he saw that Hannah wasn't

only disheveled and dusty, she had a hell of a beard burn on her chin and one cheek. Her fair skin was no match for his whiskers.

And she looked at him with such clear, fearless eyes, her tangled hair catching the rays of the sun and turning flame red.

Rico and Sullivan dropped the rope and came forward, tired smiles on their faces.

"What happened?" Sullivan asked. "Miss Winters's rented horse came back to the livery on its own; then Benedict came into town last night and said the horse you bought from him yesterday showed up at his place saddled but riderless."

Hannah stepped around Reese, and Jed placed a tired arm casually over her shoulder. "Someone lured Hannah out here with a note saying they knew who really killed Clancy. They tried to kill her."

"And you?" Sullivan asked.

"I came out here after I found this." He dug deep in his pocket and pulled out the crumpled note. "There were two of them."

Sullivan studied the note with a frown on his face. "You found this where?" he asked.

"In her room."

Sullivan glanced up and raised his eyebrows in a silent question Jed was not ready to answer.

"We tracked the horses here at sunup and saw the cave-in," Rico said as Sullivan reread the note. "Spent the rest of the morning looking for another opening." He smiled. "We should have known you would find your way out."

"Whoever lured me here is no doubt the real killer," Hannah said sharply. "Now, do you all believe me?"

The guys looked skeptical, still.

"Might not make a difference," Sullivan said lowly. "The trial is underway. It may even be over."

"I'm Baxter's counsel," Hannah snapped. "They wouldn't dare start without me."

Sullivan shrugged his shoulders apologetically.

"Where are the horses?" Jed asked, leading Hannah away from the opening in the rock.

"Down the hill," Rico said, pointing.

They all followed Rico down the rocky path, over loose stones and natural stairsteps, and down sheer, short drops. He never completely let go of Hannah.

At the base of the hill were four horses. The three the guys had ridden out that morning, and Jed's new sorrel.

Jed pointed to the grouping of rocks where the bushwhackers had hidden. "They were there, two shooters," he said. "You should be able to track them. Don't kill them when you find 'em, though. I'd like that privilege for myself."

Jed briefly patted the sorrel on the neck, then stepped into the stirrup and hoisted himself into the saddle. Looking down, he offered his hand to Hannah. Without hesitation she took it, and he quickly and easily hauled her up and dropped her in his lap, both legs dangling to one side as if he were her own personal sidesaddle.

"We're going to see if we can't stop a trial."

"It's not enough," Sullivan said as he mounted his own horse smoothly.

"What do you mean it's not enough?" Hannah asked, her voice tired but still strong enough to be piercing.

Sullivan set calm eyes on her. "What happened to you would be enough to make me think twice, but I'm afraid it's too late for that. Everything is in the judge's hands now, and he'll either claim that you're making up the story to get Baxter off, or that what happened had nothing to do with Clancy's murder."

"But why else . . ."

"Save your arguments for the judge, Miss Winters," Sullivan interrupted. "And I'd suggest you hurry."

Jed grabbed the reins and Hannah and whirled the sorrel around to race to town.

The ride from Wishing Rock to Rock Creek had been fast and furious, but Hannah had not been afraid as the ground flew past. Jed held her tight, and she felt no fear. Her mind had flown as the horse had, over what had happened last night and what was still to happen today.

It looked as if every resident of Rock Creek had crowded into the hotel lobby, which had been converted to a courtroom for the day. Eyes were trained unerringly forward; no one looked Hannah's way as she tried to make her way to the front of the room.

She ached all over, she was starving, her mouth and throat were dry, but there was no time to even think about her discomfort. Time was quickly running out. The foreman of the jury stood.

"Wait," she said, but her voice was weak, too dry to be strong enough to be heard in this crowd.

The foreman read the verdict. *Guilty.* Hannah stopped in the middle of the room as the spectators nodded in satisfaction. She was too late.

Jed stood beside her, silent and pensive. God, she wanted to fall into him; she wanted to hide her face in his chest and cry. She had come here to help her sister, and she had failed miserably.

Rose shot to her feet. "I can't let you do this," she said, her voice stronger than Hannah's had been.

Baxter, who had shown no emotion upon the reading of the verdict, rose to his feet and pointed at Rose. "Sit down and shut up."

Staring at Baxter, Rose shook her head. "No." She turned her eyes to the judge. Her face went ghostly white, and she looked as if she might keel over at any moment. She seemed to reel on her feet. "My husband didn't kill anyone. I stabbed Reverend Clancy."

"Rose, sit down." Baxter turned to the judge himself. "Excuse my wife, your honor. She's hysterical; that's all I can say. The jury had it right." He lifted his chin defiantly. "I killed Reverend Clancy, and good riddance."

"No," Rose shouted. "He's covering for me; can't you see that?"

Excited whispers made their way through the room, growing and building like a tidal wave.

"Well, I'll be damned," Jed muttered. "You were right all along."

The crowd grew louder; people no longer whispered or remained in their seats. Everyone reacted in one way or another to the outbursts. Hannah rose up on her toes, but she couldn't see anything, not even Rose. She couldn't move, as the crowd pressed around her, jostling her and threatening to push her back.

Jed took her arm and made his way through the crowd easily, guiding her alongside him. He headed straight for the baffled judge.

"Your Honor," he said as he approached the table where the judge sat.

The judge, a younger man than Hannah had expected, laid his eyes on Jed. *"You,"* he breathed with evident animosity.

Jed smiled down at Hannah. "Harry and I are old friends."

"I can see that."

He returned his attention to the judge. "Harry . . ." In apparent apology, he offered a sheepish smile. *"Your Honor,* I have something to say."

The noise from the crowd eventually died down, until all was silent but for the occasional sob from a distraught Rose.

"Your Honor, the jury has found Baxter Sutton guilty of murder, but you're the one who sets the sentence. Now, I know murder is a serious charge, and under the usual circumstances a hanging would be forthcoming."

Rose wailed.

"But the fact of the matter is, Reverend Clancy was a no-good backstabbing womanizer, and Sutton was just defending his wife and his family. I would've done the same thing in his shoes." He leaned close to the table and lowered his voice. "Of course that's the kind of man I am. I have honor, Harry. I defend my own. And I can be trusted with even the most scandalous secrets." He winked at the suddenly pale judge.

"What do you suggest, Mr. Rourke?" Harry asked, his left eyebrow twitching nervously.

"Sutton has served over a month in the Rock Creek jail. I'd say that's good enough."

There was a moment of hesitation while the judge pursed his lips and shook his head. Finally, he brought down his gavel. "Time served."

A puzzled Baxter looked at Hannah and Jed, and then at the judge. "Are you saying I'm free to go?"

The judge shook his head. "Yep. Try not to kill anyone else. And in the future keep knives out of your wife's reach. I don't want to see either of you ever again."

"You won't," Baxter promised, and then he ran through the mob to the row where Rose sat, still sobbing.

Hannah smiled up at Jed. "You're amazing," she whispered.

He grinned down at her.

"Now all we have to do is find the man who really killed Clancy," she said. That man was no doubt the one who had tried to kill her. Where would the trail the sheriff and his friends tracked lead?

Jed's smile faded. "Honey, Rose killed Clancy. Mystery solved."

Hannah could not believe what she was hearing. "She did not. When she said that she was just attempting to get Baxter off. They were covering for each other."

"No. I saw her face when she confessed. She did it."

"Did not."

"Did."

Hannah glared at him. "Then who tried to kill me yesterday?" Ha! Let him come up with an answer for that one.

"Oh, could be one of many," he grumbled. "You've managed to piss off a shitload of people since you got here."

"No one who would . . . who would"—oh, she couldn't catch her breath!—"who would go to such extreme measures."

"Hannah," Jed said, lowering his head and his voice, "you provoke *extreme* at every turn."

"You obstinate miscreant."

"Stubborn wench."

"You need a bath."

He grinned. "So do you."

Hannah spun around and stalked away, her spine straight and her chin high. She couldn't get near Rose at the moment; her sister was so completely surrounded by friends and the out-and-out curious. Besides, she felt too close to losing control, too close to hysteria. That simply would not do.

Clinging to what was left of her poise, she made her way to the stairs and her room. She scanned the faces she passed, faces most often smiling or confused. One face she spotted that did not give in to a smile belonged to the widow Clancy, who glared at Jed and then at Hannah. Sylvia couldn't be happy about Jed coming forward to see that Baxter received the lightest possible sentence, especially since she'd specifically asked him to see that Baxter hung for his alleged crime.

Baxter was safe, but that wasn't enough. Justice would not be served until the real killer was caught and Baxter's and Rose's names were cleared. If she had to continue the investigation on her own, then so be it.

In the safety of her room, she locked the door and leaned against it. So much had happened in the last twenty-four hours! She didn't think she would be able to absorb it all until she'd had a bath, a meal, a shot of whiskey, and a good night's sleep in a soft, warm bed.

She peeled off her cloak and had begun to unbutton her jacket when she caught a glimpse of herself in the mirror. Her hair stood up and fell down, tangled and shooting out in all directions. Her suit was ruined, filthy and torn in several places. Her face was pale, there were dark circles under her eyes, and worst of all, most mortifying, were the red places on her chin and cheek. The marks had been left by Jed's beard, certainly. Everyone who had seen her downstairs surely knew . . .

No. No one had been looking at her. All eyes had been on Baxter and Rose, and then on Jed.

I look horrendous, Hannah thought with dismay as she raised her hand to the mark on her cheek. No wonder Jed had called her a . . . a . . . What had he called her? A stubborn wench.

Hannah smiled at the horrid reflection in the mirror. Well, she was stubborn, and he'd called her much worse names than wench.

She and Jed Rourke had nothing in common; she knew that well. He was a self-professed wanderer, a crude man who valued his freedom above all else. She had more responsibilities than most women would know in a lifetime. She had a home, and a plantation, and a family who needed her to step in and straighten things out when they fell apart.

Hannah caressed the red mark on her cheek. All her life she'd been a dutiful daughter, a fair if stern employer, and a responsible member of the community. For the first time in her life, she felt like a woman.

It had been easy, last night, to forget who and what she was. She could forgive herself the foolishness of surrender, given the circumstances, but she couldn't allow it to happen again. There was too much at stake. She had too much to lose.

Her heart.

Thirteen

Sullivan, Rico, and Reese returned with nothing to show for their efforts. The bushwhackers had been careful, backtracking and then leading their horses over rocky terrain impossible to track. Jed told them what had happened at the trial, leaving out his parting argument with Hannah.

"You were right about one thing," Sullivan said as they walked into the deserted dining room. "There were two of them, a big man and a smaller accomplice. The second shooter could've been a kid, but I couldn't tell."

"It could have been a woman in a man's boots," Rico added.

Sullivan shook his head. "I don't think so."

"Sullivan just doesn't think a woman would be devious enough to sneak up and shoot another woman," Reese added with a tired smile.

"The second shooter was either a kid or a skinny man," Sullivan insisted.

"I think Eden has influenced your thinking where women are concerned," Reese said.

"All right," Sullivan conceded grudgingly. "The second shooter *might* have been a woman."

"Oliver Jennings," Jed said thoughtfully. "He

pulled a gun on Hannah once, when she asked him about his sister and Clancy. He wasn't happy to have that old rumor dug up again."

Sullivan shook his head. "Maybe, but then who was the larger man?"

"Coulda been anyone."

"Anyone wearing a new pair of fancy boots," Sullivan added.

"Wouldn't hurt to talk to Jennings, now would it?"

Sullivan nodded. "Tomorrow morning."

Eden, hearing the voices, rushed into the room and straight to her husband. "You must be starving," she said as she went up on her toes and gave him a hug. "You will all stay for supper."

Rico and Reese declined the offer and headed home to their own wives.

"Oh, Sin," Eden said as she took Sullivan's arm and walked with him to the nearest table. "It was so exciting! Rose stood up and said she did it, and then Baxter stood up and said he did it, and then Jed spoke to the judge and Baxter was let off with time served. I still don't know who did it!"

"Rose did it," Jed said through gritted teeth. Had no one else seen the expression on her face as she confessed? She had been terrified, but she had not been lying.

Eden looked at him, wide-eyed. "I don't think so. Not *Rose.*"

"That's right. Rose is incapable of murder."

Ah, that stern voice. Jed turned to watch Hannah walk regally into the dining room. She had taken a bath, had a nap, and dressed in a simple outfit consisting of a prim white blouse and a full plum-colored skirt. Her hair was tamed and piled on top of her head. The rash on her face had faded, quite a bit, or else she had disguised the marks with face powder.

She definitely did not look like she'd spent the night trapped in a cave, sleeping on the hard, cold ground . . . wrapping her legs around him and moaning his name.

"Everyone is capable of murder," Jed argued, "in the right circumstances. Have you spoken with Rose yet? Have you asked her?"

"No." Hannah met his stony gaze with one of her own. "I fell asleep and just woke a short while ago. It's so late, I decided to wait until morning to speak with my sister." She turned her attention to Eden, and her entire face softened, became unbearably beautiful.

"I was wondering if it's too late to get something to eat. I am positively starving."

Eden smiled widely. "How about a late supper for four. I was waiting for Sin to get home, and Jed didn't eat earlier, I know."

A touch of mild distress crossed Hannah's face. "That would be lovely."

"You two look none the worse for wear," Eden said cheerfully as they passed around butter and jam for the biscuits. Scrambled eggs and thick slices of ham finished off the full plates. "You certainly don't look like you spent the night trapped in a cave. It must've been dreadful."

Hannah had the urge to reach across the table and slap the sheriff, who looked as if he were about to burst out laughing. He contained his hilarity very well, though she imagined he would share his suspicions with his wife later. Hannah was only slightly mortified.

"It was quite dreadful," she agreed, spooning a dollop of blackberry jam onto one half of her biscuit, unable to look at Jed, who sat silently at her other side.

"You're lucky you had Jedidiah with you," Eden said softly. "He can be handy to have around in a crisis."

"Handy," Hannah agreed simply, studying the blackberry jam with great interest.

The sheriff almost choked on his biscuit.

Hannah cast a quick sideways glance at Jed. He looked annoyingly wonderful, in spite of the ordeal they'd survived. He'd bathed and changed into clean clothes, and his hair hung in waving, golden strands to his shoulders. His eyes were the most beautiful thing about him, she decided as she cut a bite-sized piece of ham. Blue and spellbinding, they were his best feature.

Of course, his nose was quite nice, too. Long and straight and lovely, a man's nose set in a harshly strong face. The hair was nice, too, she conceded silently. Unfashionable, perhaps, but lovely. And his body was . . .

"Are you all right?" Eden asked softly, laying her hand over Hannah's.

Only then did Hannah realize that she'd cut a portion of her ham into tiny, tiny pieces. "I'm fine. Just very tired, still."

"Of course you are," Eden said, patting Hannah's hand affectionately. "As soon as you've eaten, it's off to bed with you."

"I slept all afternoon"—Hannah sighed—"and I'm still exhausted."

Eden smiled and laid a hand over her stomach. "I know what you mean. It's impossible to fight exhaustion. I wasn't sick at all with Fiona, and so far I haven't been sick with this one. But sometimes I feel like I could sleep twenty hours a day!"

Jed mumbled something low and indecipherable. Hannah decided it was just as well no one knew what he was grumbling.

But Eden's rambling had Hannah wondering. What if last night or this morning had left her carrying Jed's child? She hadn't thought of the possibility until now, and strangely enough she found she was not at all distressed by the idea.

If, when she returned home, she found herself with child, she'd handle it as she handled everything else. The best she could. She might take that long trip abroad she'd always wanted to take, and while she was there she'd have her baby. When she returned home she could say she'd adopted the child on her journey.

Or she could tell the truth and the rest of the world be damned.

Eden finished eating and began to carry plates and glasses to the kitchen. Her husband helped her, leaving Jed and Hannah alone at the table, two cups of weak, sweet tea before them.

"I could use a shot of whiskey," Hannah said to herself.

"Me, too," Jed grumbled. Without another word, he stood, took her hand, and pulled Hannah to her feet. "Come on."

When Eden entered the dining room from the kitchen, Jed thanked her for dinner and continued on, practically dragging Hannah into the lobby.

"Jedidiah," Eden called, "Hannah needs to get to bed!"

"I know," he mumbled as he pulled her onto the boardwalk and into the street.

They walked across the street to Three Queens, which was by far the liveliest business in Rock Creek. Music drifted toward them, the notes of a well-played piano and a lovely voice filling the air.

"Jed, really . . ." Hannah protested.

"This is the only place in town to get a decent drink, these days."

"I don't really need a drink."

"I do," he grumbled.

The place was pretty crowded, for a Monday night. A few people drank and played cards, but most of them sat and listened to the singer, Lily Salvatore.

Lily was dressed in a fancy silk gown, her hair was elaborately styled, and she was stunningly beautiful. The kind of beauty that could make a man stop in his tracks. Was that lip rouge?

Jed nodded to Rico, who stood near the stage. They weaved around tables and past the bar, to the back of the room. There, Jed opened a door and pulled her inside.

Hannah found herself in a large storeroom. Shelves were lined with glasses and bottles and trays, cartons had been shoved against the walls, and a table with a broken leg sat in the middle of it all.

Jed lit a lantern, set it on a bare space on the shelf, and closed the door.

"Sit down," he said, tipping his head to a sturdy-looking carton.

Too exhausted to argue, she sat.

Jed grabbed a bottle from the top shelf and two glasses from just beneath. He placed the glasses on the precariously balanced table in the center of the storeroom and poured.

Her brain told her clearly that last night had been a terrible mistake. But even now, exhausted and angry and befuddled, her body told her differently. All she had to do was look at Jed and her heart beat faster. A warmth, radiating from the inside out, filled her. The world became a softer, gentler place. She wanted, more than anything, to touch Jed again. To hold him.

To shift her traitorous thoughts, she spoke. "Your sister and her husband are a lovely couple, even if the sheriff is a moron."

He snorted as he placed the bottle aside and lifted their glasses. "Lovely couple, my ass. Eden could've done better. A lot better."

She took the glass he offered, but did not take her eyes from his face. "How can you say that? She obviously adores him, and he . . ."

"He can't keep his damn hands off her," Jed interrupted, as he sat on the crate next to hers. "So here she is in Rock Creek, working too hard running that hotel, raising three kids that aren't hers, one that is, and now there's another one on the way. God in heaven, I can just imagine that hotel a few years from now. If they keep this up there won't be any room for paying customers!"

Hannah smiled and took a sip of the whiskey.

"It's nothing to smile about," Jed snapped. "She could've married someone with money"—

he took a quick drink of his own—"and a little self-control."

Hannah's smile died. "Eden is wonderfully happy here," she said. "Trust me when I tell you that money doesn't guarantee such happiness."

He cast her a suspicious glance. "I know, but . . ."

"And marrying for money is the worse kind of folly," she interrupted.

Jed reached out one big hand and caressed her cheek. "I'm sorry," he whispered.

"Don't be." She sighed when he dropped his hand. "I just have a different point of view on the subject, that's all. Do you think no one has ever proposed marriage to me? I might not be a great beauty, and I might not have your sister's charm, but I do have the one thing some men run willingly and unerringly to. Money."

She would trade everything she had for someone to look at her the way the sheriff looked at his wife. She would gladly give away the plantation, the cash, the things she surrounded herself with, for that kind of happiness.

"How can you say you're not beautiful?" Jed asked gruffly.

"I have a mirror, Jed," she said, not allowing her sentimental introspection to show on her face or in her voice. "I know well my strengths and weaknesses."

His hand wandered back to touch her cheek, there where he'd left his mark on her last night. "The only weakness you have is that you're a bit too stubborn."

"That's one of the strengths," she whispered.

"Depends on which side you're on," he said with a grin.

His fingers brushed over her mouth. "I think you need a new mirror, Hannah. Have you ever taken a good look at these lips? Perfectly shaped, soft, and full, and the color of a ripe plum."

Her heart skipped a beat.

"And your eyes," he said, staring into them. "Cold as ice when you're mad, a blue-gray sky when you're happy, and always . . . always dancing."

"Some men will say anything to get what they want," she said softly.

"What do you think I want, Hannah?"

She knew what he wanted, and for once it wasn't her fortune that drew a man to her.

"When I find the person who killed Reverend Clancy, I'll have to go home," she whispered. "I have . . ."

"Responsibilities," he finished for her. "I know."

"So it would be foolish for us to get . . ."

"Attached," he supplied when she faltered.

"Attached," she repeated, "when we know I won't be here much longer. Besides," she added, trying to convince herself as well as Jed, "you and I have nothing in common."

"I wouldn't say that," he said softly, coming closer to lay his mouth over hers, briefly and so sweetly he took her breath away.

"Well, there is that," she agreed, giving in too easily.

She took another sip of her whiskey. "Tomorrow morning I'm going to talk to Rose. Maybe once I have the real story of what happened that morning, it will be easier to find the killer."

"And if Rose tells you she really did do it?"

Hannah shook her head and took another drink. A deep one. "I can't believe it's true."

"But if it is?" Jed pressed.

"Then I suppose I can go home." Oh, she didn't want to go home. She wanted to stay here almost as much as she wanted Rose not to be responsible for Reverend Clancy's death. She finished off her whiskey and set the empty glass aside.

"In that case," Jed said, drawing her to him, "we don't have a hell of a lot of time to waste."

He kissed her again, deeper this time, and she closed her eyes and relished the way he came to her. When he pulled her head against his shoulder, a strange heat washed over and through her. She was boneless; her eyes would not stay open.

"You're tired," Jed whispered.

"Uh-hmm," she moaned against his shoulder. "Maybe that whiskey wasn't such a good idea, under the circumstances."

His arms encircled her and pulled her closer, and she melted against him. Big and hard but still soft and gentle, he made the perfect resting place.

Hannah didn't drift toward sleep, she fell. Hard and fast.

Well, this was a fine mess he'd gotten himself into. Jed sat there, his back against the wall and Hannah once again sleeping in his arms. Lily's muffled voice, singing a sappy love song, drifted through the closed storeroom door.

Come tomorrow morning, Rose would tell Hannah that she was the culprit responsible for Reverend Clancy's murder. Hannah would accept that as fact, like it or not, and pack her bags. Hellfire, he wasn't ready for her to leave.

He could always go with her, for a while. With just a little persuasion he could be convinced to escort Hannah to Alabama, maybe taking a roundabout route. He wouldn't stay, though. Jed knew himself well enough to know that was impossible.

She was going to have a hard time accepting the fact that her sister had taken a man's life. It didn't make sense to Hannah, with what she knew of Rose. What she was willing to accept.

Jed had been on the side of the law most of his life. Normally, he would insist that justice be done, but he knew Rose and he knew Clancy. The preacher deserved what he got, and Rose wouldn't have done it unless she'd been panicked. Man, and woman, would do a lot in the name of survival.

It would be interesting, though, to hear Rose's version of that morning, now that the truth had come out.

He had never thought much of Baxter Sutton, that coward, but his estimation of the shopkeeper had risen a little this morning. The man had been willing to hang to save his wife. He was still willing to let everyone in town think him a murderer, so Rose would not have to live with that label.

Hannah said her brother-in-law didn't have the guts to commit murder. Taking the blame and facing a noose took more guts than the split second it took to drive a knife into a man's heart.

Lily's song ended, the crowd clapped enthusi-

astically, and unaccompanied piano music filled
the air. Hannah slept on. Jed brushed her hair
back. How could she say she was not beautiful?
She had the kind of face a man might never forget. She didn't have Eden's girlish beauty, or Lily's
exotic flair, but she had her own beauty. Her face
was valiant and fascinating, and he damn well
knew he'd never forget it.

There was a soft knock at the door, and then
it swung open slowly. Rico stuck his head in.

"We are about to lock up. Are you spending
the night here?" He smiled wickedly.

"No." Jed shifted forward, Hannah firmly in
his grasp. With one arm behind her back and the
other scooping under her knees, he stood. She
didn't move, but to turn her head toward his
chest and sigh deeply.

"She's plumb worn out," he said softly.

"I can imagine," Rico said with a nod of his
head as he backed up and opened the door wide.

Hannah weighed next to nothing, as he well
remembered. At least this time she wasn't hitting
him with her cane or pinching like the hellcat
she was beneath her buttoned-up illusion of pro-
priety.

Her cane was still in that cave, stuck in the rock
floor with her burned up drawers hanging from
the gold head. Since he'd met her she'd carried
that cane like a weapon, as diligent and skilled as
he was with his rifle. He'd have to get her another
walking stick to replace the one they'd left behind, maybe for Christmas.

If she was still here a week from now.

He echoed Rico's softly spoken good night and
headed across the street with Hannah in his arms.

The lobby was deserted, and he climbed the stairs without being forced to answer any annoying questions from his sister or his brother-in-law. In the second floor hallway, he bent down to open the door to her room, turning it with the hand that barely extended from beneath Hannah's knees. He pushed open the door with his booted foot.

By the dim light that broke through from the hallway lamp, he very carefully laid Hannah in the center of her bed. She moaned once, perhaps missing the feel of his body against hers, then rolled onto her side and instantly resumed her deep sleep.

He lit the lamp on her dresser and closed the door. Hell, he couldn't just leave her here like this!

Sitting on the edge of the bed he removed her boots, unlacing them carefully and slipping them off with great care. She seemed not to know that he was even there, so such care was probably not necessary. Still . . .

She would choke in her sleep with that blouse buttoned to her chin, he decided, so he unfastened the buttons from her chin to the swell of her breasts. They were right fine breasts, he decided, peeking only briefly as the fabric fell back and away.

Then and there he vowed that the next time he bedded Hannah it would be in a *bed*, with lamps all around and not a stitch of clothing to spoil the view.

The waist of her skirt had to be pinching her. It would be uncomfortable to wake up at night with that waistband twisted and biting into her, wouldn't it? He unfastened the buttons there and slipped the skirt down and off, leaving her in a single petticoat.

And there was that damn garter. He lifted her petticoat just enough to glimpse the garter. Ah, she hadn't been lying. It was black and lacy, and there to the side was that little nubby satin rose he'd found with his fingers last night. He slipped his fingers beneath the garter and slid it down and off her shapely, enticing leg, absently twirling the black, lacy thing on his finger while he righted Hannah's petticoat.

If he made her any more comfortable, and in the process made himself any more *un*comfortable, he would never get out of this room tonight.

He rolled her up and into his arms, holding her against his chest with one hand while he pulled down the quilt. She didn't offer any resistance as he placed her back on the center of the bed and covered her.

The temptation to kiss her sleeping lips was great, but he resisted. He couldn't stop with one kiss, not the way he felt right now. He'd wake her, exhausted or not, and take her here and now.

Jed extinguished the lamp and left quietly, climbing the stairs to his own room, absently twirling the black garter on his finger as he went.

Fourteen

Hannah woke feeling oddly exhilarated. It took her a moment to realize that she could not remember how she'd gotten into her room and into bed, half dressed. There was just a hint of a memory of last night, and that was of Jed carrying her into the hotel.

She chose a severe dark blue suit and a matching hat, mentally preparing herself for a day of investigation as she dressed. Once Rose admitted that her confession had been a lie, there would be a murderer to catch.

Descending the stairs slowly, she laid her eyes on Jed, who paced impatiently in the hotel lobby.

"Good morning," she said, calling on her most docile voice.

He pinned his eyes on her and watched as she descended. "Almost good afternoon," he snapped.

She smiled as she reached the foot of the stairs. "Have you been waiting for me?"

He opened his mouth to deny it, she was sure, then hesitated and said, "Yes, damn it."

Wearing a pair of brown twill pants, a tan shirt, and a leather vest, his hair golden and soft, his beard a bit more closely trimmed than usual, he looked warm as toast and sweeter than Eden's blackberry jam. Tall and wide in the shoulders, massively built, he was as hard as Wishing Rock. But inside . . . Inside he was tender.

Hannah walked slowly toward him. "Since the sheriff is your friend and brother-in-law, perhaps you could report a theft to him for me," she said as she reached Jed.

"A theft?" he repeated.

"I woke this morning to find something missing from my room."

"What's missing?"

She lowered her voice and leaned slightly closer to him. "Well, it's black and has a pink satin rose on one side."

He reached into the inside pocket of his vest and withdrew her garter, spinning it on one long, brown finger. "Would this be what you're looking for?"

They were alone in the lobby, but she heard people in the dining room, people too close by. "Put that away," she whispered, covering his hand with hers and putting a halt to his lewd entertainment.

With a grin he complied, returning the garter to his vest pocket.

"Want to grab a late breakfast?" he asked, nodding toward the dining room.

Hannah shook her head. "I don't think I can eat." The very idea of the coming confrontation with her sister had her stomach tied in knots.

Jed nodded as if he understood, then took her arm and headed for the door.

"This is my responsibility. You don't have to go with me," she whispered.

"Yes, I do," he said, leaving no room for argument. "Someone tried to kill you, in case you've forgotten. You need a bodyguard."

"I do not," she protested weakly.

He pulled her just a little bit closer. "Hannah Winters, you need a bodyguard more than any woman I've ever met."

"Because I have a way of irritating people?"

"Exactly."

She didn't try to send him away, but she did defend herself as they approached the general store. "There's nothing wrong with speaking one's mind," she said primly. "I don't have time to waste pussyfooting around an issue simply to be diplomatic."

"Pussyfooting," Jed grumbled. "Well," he added, "you are definitely not diplomatic."

"Thank you."

A smiling Bertie stood behind the front counter. Her smile faded when she saw Hannah and Jed enter the store. Once they were inside, Jed released his hold on her.

"Miss Winters," Bertie said softly; then she bit her bottom lip.

"How are you, Bertie?" Hannah asked.

"Fine," she whispered.

"I hope you haven't been working too hard, here," Hannah said. "You've been a tremendous help. Of course, now that Baxter has been released, you can move back into the hotel, if you'd like."

Bertie shook her head quickly, nervously. "No, thank you. Rose fixed up a back room for me, and it serves quite nicely. And . . . and"—she seemed to have a hard time catching her breath—

"and I'm not leaving when you go back to Alabama. I'm staying here." She nodded her head with finality.

Truly surprised, Hannah raised her eyebrows. "Really?"

"Yes, ma'am," Bertie said softly but with some force. "I've met a fella, and I like the people here, and I like working in the store. Rose said I could stay." She lifted her chin as if she were ready to do battle.

Hannah smiled. "I'm happy for you, Bertie."

The girl narrowed her eyes suspiciously. "You are?"

"Of course. And I want to meet this young man who's been calling on you, before I go home."

"Oh, you've already met Oliver."

Her smile faded. "Oliver Jennings?"

Bertie nodded, her head bobbing with apparent excitement.

Hannah sighed. Well, there was nothing she could do, was there? She'd have to think on it. "Where is Rose?"

"Upstairs," Bertie said, pointing to the door at the back of the store.

Hannah marched to that door and threw it open. Before her loomed the steep, narrow stairs that led to the Suttons' living quarters.

"Now, Hannah," Jed said calmly as he climbed behind her, "calm down."

"Calm down," she repeated. "Ha! Can you see that sweet girl with that . . . that ruffian? It's preposterous."

"No more preposterous than you and me," he said softly.

She stopped before the door at the top of the

stairs. Her heart was firmly lodged in her throat, it seemed. "Are we?" she asked, afraid to turn and look at his face.

"No," he whispered.

Hannah knocked soundly on the door and waited impatiently, tapping her toe. Jed was wrong. The idea of the two of them together *was* preposterous. As ridiculous as the notion of Bertie and that . . . that gun-wielding hothead Oliver Jennings.

He didn't like this at all. Hannah looked like she might burst at any moment. Her face was pale, her spine rigid, her eyes wide and horrified.

"I'm sorry to tell you this," Rose said calmly. "But it's the truth. I went to see Reverend Clancy that morning to tell him to leave me alone or I'd go to his wife and inform her of his improper advances. He was so smug, so self-righteous." In spite of her apparent calm, Rose shuddered, visibly and deep. "He stood up and laid his hands on my shoulders, and when I tried to back away he"—the calmness wavered, and a hint of panic touched Rose's eyes—"he grabbed me and put his mouth on me; he put his hands on my . . . on my . . ."

"That's enough," Baxter said, his voice low and clear. He stood behind his wife, his hand on her shoulder.

"So I grabbed the knife from the table beside his chair, and I just . . . I swiped out at him. I just wanted him to back down, to let me go, but the knife went into his chest and he fell back into his chair. He grabbed his chest and began to curse, and I panicked and ran home."

"I went there to see if I could doctor his wound," Baxter said, when it was clear Rose was capable of saying no more. "And to tell him that if he pressed charges I'd see that everyone in town knew what he'd been up to. But he was already dead."

"I didn't mean to kill him," Rose said softly.

"Sounds like an accident to me," Jed said. "Why did you lie about what happened?"

"I wasn't going to take the chance that Rose would end up in jail," Baxter said. He laid his eyes on Jed. "I never got the chance to thank you yesterday. How on earth did you get the judge to set such a light sentence?"

Jed grinned. "Harry and I used to run together, before he became a judge. Before the word *dignified* was even in his vocabulary. Let's just say I know a few secrets the judge would rather not be made common knowledge."

"You blackmailed him," Hannah said tersely.

"Yep."

He had to get her out of here before she exploded. This news was tough on her, tougher than he'd imagined it would be. "Let's go," he said, standing and offering Hannah his hand. She took it and rose to her feet.

"I guess I'll be heading back to Alabama," she said, "now that things here are in order."

Rose's face softened, and she stood to face Hannah. "Stay until Christmas."

Hannah shook her head.

"It's just a week away," Rose added. "And we haven't spent a Christmas together in too long."

Hannah capitulated much too easily, nodding her agreement. "All right. I can manage another week."

A week. It had been years since he'd spent that long with a woman, and yet he was certain it wouldn't be enough with Hannah.

He followed her down the stairs, watching the set of her back and the tension in her neck. A few tendrils of dark red hair had escaped and trailed softly across that creamy neck. Her shoulders were squared, and when she reached the foot of the stairs and he got a good look at her face, he could see that escaping the confines of Rose's rooms had not eased her distress one bit.

Ah, he knew just how to make her forget this bad news. For a while, anyway.

On the boardwalk, she headed with clipped steps back toward the hotel. "I don't know why I agreed to stay for another week," she snapped. "I'm not needed here. There's nothing for me to do."

"Now, Hannah," he said, easing up beside her and taking her arm in his.

"Don't you *now Hannah* me," she cracked.

"Are you pissed because Rose killed Clancy or because you were wrong?"

She stiffened, and refused to so much as glance at him. "Dunderhead," she mumbled.

"Obstinate female."

"Mannerless . . ."

He cut her off, drawing her into the alley that ran between the hotel and an abandoned storefront. He pressed her back against the wall and kissed her, hard and deep. She kissed him back, parting her lips, yielding to him instantly.

"Mannerless . . ." she began again as he took his mouth from hers. Her voice had weakened somewhat, he was happy to see.

He stilled her insult again, in the same way, and she wrapped her arms around his neck and kissed him back.

This time when he took his mouth from hers she said nothing.

"Mannerless what?" he asked lowly.

"I forgot," she whispered.

To his horror, her lower lip began to tremble. Even worse, her eyes filled with tears. She didn't lower her arms from around his neck, but held on tight.

"I can't believe it," she said softly, one of those tears trailing slowly down a pale cheek. "Not Rose. She was always the sweet one. Sweet, beautiful Rose who could do no wrong, until she met Baxter and committed the horrible sin of falling in love."

Hannah trembled from head to foot, so Jed pulled her closer and held her tight. "It was an accident."

"I know that," she whispered.

"It could've happened to anyone," he said, stroking her back.

"But it happened to Rose."

He held her while she wept softly, trying so hard to pretend, as she held her face against his chest, that she wasn't crying. When she stopped shaking and sniffled softly, he took her chin in his hands and made her look at him.

"And as for you leaving Rock Creek right away, forget it. Not needed here? Honey, *I* need you."

"Yeah, but that's"—she sniffled again—"that's different."

He kissed her again, softer this time. "Dinner tonight," he whispered. "Eight o'clock, in the hotel dining room." He grinned at her. "Wear something pretty."

Hannah paced in her room, wishing she had her cane so she could hit *something*.

She should be concerned, still, about the news that Rose had truly killed a man, but Jed's reasoning had calmed her. It had been an accident. It could have happened to anyone.

Instead, three damning words echoed in her head. *Wear something pretty.*

She owned an obscene number of sensible, good quality, expensive clothes. None of them were *pretty*. It seemed a shame to waste a frivolously splendid dress on a plain girl. You could wrap the plainest stone in gold paper, but underneath the gold wrapping what you held was still just a rock.

Jed thought she was pretty. What did he know? He was a large, hairy, often unbathed miscreant.

But he liked her lips. She remembered that from last night. And her eyes, he'd said. He thought her eyes were pretty.

The pace of her step increased. She'd rather balance the plantation books three times than try fruitlessly to be *pretty*. She'd rather be lost in a dark cave than dress in an enticing gown and present herself for a man's inspection. And rejection.

But what did she have to lose? This was Rock Creek, a homely little town. And the man in question was Jed, after all, who was an unassuming, uncomplicated, straightforward man. All he'd asked for was a simple dinner. Maybe a not-so-simple evening to follow, in her room or his. She knew, if she knew nothing else, that he did *want* her. For the next week or so.

She left her room with the same determination she'd called upon during her time in Rock Creek. Only now she wasn't looking for a murderer, she was on a quest for *something pretty.*

She stepped into the December sun, and experienced a moment of complete despair. There was one decent dress shop in Rock Creek, but there was no time to have anything made. All Rose carried in the general store were a few plain calico dresses and blots of fabric. She couldn't very well drape herself in unsewn yards of silk, and she would not meet Jed wearing anything as ordinary as calico.

Her gaze fell on the establishment across the street, and her calculating eyes narrowed. Lily was always well dressed, often in gowns that were cut provocatively and hugged her figure. That was surely the kind of thing Jed would like. Exposed cleavage was probably his idea of *pretty.*

Hannah took a deep breath and straightened her spine. If anyone in Rock Creek could wrap this plain little stone in gold paper, it was Lily Salvatore.

Jed interrupted Eden as she was cleaning up after lunch, wiping down dishes alongside the new hired girl. She was, as always, happy to see him.

"Jedidiah," she said, "are you hungry? There's plenty of stew left."

He shook his head, glancing at her still-flat stomach. Damnation, another baby. "Have you been feeling all right?" he asked.

"I've never felt better," she assured him.

"You're . . . happy, aren't you?" he asked, remembering Hannah's words from last night.

"About the baby? Of course . . ."

"About everything," he interrupted, his eye catching and holding hers.

Her smile muted but did not fade and, damn it, her face glowed. "Oh, Jedidiah, I never thought I would be so lucky, or so happy."

He had never thought his little sister could fit in here in Rock Creek. She was too tender, too . . . too damn sweet. But she had made this place her home and the people in it her friends.

"And Sullivan," he said gruffly. *"Sin,* he's . . . He's good to you?"

"You know he is," Eden said, taking Jed's arm and leading him into the deserted dining room. "And you know, too, how very much I love him."

Jed sighed. "I do."

"What's this about?" she asked.

He looked down at her, his little sister. "All I ever wanted was for you to be safe and happy."

"I am."

Jed took a deep breath. Why was this so damned difficult? "Then I'm glad you married Sullivan," he said quickly, before he chickened out.

Eden grinned and came up on her toes to kiss him on the cheek. "Are we finally getting your blessing?" she teased.

"Yes," he said, stroking his rough beard. "I guess you are."

"What caused this sudden change of heart?" she asked suspiciously.

Jed shrugged. Hell, he wasn't sure, himself. And right now he just wanted to change the subject. "You know that suit you made me buy last year?"

She nodded enthusiastically. "I packed it away, instead of burning it like you suggested."

"Good," he said lowly. "I think I'm going to need it."

Fifteen

Well, if he wasn't the biggest fool this side of the Mississippi River. Jed scowled at his reflection in the mirror above the dresser in his room on the third floor of the Paradise Hotel. Hannah would laugh at him. So would anyone else who got a good look at him in this condition.

All he wanted to do was sweep Hannah off her feet. Was that too much to ask?

The knock on his door interrupted his musings, but didn't improve his worsening mood.

"Come in," he grumbled.

The door opened slowly, and Sullivan, wearing a scowl of his own, stepped into the room and closed the door behind him. "What the hell is going on?"

Jed glared silently at his brother-in-law. Hell, it had already started.

Sullivan's scowl softened and changed to an expression of complete befuddlement. "Dear God," he mumbled. "Maybe she's right."

"Maybe who's right about what?"

Sullivan looked Jed square in the eye. "Eden is a wreck. She thinks you're dying."

"Dying?"

"She was cooking supper when it hit her. The belated blessing, the request for the suit, the . . . the . . ." He waved a hand at Jed's newly cut hair and smooth face. "That. And then you asked her to make all your favorites for a late dinner. Roast beef, boiled potatoes, biscuits, overcooked greens, and blueberry pie."

Jed smiled softly. "Bless her heart. She thought I was requesting a last meal?"

"Yep."

Jed shrugged his big shoulders. "I'm not dying, I've just got a dinner engagement with a lady. That's all." Unimportant. Easy. Happened every day. "Give Eden a big hug for me and tell her I'm just fine."

Sullivan's eyebrows shot up. "You want me to hug her for you? You mean, I'm now allowed to *touch* my wife?"

The sarcastic comment was grounds for an argument, not the first he and Sullivan had had, but Jed let it slide. "Well, I reckon you are married," he conceded.

"Yes, we are."

"And she's crazy about you."

Sullivan smiled. "Yes, she is."

He had never, never understood what his sister and Sullivan saw in each other. The match just didn't make sense. But somehow . . . Somehow they made it work. "And you take good care of her."

In an instant, Sullivan's mood changed. He was no longer smiling softly. "You are dying, aren't you?" he said, taking a step forward and narrowing his suspicious eyes.

"No," Jed snapped. "But if you don't wipe that

sappy expression off your face, you just might be requesting your own last meal before the night is over."

With a shake of his head, Sullivan looked Jed up and down once again. "So, all this is for a woman?"

He was right. This had been a *very* bad idea. "Can't a man clean up now and then without people thinking the world has come to an end?"

Sullivan shook his head and backed out of the room. "I reckon. I'm going to go tell Eden that you're not going to kick the bucket anytime soon."

"I'd appreciate it," Jed grumbled.

After Sullivan was gone, Jed turned back to the mirror. Five minutes. He was supposed to meet Hannah in the lobby in five minutes. Time to change clothes, if he had a mind to. He stroked his smooth jaw. Nothing to be done for this, though.

He grabbed the lapels of the black frock coat and tugged, settling the coat more securely over his shoulders. "Dying my ass," he grumbled as he left his room, slamming the door behind him.

He didn't run into anyone on his way down the stairs. Just as well. His mood had not been improved by Sullivan's visit. If anyone else thought he was dying just because he decided to put on a suit and get a shave and a haircut, he might just give up on this evening before it got started. As he passed Hannah's door he glared at it, willing her to feel the heat of his gaze. A *woman* had done this to him. She'd turned him upside down and inside out. He had never thought it possible.

The lobby was deserted. Again, he took this as a good sign. He could pace unimpeded.

All he really wanted was to screw Hannah again, right? In a bed this time, with a little light to see by. That wasn't too much to ask, and the prospect certainly shouldn't make him so damn nervous. It definitely didn't require a suit and a boiled shirt and a string tie that was about to choke the life out of him.

A kiss and an invitation, that was all he really needed. But he wanted this night to be special. Hannah deserved special.

The rustle alerted him to a presence on the stairs, and he turned his head. And almost quit breathing.

He had told Hannah to wear something pretty, but he had never dreamed . . . He hadn't even imagined . . .

Her silk dress was a brilliant blue, not pale, not dark, but a jewel-like color in between. It was cut low to reveal the swell of her breasts, and snugly followed her curves down to a tiny waist before swelling over shapely hips. Her dark red hair was piled atop her head, a mass of soft curls. A small silk flower, a paler blue than the gown, had been tucked behind one ear. Her lips were just a little redder than usual, and as tempting as any sight he'd ever seen.

His mouth went dry, his necktie grew tighter, and his heart beat so hard he could feel it pounding in his chest.

And Hannah didn't move from the top of the stairs. She stared at him with wide eyes set in a beautiful, creamy pale face.

"Jed?" she whispered, taking the first step down the stairway.

It wasn't possible that the man waiting at the foot of the stairs might be Jed Rourke. He was much too gorgeous.

But it *was* her Jed, and she had known it from first glance. No one else was so tall and broad in the shoulders, and she'd know the way he moved from a mile away. Sensual and powerful, strong and masculinely graceful. Even cut short that honey golden wavy hair was unmistakable. And even if that hadn't given him away . . . the blue eyes he laid on her were definitely Rourke eyes.

Her heart sank as she walked slowly down the stairs. This man could have any woman he wanted. *Any woman in the world.* What would he want with a disagreeable old maid like Hannah Winters when he looked like *this?*

The corset Lily had insisted she wear pinched her waist, reminding her that for tonight, just for tonight, she wasn't old maid Hannah Winters. Just for tonight, she was beautiful, and seductive, and daring. And she was Jedidiah Rourke's woman.

As she reached the foot of the stairs, Jed offered her his hand. "Goddamn, Hannah Winters," he said softly. "Are you trying to kill me on the spot?"

She smiled as she laid her hand in his, taking his gruff comment as the compliment he'd intended. "That would spoil the evening, wouldn't it?"

Jed smiled, and she discovered that without the beard he had a small, endearing dimple in one cheek. She reached up and touched his smooth jaw with her fingers. "Look at you," she said softly.

"I never would've known there was such a hand-some man beneath all that hair."

He winked at her and glanced down, not very discretely, at her exposed cleavage. "All of a sudden, I'm not very hungry. I wonder if Eden would mind if we skipped dinner."

Hannah slipped her arm through his. "Oh, no. You're not getting off that easy." She wanted it all. The dinner, the conversation, the waiting. The anticipation.

They walked, arm in arm, slowly and quite happily, toward the dining room.

A small voice stopped them. "Uncle Jed?"

They turned and discovered Millie on the stairs, adorable in her white nightgown, with fair curls falling over her shoulders.

"What are you doing up, sweetheart? Isn't it past your bedtime?"

Millie nodded. "Uncle Jed, you're *purty*."

The child made the compliment sound like a condemnation.

"Not nearly as purty as you," he said, patting Hannah's hand before releasing his hold on her and heading for the stairs.

"Tuck me in?" Millie asked, in a voice no man could resist.

"Of course." Jed spun around and pointed a finger at Hannah. "Don't move. I'll be right back."

She watched, her heart swelling, as Jed ran up the stairs and lifted a squealing Millie into his arms and tossed the little girl over his shoulder.

If she were a different woman, if she led a different life, she would definitely set her sights on Jed Rourke. The longer she knew him the more perfect he became. When he did decide, as he surely would, to marry, he would have his pick of women. The thought did not cheer her. When it came to competing with other women for a man, she knew she didn't have a chance. She always managed to scare or annoy people, eventually, by speaking her mind and insisting on having things her way. In that respect, she was too much like her father.

Oh, she did not want to be like her father. She certainly didn't want to end up like him, alone and bitter and unloved.

Two men burst into the hotel lobby, and Hannah turned her head to watch them saunter into the room. Like most of the men she'd encountered in Texas, they were rough, dusty, and armed. One of them, a plainly dressed man with very short hair, weaved drunkenly. The other removed his flat-brimmed black hat and beat it against his leg to remove the dust. Dressed in a tailor-fitted black suit and a ruffled shirt, well groomed with neatly cut dark hair and a small mustache and goatee, he still managed to look mean.

He lifted his head and laid piercing, dark eyes on her. The cruel mouth curved into a smile as he walked toward her. "Well, well. You're new," he said, tossing his hat onto the green sofa.

"I'm hardly *new,*" she said, calling upon her most dignified voice.

The other one, the man who was most definitely drunk, headed up the stairs without a word.

"Well"—the remaining newcomer looked her up and down audaciously, his dark eyes sparkling when they lit on her exposed cleavage—"you definitely weren't around the last time I came through Rock Creek. I would've remembered someone as gorgeous as you."

Hannah sighed. "If you insist on speaking to me uninvited," she snapped, "would you kindly look at my *face*. It's common courtesy, even among scoundrels."

He was unbothered by her rebuke. "There's so much magnificence to look at, I just don't know where to start." He hummed to himself, as if content, and continued to rake his eyes over her. "Sweetheart, a woman like you is wasted in a hell-hole like Rock Creek. Let me take you to New Orleans. We could have a great time there."

Hannah shook her head and placed her hands on her hips. "Are there women out there who actually *believe* you when you ramble on like this?"

He lifted his eyes to hers. "I like you already," he said with a grin that was as cold as his eyes. "Let me buy you a drink across the street. It's not New Orleans, but it'll do as a place to start."

Without waiting for her response, he took her arm.

"Unhand me," she said, jerking her arm back and wishing she had her cane with her. The man definitely deserved a good smack! "I have no desire to have a drink with you, you ill-mannered, black-eyed, grimy wretch."

He dropped her arm, and his smile faded. "Grimy wretch?"

"Touch me again," she said, leaning slightly forward and giving him a glare to match his own, "and I'll give you the thrashing you so richly deserve." *As soon as I get my hands on another cane.*

"Mighty big talk for such little thing," he muttered, insolently raking his eyes over her once again.

Angry at his impudence, she grabbed his chin and forced him to lift his face to hers again. She would not have him gaping at her as if she were on display for his lascivious amusement! She had every intention of ordering him to leave her alone, when those black eyes latched on to hers and she knew she had made a terrible, terrible mistake.

Dropping his chin, she took a single step back. His fingers seemed to twitch as they hovered over the matching, fancy six-guns he wore.

When she heard Jed's heavy footfall on the stairs, relief rushed through her. She turned her head and looked at him, and he, unsmiling, stared at the man who had irked her.

"Cash," Jed grumbled.

The black-eyed man turned his head to the stairs. Eyebrows lifted in surprise. The unmistakable danger that had lurked on his face disappeared. "Jed?" He looked Jed up and down almost as audaciously as he had her. "Is that you?"

"Hannah," Jed said, stepping quickly down the remaining stairs, "what have you been up to?" He glanced at Cash. "I can't leave her alone for a minute."

"She's *yours?*" the man Jed called Cash said incredulously.

To Hannah's dismay, he hesitated before answering. "Yep."

Cash lifted his hands in surrender and backed away, smiling once again. "I should've known."

Jed placed himself at her side, almost protectively, she thought.

"When did you get back?"

"Just now."

"Nate?"

Cash nodded his head toward the stairway. "Upstairs."

"Staying for a while?"

Cash shrugged his shoulders. "I reckon." He turned to Hannah, winked at her, and bowed in a courtly manner. "Sorry to have bothered you, ma'am," he said, more than a hint of sarcasm in his smooth voice. "But to be honest, any woman who can get Jed Rourke to shave and wear a suit is too much woman for me."

Jed took her arm and they turned their backs on Cash. She wasn't certain that was a good move, but decided to trust Jed's judgment in the matter.

"That cretin is your friend?" she asked as they entered the deserted dining room. One table, in the center of the room, had been prepared for the late diners. It was lovely, with a spotless white tablecloth, two burning candles, and Eden's best china and silver.

"Yep. He's also the one man in Rock Creek you really don't want to take on," Jed snapped. He was obviously disturbed. Maybe even angry.

"And why is that?"

"Because if he ever does draw one of those guns on you, he will kill you without so much as blinking." Yes, he was definitely angry. His smooth jaw was tight, his eyes piercing.

"Why is a man like that your friend?" she asked as he pulled her chair out for her.

Jed took his seat, shaking his head dismally. "You fight long enough with a man and he becomes like a brother. You can't turn your back on him just because what happened marked him more than it marked you."

She nodded. The war. "Is that why you're so angry? Did you think he'd really shoot me?"

The expression on his face hardened. A muscle in his jaw twitched. "No," he muttered reluctantly. "I got angry because I came downstairs and found you talking to a man who could charm the drawers off a nun."

He was jealous! No man had ever, *ever* been jealous of her before. Hannah leaned slightly forward, moving herself closer to Jed and staring at him through the soft light of two flickering candles. The new position practically offered her exposed cleavage for inspection. "Lucky for you I'm not a nun," she whispered.

His eyes lit up. "Lucky, indeed."

This was a night to end all nights, a night to take what she wanted without reservation. "Doubly lucky for you," she said, lowering her voice to not much more than a breath, "I'm not wearing any drawers."

Jed grinned at her, bringing that dimple into play. Any anger he had been harboring a moment ago was gone. The emotion on his handsome face was not hostility. It was passion, pure and simple.

"Are you really hungry?" he asked, just as Eden emerged from the kitchen with a tray laden with food.

"Yes," she said, leaning back in her chair and smiling.

Eden sniffled as she placed the food on the table. She'd obviously been crying.

Hannah's smile faded. "Are you all right?"

Eden sniffled some more, and laid weepy eyes on Jed. "I'm fine."

Jed squirmed, just a little. "Sullivan did tell you everything's okay, didn't he?"

Eden nodded quickly. "I'm sorry. I'm just overly emotional these days. I was the same way when I was carrying Fiona."

With the food on the table and no other customers, Eden could've returned to the kitchen or headed upstairs. But she seemed determined to stay in the dining room, and near the table, until Jed called her over with a crook of his finger and placed an arm around her waist. "Nate and Cash are here. They just headed upstairs."

In spite of her continuing emotional affliction, Eden's face lit up and she smiled down at her brother. "They are? Oh, I haven't seen Daniel and Nate in ages."

"I bet they'd be grateful if you took 'em up some leftovers and a pot of coffee."

She hurried to the kitchen, and Hannah laid her eyes on Jed. He had purposely run his sister out of the room. Just as well. She wanted to be alone, even now as they shared dinner.

Something nagged at her, something coming together a small piece at a time.

"Daniel Cash?" she asked, as Jed poured her a glass of wine.

"Yep," he said simply.

"Bertie has a dime novel about a gunslinger named Daniel Cash. What a coincidence."

His eyes found and held hers. "Nope. Not a coincidence," he said lowly.

Hannah felt herself pale. She had called a

deadly gunslinger a grimy wretch and threatened to *thrash* him. "Oh."

"If it makes you feel any better, I'm almost positive some of those stories are exaggerated. Some might even be out-and-out fiction."

Some. She shook her head, then took a long swig of the wine. If even a fraction of what she'd read were true . . . "I suppose I should be more careful who I antagonize in this part of the world," she said. "You do things differently here."

"That we do," he agreed.

"The story about Dallas . . ." she began.

"Oh, that one's true. I was there." He shook his head and grimaced slightly.

"And Kansas City?"

"Mostly true."

She had grabbed his chin and called him . . . several nasty names. "And . . ."

"Hannah," Jed interrupted, lifting his glass to her, pinning intense blue eyes on her face. "I don't want to talk about Cash tonight. You're beautiful. You're mine. Can't we talk about your drawers some more?"

She smiled at him, more than happy to dismiss all unpleasantness and move on. "What drawers?"

Sixteen

Hannah couldn't eat more than a few bites, and the problem with her appetite had nothing to do with the tight corset she wore. Her heart fluttered, and her insides tightened and quivered. And Jed stared at her like he wanted to eat her up. No one had ever looked at her this way before.

It was the fancy, revealing dress, she reasoned, or the touch of lip rouge Lily had insisted upon that stirred Jed so completely. He couldn't possibly want *her* this much.

In the darkness of a cave, lost with possibly no way out, he had made love to her. She remembered every sensation, would always remember the way it had felt the first time he'd kissed her, the first time he'd touched her, the moment he'd become a part of her.

Wonderful as those memories were, one night to remember wasn't enough. She craved more, with her heart and with her body.

"You're not going to finish your pie?" he asked, nodding at her untouched dessert.

She shook her head slowly. She could not eat with this lump in her throat.

Jed stood and rounded the table to pull out her

chair and help her to her feet. Oh, she needed help. Already her knees wobbled uncertainly.

With his big hand on her chin, Jed tipped up her face and kissed her briefly, his mouth barely touching hers. "If you're having second thoughts, now's the time to tell me," he said, his voice low and gruff. That soft, warm voice shot through her, crept under her skin and into her heart.

"No second thoughts," she whispered, the lump in her throat dissolving.

Jed took her hand, threading his fingers through hers, and led her from the dining room, up the stairs, and down the hall to her door. With every step her heart beat harder.

Outside her door, Jed hesitated with his hand on the knob. He glanced up and down the deserted hallway, then pushed open the door and whirled her inside.

With the door closed behind him, the room was dark, lit only by moonlight through the lace-curtained window. After the complete darkness of the cave, the soft moonlight was comforting, friendly, and gentle.

Apparently it was not sufficient for Jed, who lit the lamp on her dresser and turned it low. There would be no hiding this time, no cover of darkness.

In the center of the room, he held and kissed her. There was no rush to tumble to the bed, no instant demand. Instead, Jed kissed her deep and held her close, his hands comforting at her back, his mouth enticing and promising, arousing and possessive.

When he took his mouth from hers he smiled

wickedly and removed the flower from her hair. "Did I tell you how beautiful you are?"

"Once or twice," she whispered.

"Did I tell you that I wanted you the moment I laid eyes on you tonight?" he asked gruffly. "That if I'd had my way I would have had you there on the stairs?"

Her heart lurched, and at her very core she shimmied. "No, I don't believe you did."

His fingertips brushed the swell of her breasts, setting off a powerful new surge of desire with the simple touch.

Hannah reached up and loosened his tie. "Did I tell you that you're strikingly handsome tonight?"

"Once or twice."

She stared at his tempting, masculine neck and licked her lips in anticipation, as she wondered what it tasted like. "Did I tell you that if I didn't still have some shred of decency buried somewhere deep inside me, I would've done my best to seduce you right there in the dining room?"

"Decency's highly overrated," he said lowly, his able hands finding and releasing the fastenings at the side of her dress, loosening the gown one hook and eye at a time.

"So I'm discovering," she said as she ran her hands up his chest and to his shoulders, pushing his frock coat off and to the floor.

He gently tugged the neckline of her loosened gown lower and bent his head to kiss the swell of her breast. With her hands in his newly shortened hair, she closed her eyes and savored the pleasure that shot through her. Ah, he really *did* want to eat her up. One nibble at a time, apparently.

One thing was clear as Jed touched her: this

would be no quick tumble, no fast coming together simply to satisfy their mutual physical
need. He took his time as he devoured her, moving his mouth over the swell of her breasts with
slow deliberation.

When he took his lips from her flesh and stood
tall once again, she reached out to unfasten the
buttons of his boiled shirt and slip her hand inside the opening to touch his bare chest. She
found and held her hand over his heart, then
flicked her thumb over a small tight, flat nipple.
While she circled her finger around the nipple,
she rose up on her toes and laid her mouth over
his neck, lips slightly parted as she tasted and
teased with her tongue.

While she raked the tip of her tongue over his
salty skin, he let down her hair and threaded his
fingers through the strands.

Hannah nibbled and kissed and sucked on Jed's
suddenly intriguing neck, and she was rewarded
with a low growl from deep in his throat, a sure
sign that he was losing control. Oh, she liked the
sheer power of making a man like Jed Rourke
shudder and moan with something so simple as
a flick of her tongue.

He tugged her gown off her shoulders and
pushed it down past her waist and to the floor.
She stepped out of it and kicked away the pile of
silk and lace. All that was left was a black silk petticoat, dainty satin slippers, a low-cut chemise over
the too-tight corset, black stockings . . . and a
small surprise for Jed.

She pushed gently at his chest, and he obediently backed up a step. With a short distance between them, she grabbed the petticoat in her

hands and lifted it, an inch at a time, revealing a black-stockinged leg and, as the petticoat was raised to above her knee, a shockingly red garter.

"Oh, honey," Jed whispered, his eyes on the garter. He groaned and whipped his shirt off and over his head.

She had seen men's chests before, on a working plantation, but she had never seen anything like this. Wide and muscled and dusted with fine brown hair, there was not an ounce of wasted flesh on Jed's torso. He was perfection; she should have expected no less.

She scooted out of the petticoat, kicked off her shoes, and unbuttoned the chemise to reveal the corset beneath.

"You are wearing entirely too many clothes," Jed said, reaching out to unfasten the tight corset.

While he unfastened the restraining undergarment, she boldly unbuttoned his trousers, her fingers dancing down the front opening as his danced down her torso. What clothes remained on their bodies, loosened and all but falling off, they stopped to kiss. It was a need, Hannah realized with complete surrender, a need too fierce to fight. She had never truly needed *anything*, but she couldn't kiss Jed long enough or deep enough.

With the corset peeled away, Jed lifted her off her feet and laid her on the center of the bed. He landed gently on top of her as she fell, his hands and mouth caressing her exposed breasts with hunger and tenderness. When he took a nipple deep into his mouth, the tug deep inside took her breath away, made her quiver from head to toe.

Jed removed his boots and shucked off the trousers, and when he returned to her the only items of clothing worn by either of them were her black stockings and the red garter. His fingers teased the garter and her inner thigh as he hovered above her, golden and muscled and exquisitely male. Hard and warm, long and powerful. And aroused.

He lowered his head to kiss her while he fondled the garter, and when his fingers inched higher he took his mouth from her to rub his smooth cheek against hers, to nuzzle and caress and kiss while his fingers stroked and teased.

Her body throbbed with need, her legs trembled and parted wide. She had never needed anything the way she needed Jed right now. She had never felt desire this way before.

Just before she broke down and begged him to fill the ever-increasing void he had created, he guided himself to her and pushed inside. She stretched to accept him, held on tight, and lifted her hips. He slipped one hand beneath her leg and raised it, and she obediently draped her leg over his hip, bringing him closer, deeper, as he pushed into her again. She raised the other leg as well, wrapped it around his long thigh, lifted her hips, and waved up and into his ever-increasing thrusts.

She closed her eyes and listened only to the demand of her body and his. They danced, coming together and moving apart. What began as a warm, tender coming together swiftly turned into a fierce, hot mating.

The bed rocked and creaked, the very air in the room was charged with their shared lust for

each other. The room shook; the world trembled.
Hannah opened her eyes to watch Jed's face as
he loved her. She wouldn't hide in the dark, not
this time. Beads of sweat broke out on his skin
and hers, and they gleamed by lamplight. She laid
one hand against his chest, so close, and ran her
fingers over his damp, muscled skin. She loved
the feel of him, everywhere. Could never get
enough, could never be close enough. She lifted
her breasts so they pressed against his chest, and
raised her hips to meet his increasing surge.

A wave of release hit her when he pushed deep
inside once more, coming as a force of intense
pleasure that made her cry out, and then billow-
ing through her entire body. She felt her inner
muscles squeezing Jed, milking him as he gave
over to the same release, a powerful culmination
that made him moan and growl and whisper her
name.

He collapsed to cover her, resting his head on
her shoulder and covering one of her trembling
hands with his. Again, his fingers threaded
through hers. His breath came as hard as hers
did, and his heart beat so hard she could feel it
pounding against hers.

How was she going to walk away from him in a
week? A *week!* How was she supposed to ever again
be satisfied with anything else when she knew
what it was like to depend on another person, to
open herself to him, to look forward to every moment he was with her and dread the moments
when he was not? How was she supposed to keep
pretending that she didn't love him?

She raked her fingers through his waving hair.
The last thing she wanted or needed was to fall

in love! A brief affair was one thing, but love? Surely not.

When he lifted his head and smiled at her, she knew it was much too late to fight what she felt. "You do have a weakness for red, don't you?" she whispered.

"I have a weakness for you," he said, kissing her sweetly, lazily.

"Sweet-talker," she cooed.

"Temptress."

"Shameless rogue," she said, draping one arm around his neck.

"Lover."

Oh, she liked the sound of that word on his lips. "Lover," she repeated.

He'd never been one to need much sleep. Not since the war, anyway. Not since he'd learned to never completely let down his guard, even for a full night's rest.

The sun would be up soon. Soft, gray light lit the sky and Hannah's room, Hannah's face, and the bed they shared.

He had never known anyone like her. The women in his life had been sweet and naive, like Eden, or calculating and weepy, like Sylvia, or coarse and raunchy, like the women who worked in the saloons he frequented.

Hannah was none of that. She was honest and open, smart and straightforward. And he never looked at her and wondered what was going on in that head of hers; she told him without reserve what she thought.

In bed she was completely and totally a woman.

Curious and not shy, she met him with the same honesty and intensity that was so much a part of her.

She was the kind of woman who would make some man a great partner, he decided as he watched the light of the rising sun on her face and the tangle of dark red hair around it. And she would be a partner in everything. In bed, in life. This was not the kind of woman a man married and then left behind.

She stirred, wrinkling her nose and rolling her bare shoulder. He had slipped off the stockings and discarded the garter hours ago, so beneath the quilt they shared she was completely, totally bare. He grabbed the quilt and inched it downward, just an bit.

Hannah came suddenly awake, grabbing the quilt and drawing it to her chest, sitting up and staring at him wide-eyed. *Great,* he thought. *Here it comes, the inevitable "what-have-I-done?" lament.*

Hair a tempting red tangle falling over bare shoulders, eyes coming quickly awake, Hannah stared at him. Her lips were as lush as a man could ask for, her eyes smoky and direct.

"If Rose swiped out at Reverend Clancy with the knife, how did it pierce his heart?" she asked softly. "Wouldn't that require a more direct plunging motion?"

"Good morning to you, too," Jed said, rising up on his elbow.

"I just thought of it," she said, "as I was coming awake. It's as if my head is clear for the first time in days, and it all came together. Rose said she *swiped* the knife at Clancy. If that's true, then maybe she didn't really kill him."

Jed reached out and brushed a strand of hair away from Hannah's face. "Honey, that doesn't make sense," he said gently. "There were just a few minutes between the time Rose left and Baxter found Clancy dead. I doubt someone was standing nearby, just waiting for such an opportunity to arise."

She leaned in to him, resting her cheek on his hand. "Well, it wouldn't hurt to speak to the undertaker, just in case."

"The undertaker," he repeated.

"Simply to make sure that the wound that killed Reverend Clancy was a swipe, not a stab."

"Honey, Rose probably cleaned up the story a little bit for you. She didn't want you to know that she was responsible for Clancy's death. She might very well have tidied up the details on your account." He trailed his fingers down her smooth cheek and over her neck. "It's over. Forget it."

She scooted closer to him. "I have to be sure," she whispered, laying her hands on his shoulders and pressing her bare body against his.

With his fingers, he combed the hair away from her face. Hellfire, he couldn't touch her enough, couldn't keep his hands off her. "Just let it go," he said gently. "Rose confessed, Baxter is free, and everything's fine."

"But I need to know." She draped her arm around his waist, the move familiar and intimate. "Something is just not right about this whole business."

Hannah didn't want her sister to be responsible for Clancy's death, no matter what the circumstances might have been. He wondered if she'd ever let it go.

"I can think of better things to do with our
time than hunting down that creepy old undertaker," he said, scooting the quilt down and laying
his hand on the pale curve of her hip.

"Oh, you can, can you?" she whispered, lifting
her face to his and lightly brushing her lips across
his mouth.

"Yes, ma'am," he breathed, pulling her against
him so she could feel his erection pressing into
her soft flesh. He wanted her to know that he
needed her, that she roused him in ways no
woman ever had.

Mouth still against his, she smiled. "You are in-
satiable, Jed Rourke."

"Yes, ma'am."

She didn't shy away from him as he trailed his
fingers down her collarbone to her exquisite,
rounded breasts.

"You can take me to the undertaker's, can't
you? Surely you know him, and he'll most likely
be more willing to talk to you than to me.
Please?"

He couldn't help but smile. "You know, most
women cajole for flowers, or jewelry"—*or a wedding dress.* "But Hannah Winters? No, she wants
a personal introduction to the undertaker."

"Flowers belong in the garden, where they'll
last and last, and I have all the jewelry I'll ever
need." She laid her hand on his hip, her fingers
sure and bold.

"I know how to make you forget all about that
undertaker," he whispered, sliding his hand between her warm, soft thighs.

"Do you?" she breathed.

"May be."

He kissed her deep and touched her. Had he really been afraid, for a moment, that she'd come awake regretting last night? He should have known better. Hannah parted her thighs and reached for him, touching him as intimately as he touched her, closing her eyes and shamelessly reveling in the sensations they shared.

A *partner.*

She wrapped one leg around his hip and pulled him closer.

"What are you thinking about now?" he whispered in her ear.

"I'm thinking about you, but I haven't forgotten that undertaker." There was passion and humor in her voice, a lighthearted teasing.

"Well, we can't have that."

He rolled Hannah onto her back and tossed the quilt to the floor, baring her beautiful body for him to peruse. Creamy and smooth and shapely, she was flawless.

He lowered his head to take one nipple into his mouth, deep and gentle. She quivered, tossed back her head, and closed her eyes. He teased her with his hands and his mouth while the sun came up, tasting and stroking, licking and nibbling until he could almost feel her coming apart in his hands.

She touched him boldly, arched against him, licked her lips, and moaned softly.

As he rolled atop her she spread her legs and pulled him against her. His erection touched her, where she was wet and hot and pulsating.

"What are you thinking about now, Hannah?" he whispered, waiting.

"Nothing," she whispered.

"What about the undertaker?"

"What undertaker?" she breathed, resting her hand at the back of his head and spearing her fingers through his hair. Down the length of her body she held him as he held her, possessive and tender. And as he buried himself inside her the word came to him again.

Partner.

Seventeen

"You didn't think I would really forget about the undertaker, did you?" Hannah asked with a smile as she and Jed walked down the boardwalk, side by side.

"Yep," he said sourly.

She wound her arm through his. "I did forget, for a while," she said softly.

This time with Jed was temporary; she knew that, but she refused to spoil what they had by constantly dwelling on the fact that it was not a lasting relationship.

"When the undertaker explains what happened and you're satisfied, then we're going to let this murder business go, right?" he asked, pulling her against his side without slowing his step.

Hannah took a deep breath. Letting go of anything was not easy for her. Never had been. "Yes," she said softly, meaning it.

"Then I can spend the rest of the week distracting you," he said softly.

She smiled. He could distract her all he wanted.

For some reason, she had expected a tall, thin, cadaverous-looking man to be in the position of undertaker, but Mr. Timmons turned out to be a

short, round man with a jolly, pale face. Jed had
been right, though. There was something decidedly creepy about him. It was the eyes, she decided. They were much too . . . wide and
intensely cheerful.

He was happy to greet them. Apparently he
didn't get many living visitors.

They sat around a small, rectangular table.
Once they had declined Mr. Timmons's offer of
coffee, they got right to business. As agreed be-
forehand, she sat back and let Jed do the talking.

"Tell me about the stab wound that killed Reverend Clancy."

Timmons's eyes lit up. "Oh, the blow that killed
him was classic. Knife wound directly into the
heart. Deep and clean, powerful and to the hilt
and"—he looked heavenward as he searched for
the right word—"decidedly lethal. Instantly fatal."

Jed narrowed his eyes. "Instantly?"

Hannah took a deep breath. That didn't match
Rose's latest version of the story at all!

Timmons nodded his head. "Oh, yes. Someone"—he glanced at Hannah with obvious suspicion and curiosity, perhaps wondering which of
her relatives had delivered the blow—"put quite
a lot of force into that attack."

It made no sense. For Rose to deliver such a
blow, she would've had to draw back and put all
her strength into the strike. She would surely have
known, before she went to fetch Baxter, that
Clancy was dead.

Did she really know her sister and what the
woman was capable of?

Hannah leaned forward, hopeful, searching for

an answer, still. "Were there wounds other than the fatal stabbing?"

Timmons laid his peculiar, lively eyes on her. Yes, he was definitely a strange man. "Well, there was one other injury to the upper torso, but it was not much more than a deep scratch. It was the blow to the heart that killed him."

Hannah looked at Jed in triumph. Now, he would admit she was right!

He didn't appear to be at all relieved, or even curious. "This doesn't mean . . ." he began.

"Yes, it does," she interrupted. "Someone else came in after Rose left."

He took her arm and assisted her from her chair as he nodded good-bye to Timmons, who again offered them coffee and volunteered to tell the fascinating tale of the last man who'd been shot in Rock Creek. Jed closed the door on the undertaker's offers.

"I know what you're thinking," he said as they headed back toward the hotel. "Just put it out of your mind. Either Rose lied about what happened, leaving out the second blow, or Baxter finished the job for her. Either way, it doesn't matter. It's over and done."

"There is another possibility," she offered.

He sighed, deeply and with obvious reluctance.

"What if Sylvia found her husband wounded and decided to finish him off herself?"

Jed shook his head. "She wouldn't . . ."

"Just because she's an *old friend*," Hannah interrupted, "doesn't mean she's incapable of murder."

"I was going to say . . ."

"I can't dismiss my suspicions because Baxter

is no longer in danger," she snapped. "And I have no desire to listen to you defend that . . . that woman." Oh, she was jealous! She knew Jed and Sylvia had once been much more than friends. Was that why he defended her now?

Jed stopped and hauled her around to face him, placing her back against the wall of the barbershop and leaning into and over her. "Give me one good reason why she would kill her husband. She's a widow now, and she has nothing. Sylvia always wanted to be taken care of. She didn't ever want to be on her own. The idea that she would do away with the man who kept a roof over her head and food on her table just doesn't fit with the woman I know."

She stared up into his handsome face, at his startling blue eyes and smooth cheeks. He'd shaved for her, she knew, because this morning as they'd dressed he'd commented on the lack of red beard-burn marks on her face, this time.

"Remember the morning I thought I heard you in her bedroom?" she asked softly.

"Yes."

"What if Clancy, reprobate that he was, found out that Sylvia had a paramour of her own? Men like that don't accept infidelity in their wives just because they practice it themselves."

"Are you sure someone was there?" he asked, narrowing his eyes.

"I heard something in her bedroom hit the floor and break," she explained.

"She used to have this little dog. Maybe he's still around and that's what you heard."

"Unless this little dog can mutter *goddamn it* in a rather deep voice, that solution doesn't work."

He narrowed his eyes, obviously not liking what he heard. "She wouldn't kill him," he said lowly.

"Not even if he threatened to kick her out? Would your Sylvia enjoy being booted into the street with nothing to her name?" It annoyed her that Jed insisted on defending the woman!

"You're suggesting that she stood over her wounded husband and . . . and coldly plunged the knife into his heart."

"Well, you're suggesting that my sister did the same thing," she snapped. "Why can't you even consider the possibility that Sylvia did it?"

"Rose had cause."

"So did Sylvia."

Jed glared at her. "Clancy was a no-good lying womanizer who got exactly what he deserved. I don't care who killed him."

"I don't believe that," Hannah whispered. "You're too honest to accept the possibility that someone is going to get away with murder."

He glanced down the street, toward the general store. "Hannah, someone already did."

She wanted to lash out at Jed, to blame him for everything that had gone wrong. But she couldn't. Falling in love with him had ruined everything.

"Not Rose," she said softly. "Not Baxter."

He looked down, sighed deeply, and reached out to tuck a strand of loose hair behind her ear. "If I can prove to you that Sylvia didn't kill her husband, will you let it go?"

"I'll try," she whispered. "But I can't make any promises."

He took her arm and resumed walking toward

the hotel. "You're a lot more agreeable when you're naked," he said softly.

"Is that a fact?" she asked, glancing around to make sure no one was close enough to hear. Fortunately they had this portion of the boardwalk to themselves.

"Yep."

"Oddly enough, you're a lot more persuasive when *you're* naked," she countered, her voice low.

"Care to prove it?"

"Now?"

"Why not?"

She glanced up at his handsome profile, at the dimple in his cheek. "For one thing, I'm starving. We rushed out without breakfast and I feel absolutely weak from lack of food."

"I'm ravenous, myself," he said with a small, reluctant smile.

"Persuasion is hungry work, I imagine," she said almost sweetly.

"That it is, Hannah. That it is."

Hannah could not understand why Jed insisted on speaking to Sylvia alone. She nervously paced the hotel lobby waiting for him to return. He said Sylvia wouldn't open up if anyone else were present, not the way she would with him alone. Ha! Of that Hannah had no doubt.

She had cautioned him against openly confronting Sylvia with the suspicions, but Jed wasn't one to play games. He had probably arrived at the rectory and was right now telling the widow how Hannah just couldn't let go of the idea that someone else had killed Clancy. He would probably even tell Sylvia that she was Hannah's prime suspect. They'd have a good laugh, and the widow would drape herself all over Jed and try to convince him that she was innocent.

Hannah had no illusions about herself. Stand her up against Sylvia Clancy and she didn't have a chance. Not even with Jed.

She wondered how many red garters Sylvia Clancy owned.

Hannah stormed toward the hotel entrance. She couldn't stand by and allow this to happen! Once she was gone, she'd have no claim to Jed Rourke, but after last night she *did* have a right to make sure he wasn't being taken in by that brazen hussy.

She was almost to the doorway when a dark shadow filled it. Recognizing Daniel Cash, she stopped in her tracks, then backed up a single step. She held her breath as she waited for him to enter, leaving the entryway free. Once Cash had cleared the doorway she'd escape and rush over to the rectory. She'd come up with some excuse for her intrusion on the way.

But Cash didn't enter. He stopped and leaned his shoulder against the doorjamb, blocking her avenue of escape.

"Well, well," he drawled. "Good morning, Miss Winters."

"Mr. Cash," she said, nodding her head once.

He had removed the road dust and was dressed in yet another very nice black suit and a white shirt with a ruffle down the front. His black hair had been washed and combed and positively gleamed. And he still looked dangerous.

It was the eyes, she decided. Jed could yell and

stomp and rage, but his eyes were always dancing. Sometimes with anger, sometimes with passion, but always vital and expressive. Daniel Cash's eyes were dead. Black and cold and lifeless.

And he showed no sign of removing himself from her path. He raked his eyes over her, up and down, taking in her plain skirt and prim blouse. Those dead eyes landed and dwelled audaciously on her face. He was probably wondering why he'd ever been so foolish as to ask her across the street for a drink.

"Where's Jed?"

"Running an errand," she said primly. "I expect him back at any moment." If he knew Jed was on his way, surely he'd remove himself immediately.

Instead, he grinned. "I just saw him heading into Sylvia's house. Unless the circumstances have changed, I doubt he'll be back *at any moment.* Did things not go well last night, Miss Winters?" he asked insolently.

Daniel Cash was armed, a gunslinger, a dangerous man. But she was not going to stand here and be insulted.

"What a vile excuse for a human being you are," she said, lifting her chin defiantly. "I can't believe a man as fine as Jed Rourke would tolerate someone as wretched as you, much less call you a *friend.*"

Her insults didn't seem to vex him at all. "Sweetheart, everyone tolerates me. It's risky not to."

"Do you think that because you know how to use those six-shooters," she said, pointing at the matching pair he wore, "that it gives you free rein to be a boor and a menace?"

"A boor?" he asked, obviously amused.

"And a menace." She looked him up and down as audaciously as he had when he'd done the same to her. "I feel sorry for you," she said softly, meaning it. "One day you're going to end up dead on a street somewhere, and no one will mourn your passing."

His smile faded.

"Oh, Jed and the others here will probably shake their heads, and some might even say a prayer for your soul, but at the same time they'll know that you asked for what happened to you." She found herself curious about this annoying man. Jed said Cash had been marked more than he had. By the war? By something else?

"You're a nosy bitch, you know that?"

She imagined she was supposed to be offended. To stomp off, indignant, and leave the man alone. "I've been called that before, I'm sure. Behind my back, though. Never to my face."

"In Rock Creek, being nosy can get you killed."

"So I've heard."

Cash's pose remained casual, while the expression on his face was anything but.

Hannah looked him over as audaciously as he had her, unbending and annoyed. "You know, I thought you would be taller."

Cash raised his eyebrows rakishly. "Aren't you going to push me out of the way and rush out of here to knock down Sylvia's door and make sure Jed is behaving himself?" he goaded, trying to change the subject, trying to get rid of her.

That had been her intention, hadn't it? Until

just a few moments ago. "No," she whispered. "I have no right and no need to make sure Jed is *behaving himself*. He's always been honest with me. I have no reason to think that will change this morning."

"He and Sylvia have a history, you know."

"I know."

The smile came back, but it was no longer audacious and dangerous. This time the grin was weak, maybe even a little sad. "Hell, woman, aren't you afraid of anything?"

"No," she answered without hesitation. "Are you?"

"Nope."

He was the one who walked away, pushing away from the doorjamb and heading calmly for the stairs. Eden intercepted him, as she descended those same stairs with a lively, light step.

"Daniel," she said, real joy in her voice. "Are you hungry?"

Cash offered his arm at the foot of the stairs, and Eden took it with the ease of a familiar friend. "For your cooking? Always."

Eden smiled at Hannah. "Would you like to join us for coffee and a bite to eat?"

"No, thank you."

Cash leaned closer to Eden and grinned lasciviously. "Miss Winters has an urgent errand to run."

Hannah lifted her chin and steeled her spine. She would not allow this common man to scare her into rushing after Jed as if she didn't trust him. "No, I don't. I would love a cup of coffee."

The insolent gunslinger winked at her.

***

Even here, at a table with Eden and the annoying Hannah Winters, Cash sat with his back to the wall. His eyes were aware of every movement in this room and beyond, every person passing by the doorway to the lobby and the window that gave him a visual access to Rock Creek's main street.

While Eden told him about the kids and how they'd grown, he stared at Hannah Winters. Damn her nosy hide, she was right. If he kept living the way he'd been living the past couple of years, he wouldn't last much longer. No one was glad to see him come riding into town, and they all breathed a sigh of relief when he left.

Everywhere but here.

He was tired of never getting a good night's sleep, of never trusting anyone he met. Hell, if he didn't have Nate to watch his back, someone would've put a bullet into it long ago.

Miss Winters's eyes kept cutting to the doorway, too. She wasn't looking for trouble, though. She was waiting for Jed.

Jed Rourke was always trouble.

Cash turned his attention to Eden when she asked, "How long are you going to stay?"

He lifted his coffee cup and silently toasted her. "For good."

She rewarded him with a huge smile. "Wonderful. I worry about you traipsing about the way you do."

Eden Sullivan was too well mannered to point out his growing reputation, unlike Jed's Hannah, but he could see the worry in her eyes every time he came home. Every time he left.

"I'm opening my own place. God knows this town needs a decent saloon."

"Three Queens is very nice," Hannah said.

"My place will have no singing, no entertainment. No women at all. This will be a man's place. Whiskey and cards. That's it."

"No women?" Hannah asked, raising her eyebrows.

"I would bring in a couple of prostitutes," he said, glaring at the irascible Miss Winters the same way she glared at him. "But it would be a waste of time. Eden or Lily would reform them before the week was out." Besides, he was getting tired of painted ladies with false smiles, high-pitched laughter, and busy beds. Mostly, he was just getting tired.

Hannah's head turned, as Jed's tall form filled the entryway between the lobby and the dining room.

Jed nodded absently at Cash, smiled at his sister, and crooked his finger at the nosy Miss Winters. Hannah didn't hesitate before rising to her feet and answering the silent call.

Eden dismissed the couple without a second thought. "So," she said, leaning across the table.

Ah, she was so damnably easy to read. He saw suspicion, a hint of disapproval. "A saloon."

Jed tried to reason with Hannah, but it was an impossible task. Damn, she was the most unreasonable woman he'd ever met.

She sat on the bench in the deserted garden, and he paced before her, taking long, restless strides.

"If you could've seen her . . ." he began.

Hannah shot to her feet. "Let me guess." She laid the back of her hand on her forehead, placed a falsely moony expression on her face, and sighed dramatically. "Oh, Jed, how could you think such a thing," she said, her voice breathy and too high. "I would never . . . I could never . . ." She fell against his chest, looked up, and fluttered her lashes. "Oh, hold me, darling. I feel faint."

Ending her charade, she slapped him on the chest and stood up straight. "Is that about right?"

Closer than he cared to admit. "She's not as strong as you are, Hannah."

"Did you ask her about the man in her bedroom?"

He nodded. "She was just lonely, and she gave in to temptation that one time. It was a mistake."

Hannah rolled her eyes in open disgust. "I can't believe you fall for everything that woman tells you. I should've gone along to question her myself. So, who was this mistake?"

"She wouldn't tell me," he admitted.

She threw her hands in the air, displaying her total disgust.

He took Hannah's hands and made her sit again. This time, he sat beside her.

"It's not in Sylvia to kill a man."

"It's not in Rose or Baxter, either," she said tersely.

"I don't want to spend what little time we have left chasing after shadows and suspicions." He leaned close, as if to kiss her, but stopped with his mouth an inch or so from hers. "We have better things to do."

She laid a hand on his cheek and sighed. "Jedidiah Rourke, you must think I'm as silly and gullible as Sylvia Clancy knows you to be. I don't give up easily."

"I know that."

"So stop trying to seduce me into admitting that my sister is a murderer."

"Hannah," he said through gritted teeth, "she admitted it herself."

"She was mistaken."

He took a deep, calming breath. Surely there were more agreeable women in the world who would make him feel this way, women who were reasonable, who yielded now and then, who knew when something was over and done with!

"Hannah Winters," he said softly, leaving no room for argument, "this is finished. Do you hear me? Clancy is dead. Baxter is free. Rose did it, and it was an *accident*. Let it go, and let's just enjoy the rest of your time in Rock Creek."

Her calm response, the lack of an argument, was damned unnatural.

"I hate to put my foot down, but you leave me no choice," he said firmly.

She smiled, took his hand in hers, and placed it on her thigh. Finally! This was more like it.

"Feel that?" She guided his fingers over a soft, pliable lump beneath her skirt.

"Your garter?"

She nodded. "White," she whispered, "with an edging of lace, a thin blue stripe, and a lavender rose."

He grinned, for a moment, until she lifted his hand by the wrist and dropped it as if she'd touched something dirty and distasteful.

"I hope you found the description adequate, because you will never see it."

She stood and walked away, head high.

"Hannah . . ." he began, rushing after her.

"Put your foot down," she muttered. "I'll have you know I don't need or want another father to make my decisions for me. Put your *foot* down!"

"It's just an expression."

"No one condescends to me," she snapped, rejecting his argument. "Not even you."

Jed stopped in his tracks. He did not run after disagreeable women! Not even Hannah.

"Why do you have to make everything difficult?" he bellowed.

She didn't answer. Just kept stalking toward the door to the hotel, crisp and stern.

"You're not the only woman in the world," he said, his voice lower as Hannah reached the door and laid her hand on the knob.

"I know that very well," she said, her voice so soft he could barely hear her.

"And I'm not going to chase after you like some lovesick calf and keep up this ridiculous investigation into a murder that's already been resolved just to make you happy!"

"I don't expect you to," she said calmly.

She slammed the door with a solid thud of finality. Hannah didn't give up and he didn't back down. Where did that leave them?

Eighteen

Did the man think that just because she had slept with him, he could now tell her what to do? That after last night he controlled her? Put his foot down, indeed.

Spine straight, head high, Hannah stalked through the hotel lobby and kept going, onto the boardwalk and into the street. A chilly December wind lashed her face. Odd, she hadn't felt so cold before, sitting in the garden. Tears stung her eyes, tears brought on by the harsh wind, she told herself, even though she knew deep down that wasn't entirely true.

Why had she ever thought Jed was different? All her life her father had been her dictator, commanding her behavior and feelings. Richard had tried to do the same, hadn't he? Since then, the men who had been so foolish as to think they could rule her life, thanks to the simple gift of male superiority, had been quickly sent packing.

No one would rule her life again, no one would tell her what to feel and how to live. Put his *foot* down!

People up and down the Rock Creek street walked and talked and went about their business.

Some of them nodded politely as they passed; a few ignored her. As she stood there, at the edge of the street, her heart sank; the wind-induced tears filled her eyes. She had never felt as lonely as she did at this moment, even though she had been alone most of her life. Had she begun to rely on Jed, so quickly? How foolish.

She had known all along that what they had was physical and interesting and . . . temporary. A few days together, no more. Even if she *had* begun to love him, that didn't change the facts.

Finding the murderer was her only goal. Hannah shook off her melancholy and headed for the general store. First she'd confirm the fact that the slashing blow was the only one Rose had delivered; then she'd begin asking questions again. Someone in this town had murdered Reverend Clancy, and she was going to uncover the truth before she returned to Alabama.

Jed stuck his head into the dining room, hoping he'd find Hannah there drinking coffee with Eden and Cash as she'd been when he'd found her earlier. Instead, he saw his sister and the gunslinger talking in low tones and laughing. Well, Eden laughed.

Cash turned his head to the doorway. "Miss Winters is not here," he said, instantly sensing what Jed wanted to know. "She stormed out of the hotel like a soldier on a mission."

"That's what I was afraid of," Jed mumbled. What kind of trouble would she get herself into now? Lord, when the woman got a notion she just would not let it go!

Nodding to Eden, Cash rose from his seat, grabbed his black hat, and headed toward Jed. "What's going on?"

As they walked outside the hotel to be blasted by a gust of wind, Jed saw Hannah down the street, entering the general store. He kept his eyes on the spot where she'd emerge when her business there was done, leaning against the outer wall of the hotel as he told Cash what had happened since his return to Rock Creek.

Cash knew about Clancy's murder and Baxter's trial, since that was the hottest gossip in town, but he didn't know about Hannah's suspicions.

Ridiculous suspicions, Jed thought angrily. Just like a woman!

Adjusting the flat-brimmed hat on his head, Cash leaned against the wall beside Jed, seemingly at ease. Still, the man was never completely relaxed.

"What if she's right?"

Jed jerked his head around. "What?"

"Well, it's not like there's not a dozen people in town who couldn't have done it."

He couldn't believe what he was hearing. "Rose confessed."

"So did Baxter," Cash reasoned. "They were covering for each other, right?"

"Whose side are you on, runt?" Jed bellowed.

Cash smiled, crookedly and easily. "I didn't know we were taking sides."

"I just want Hannah to get this fool notion out of her head," Jed said more calmly.

"So you can keep her in your bed instead of following her all over town like a faithful watchdog while she plays at being a Pinkerton?"

Jed didn't dignify that presumption with a response.

Cash's eyes cut up and down the main street. "It's the second wound that muddies the waters," he said lowly and thoughtfully. "I can see Rose striking out at Clancy in the right circumstances." He shook his head smoothly. "I can't see her taking the second stab. It's too cold. Too calculating for Rose."

"Then Baxter did it."

"*Our* Baxter Sutton?" Cash asked incredulously. "The man wouldn't squash a bug if he thought there was a chance the thing might lift its tiny, dying head and bite him on the ankle. He wouldn't even defend his family when El Diablo was terrorizing this town. Do you think he's changed that much in four years?"

Gritting his teeth, Jed turned his face away from Cash. He kept his eyes on the general store down the boardwalk. "Maybe he has."

"Okay, so who lured your Hannah out to Wishing Rock and tried to kill her?"

He could reason with Cash. Hannah wouldn't listen, but Cash was a reasonable man. Usually. Well, sometimes. "She had a run-in with Oliver Jennings, and half a dozen other people since she got here. Coulda been any one of them."

"Miss Winters does have a way of getting under a man's skin, doesn't she?" Cash asked softly.

"Leave your skin out of this, runt," Jed grumbled.

Cash sighed and shuffled his feet. "Any other man in Texas who had the nerve to call me *runt* would get their fool head blown off for the trouble." He shook his head and gave into a half smile. "That woman of yours said she thought I would be *taller.*"

At five-foot-eleven, Cash was tall enough in most crowds, but among their group, the six of them who had fought together on and off for more than ten years, he was the shortest. By about half an inch.

"Yes, well, grow a little bit and you won't have to worry about it."

"You I can understand. We've run together long enough you know I won't shoot you. But your Hannah"—he shook his head—"she's either got balls or absolutely no common sense."

"No balls," Jed mumbled, and Cash snorted a laugh in response.

But no common sense sounded about right. Sure, Hannah seemed sensible enough, but when she got an idea in her pretty little head . . .

Cash nodded. "There she is."

Jed shifted his head to watch Hannah as she stepped onto the boardwalk. The wind whipped her skirt and strands of her normally well re-strained red hair.

If she was determined to continue this foolishness, he had no choice but to keep an eye on her. She wouldn't like it, not after their recent spat, but what choice did he have? He'd just have to keep his distance while he watched.

Hannah clutched a new cane, an unadorned walking stick, as she set her eyes on something down the street. The rectory, perhaps.

"This can't be good," Cash said softly. "She's armed."

* * *

Since Rose had cried with relief when she'd learned there was a second stab wound, Hannah had no doubt that her sister was innocent. Baxter had been unarguably relieved as well, so Hannah was just as sure he wasn't responsible for Clancy's death.

Sylvia Clancy was the obvious suspect. Not because Hannah didn't personally like the woman, but because she had been nearby and would have had easy access during the short period between the time Rose left the rectory and Baxter arrived. During those few minutes, someone had taken the knife and delivered the fatal blow.

Hannah gripped the head of the cane she'd purchased from Rose's store. It was too plain for her tastes, but would suffice until an appropriate replacement for the cane that had been transformed into a torch could be ordered. She needed something to hold on to right now, something solid to grasp in her hand. Without it, she felt defenseless.

She used the head of the cane to rap soundly on the rectory door.

Sylvia answered quickly. She was fully dressed and prepared for company, unlike the last time Hannah had called on her.

"I have nothing to say to you," Sylvia said, trying to swing the door shut in Hannah's face.

The cane swung out and stopped the progress of the door. "I just have a few questions."

"Jed told me about your suspicions," Sylvia hissed. "You're a crazy woman."

Two ladies passed behind Hannah, not terribly close, but certainly near enough to hear every word that was spoken.

"We can discuss this here," Hannah said politely, "or we can discuss it in the privacy of your home. But I'm not going to simply walk away. Not until I get some answers."

With a scowl, Sylvia threw open the door. "Your sister murdered my husband and got away with it," Sylvia said as she closed the door. "What do we have to talk about?"

"Rose did not kill your husband," Hannah said sensibly. "She did injure him, after he made an improper advance and she felt she had no choice but to defend herself, but someone else delivered the second, killing stab."

Sylvia flinched. "Do you think I don't know what my husband was like?" she asked softly. "That I didn't see how he took any and every opportunity to lay his hands on other women? He was a wolf, Miss Winters, who preyed on everything in skirts and used his vocation to lure them into his confidence and then . . . and then . . ."

"Is that what he did to you?" Hannah asked softly.

"Yes," she snapped. "I thought Maurice loved me. After I married him, I found out differently. He needed a wife, and apparently thought I would be . . . easy to manipulate. I had no family to run to, no options, once I was his wife and discovered what he was really like."

Perfectly solid reasoning for murder, Hannah thought. "Is that why you took up with another man? To get back at your husband for being unfaithful?"

If looks could kill, she would surely fall dead on the spot. Sylvia glared at Hannah with hate flashing in her eyes.

"Jed told me what you said, about it being a one-time mistake, but it just makes sense to me that if your husband was such a despicable man you would need the comfort of someone loving in your life." Hannah tried her best to sound sympathetic, as if she understood the infidelity.

Sylvia's face fell, and she looked, at that moment, a good ten years older and not so beautiful at all. "Virgil made me feel good again. I've been seeing him for the past two years. Since Jed"—her eyes hardened again—"since Jed refused to come back into my life because his morals wouldn't allow him to sleep with a married woman."

Hannah felt a rush of relief that weakened her knees. She should have known. . . . "This Virgil"—the name was familiar, but at the moment she couldn't place it—"could he have killed your husband in order to have you all to himself?"

Sylvia shook her head. "He wasn't in town when Maurice was killed." She cast Hannah a wry, sad smile. "Besides, he hasn't exactly asked me to run away with him since Maurice is gone. In fact, I've only seen him twice since my husband died, even though he's been in town for a good while, this time. I think he liked it better when I didn't need him so much, when what we had was quick and illicit and . . . undemanding."

Hannah could almost feel sorry for the widow. Jed was right. Sylvia Clancy was not a strong woman. She needed someone to take care of her.

Since she'd pushed Jed away, and Sylvia was no longer a married woman, would the two of them end up back together? She couldn't see Jed and Sylvia as a couple. He was too strong; she was too needy.

Maybe she didn't want to see them as a couple. The very idea hurt.

"Please think back," Hannah said calmly. "Did you see or hear anything suspicious that morning?"

Sylvia shook her head. "It happened just as I said it did. I had been working in the winter garden, and when I came inside, through the kitchen and into the parlor, I found Baxter standing over Maurice with a knife in his hand."

Hannah nodded her head, disappointed but not terribly surprised. "Well, thank you. If you think of anything else . . ." She stopped, almost startled as she remembered where she'd heard the name *Virgil* before. "Virgil Wyndham?" she asked belatedly. "The gambler?"

Sylvia nodded her head.

"Was he here the morning your husband was killed?"

Sylvia's eyebrows arched in surprise. "No," she said, opening the door to all but shove Hannah out. "I already told you, he wasn't here."

Hannah practically ran down the street, her step brisk as she approached. At first Jed thought she had discovered that he and Cash had been following her and was out for blood, but when she came near and he saw the sparkle in her eyes, he knew it wasn't anger that put color in her cheeks and a spring in her step.

He almost grinned and stepped forward to greet her, until her eyes swept unthinkingly past him and landed on Cash. And she smiled.

"Just the man I wanted to see," she said.

Cash raised his eyebrows and lifted an innocent hand to his chest. "Me?"

Hannah stopped a mere two feet from the gunslinger. "When will your saloon be open?"

Saloon?

Cash shrugged his shoulders. "A couple of weeks. The place I'm looking at is in pretty bad shape."

"Saloon?" Jed asked softly. They both ignored him.

With color in her cheeks and that light in her eyes, Hannah looked radiantly gorgeous. Cash saw it, too; Jed could tell by the way the man's eyes raked insolently over her. The prim blouse and jacket and plain skirt couldn't disguise her figure, the way her breasts heaved as she breathed heavily.

"I know who killed Reverend Clancy," Hannah revealed in a lowered voice.

"You do?" Cash asked, as if he were truly interested in her fantastic theories.

"Sylvia did not . . ." Jed began.

Hannah cut him a quick glance, her smile fading quickly. "No, she didn't. You were right about that."

"Then who?"

Hannah hesitated. "I don't know why or how just yet, but I think it was Sylvia's lover"—she hesitated, and her eyes danced—"Virgil Wyndham."

"The gambler who was on the stage?" Jed almost recoiled in horror. *That* was who Sylvia had taken up with?

"When I spoke to Rose earlier, she said there was a man skulking about when she left the rectory that morning."

"Skulking," Jed snapped. "And she just now remembered? How convenient."

Hannah laid long-suffering eyes on him. "Well, she didn't *say* skulking, and she couldn't identify the man, but she did say she passed a well-dressed man with a potbelly on her way to fetch Baxter. She didn't pay enough attention at the time because she was distraught."

"That doesn't mean . . ."

"Sylvia says Virgil was not in town that morning," Hannah interrupted, "but she might be protecting him. She has a very strong fear of being alone, I suspect," she added thoughtfully.

"What do you propose?" Cash asked, pretending to be interested again.

Hannah turned to face the gunslinger, and the smile came back. "A trap," she whispered. "And what better place to trap a gambler than in a saloon?"

"I had planned to take my time, but if we worked at it, the place could be ready in two days," Cash said, humoring Hannah.

"Marvelous," Hannah breathed.

"The only problem is," Jed snapped, "Cash doesn't believe in physical labor."

"I've got nothing against hard work," Cash said defensively, "as long as someone else is doing it."

"Jed will help," Hannah insisted.

"I will?"

"And Rico, and maybe even the sheriff."

"Reese might not mind lending a hand," Cash added.

Hannah smiled. Not at him, but at Cash. "I don't mind rolling up my sleeves and getting dirty in the name of a good cause."

Cash ignored a scowling Jed and offered Hannah his arm. She *took* it.

"You and I got off to a rather poor start," Cash said in his most charming voice.

"We did, didn't we?" Hannah agreed. "Well, I'm sure that can be remedied. First impressions are not always correct. I do apologize for . . . well, for saying some most inappropriate things to you in the heat of the moment."

"As do I," Cash said formally, a sparkle in his black eyes.

"And of course, you are quite tall," Hannah said sweetly, "compared to men of normal height."

Jed groaned out loud and cursed beneath his breath.

"So," Cash mused as he started down the boardwalk, Hannah comfortable and quite at ease on his arm, "what kind of plan is this?"

Jed stayed close behind.

"The details are sketchy," Hannah confided, "but I should have everything worked out in two days."

"I do love a good scheme," Cash said conversationally.

"So do I," Hannah said brightly.

Jed leaned forward, practically placing his head between theirs. "It's so nice that you two have found something in common. Something besides the fact that people flee in terror when they see you coming."

He didn't think that was funny, but Cash and Hannah both laughed.

Nineteen

The place looked as much like a saloon as the inside of the cave he and Hannah had been lost in. Vast, dirty, and literally falling down, the building was sure as hell nothing special.

But Cash seemed proud of it. The place was his.

Afternoon light shot through dirty windows, lighting the bare floor. "I was thinking of calling it the Golden Palace." Cash said, perfectly serious.

Nate, still sober enough at this time of day to have a sense of humor, laughed out loud. "Fancy name for a hole in the wall."

"I like it," Hannah said primly, casting a disapproving glance at Nate. "It has class."

Cash bowed in her direction, a small, sardonic grin on his face. "Thank you, Miss Winters."

She rolled up her sleeves and shoved them to her elbows. "If I'm going to spend the better part of the next couple of days scrubbing your establishment, you might as well call me Hannah."

"Hannah it is," he said, waggling his eyebrows.

Jed scowled. He'd rarely seen Cash so damned *agreeable*.

Hannah swept and vigorously washed the windows, putting everything she had into her menial chores. Nate and Jed moved broken boards and replaced them, hauled out collapsed furniture and an old moldy rug, and repaired two bullet holes in the wall.

Cash watched from a chair in the corner, supervising each task.

Rico arrived when they'd been at it an hour, telling them that Lily hadn't been happy about his assisting in the preparations for competition, but when she'd learned they planned to lure Virgil Wyndham into the new place she'd almost forced him out the door. She didn't care for the gambler all but living in her place.

By the time Sullivan and Reese arrived, they'd made apparent progress. The place didn't look like a saloon, and it sure as hell didn't look like any *palace*, but it was clean and almost habitable.

Hannah, obviously exhausted, excused herself. Cash rose to thank her for her assistance and see her out. That scoundrel.

Once Hannah was gone, the atmosphere changed subtly. Cash reclaimed his seat, and the rest resumed their chores. But the truth of the matter was, the six of them hadn't been together like this in a long while. Here they were at long last . . . and Cash had them all doing his dirty work.

"You had best be cautious," Rico said quietly, but loud enough for everyone to hear, as he leaned over a seated Cash. He shook a hammer at the gunslinger. "I do not think Jed cares for you being so courteous to his woman."

"*His* woman?" Cash, leaning back and balancing his chair on two legs, asked as if he didn't have a clue.

"She's not mine," Jed said as he pulled up a rotten board, a board that had once been the bottom of a long stairway of rotten steps. "Cash can be courteous to whoever he damn well pleases."

Sullivan, his damnable brother-in-law, laughed. "You can cut the sour act, Jed. She's gone." He turned his head to Reese and lowered his voice—again not enough to make a difference. "First time I saw the woman, she called Jed a ruffian. I swear, his eyes lit up like a kid who's just been handed his first puppy."

"Look at him," Cash said, lazily waving a hand in Jed's direction. "He shaved and cut his hair, and I think he's already had *two* baths this week."

"Cut it out."

"The mighty has fallen," Nate said, lifting a glass of whiskey, silently saluting Jed, then tossing it back, the first to be consumed in the Golden Palace.

"I have not fallen."

"Come on, Jed. It's not so bad. Admit it."

The last thing he wanted to do was snivel over a woman in front of these men. They were his friends, his family, his comrades. And Hannah had made it clear she didn't want anything to do with him, right? Not unless it was on *her* terms. Her way or not at all.

He gave the new bottom step he was hammering into place all his attention as he said calmly, "Y'all should know me better than that. Hannah Winters is a stubborn, difficult, cranky old maid. Maybe I did pass some time in her company, but she's not my type. She's too damn troublesome.

A man shouldn't have to work so hard just to get along with a woman."

"Jed," Reese said, his voice lowered.

No arguments, Jed thought as he hammered at the nails in the step. He was too damn close to caving in as it was. "Hell, it's no wonder she never got married," he began. "She's . . ."

"Jed," Sullivan said, his voice more urgent than Reese's had been.

"No," a soft voice whispered. "Do let him finish. I really would like to know why I've never married."

He turned and laid his eyes on Hannah, who stood in the doorway holding a tray laden with a pot of coffee and a pile of Eden's tea cakes.

Her eyes hardened. "No one's ever been so kind as to explain it to me before. Please continue."

Her heart beat too hard, her gut twisted and ached. She wanted to run, but she didn't. Hannah Winters didn't run, not anymore. She sure as hell wasn't going to run from Jed Rourke.

She placed the tray she and Eden had prepared together on the single table in the room, where Cash and Nate sat, but she never took her eyes off of Jed. "Let's see. I believe I've heard everything pertinent thus far. I arrived just in time to hear that I am a cranky old maid. Did I miss any significant criticisms?"

Jed dropped his hammer and stood, tall and broad and much too large. She refused to back down, though, no matter how intimidating he might be.

He actually had the gall to reach out and take

her arm. "Let's go for a walk and discuss this in private."

She shook off his hand and glared into his eyes. "Oh, no. Let's not deprive your pals of their entertainment. That's what this is all about, isn't it? Entertainment. For you, for your friends. I'm so happy I could be of service. Please continue. I'm anxious to hear why I haven't yet been able to land a husband."

Jed took a deep breath, squared his shoulders, and balled his fists. "You make everything so damn difficult," he said softly. "More difficult than it has to be."

"Perhaps I do, on occasion. But you should consider the possibility that the reason I'm not married is because I choose not to be." She gave him a tight smile. "Really, look around you." She turned her back on him and surveyed the room and its inhabitants.

"Here we have Rock Creek's finest," she said with a wave of her hand. She walked forward to stand before Nate. "A pathetic drunk who quotes scripture and wallows in self-pity." In response, he raised his glass to her in silent salute and took another long drink.

"And Daniel Cash," she continued, looking down at Cash's unsmiling face, "who shows poorer judgment than any grown man I've ever met. Are you trying to get yourself killed or are you simply incredibly stupid?" She didn't wait for a response, but moved on to the sheriff. "And you. Good heavens, the simplest, feeblest brain could've deduced that Baxter was innocent, and yet the fact somehow bypassed you. How is that?"

Rico and Reese stood together, near the door.

She trained her eyes squarely on Lily Salvatore's husband, who lifted his eyebrows in question. "Here we have a pretty boy, who has no doubt charmed his way through life and will continue to do so for as long as his face will allow," she said without flinching.

Hannah turned her critical perusal to Reese, who watched her stoically. She shook her head in dismay. "You have a lovely wife and child at home, a woman and a daughter who, for some unknown reason, adore you. And where do you spend your time? Hanging around with these large children. Which, I must point out, makes you no better than a large child yourself."

Hannah came full circle and stood before Jed. "And you." Her heart caught in her throat, but she fought hard not to show it. She had to walk away from Jed, but she would not do it with her head hanging. "You disappoint me most of all, because I thought you were different. And all along you were no better than the rest. An overgrown boy with a sadly inadequate character and the temper of a spoiled brat."

Jed glared down at her. He looked hurt, angry, and for a heartbeat she wanted to take back everything she'd said.

"There's not a man in Texas stupid enough to do what you've just done," he said gruffly. "You insulted all six of us in less than two minutes."

"All I did was tell the truth," she whispered. "If you can't take it, you don't have to listen."

Jed waited for the explosion that was sure to come from the men around him. They didn't take insults lightly. But no one spoke up. They all waited.

"If you don't have anything interesting to add," Hannah said softly, "I'm leaving. I think I've heard more than enough."

She glanced down at Cash as she walked past. "I'll be by in the morning ready to work. I really am in no mood to do more today."

Cash tipped his hat and said he understood completely. At the door, Rico and Reese stepped apart and allowed her to pass between them.

Jed was just about to apologize for her when Nate spoke up, lifting his glass high once again. " 'Fair as the moon, clear as the sun, and terrible as an army with banners.' "

"You just proved her right," Sullivan said. Nate shrugged nonchalantly and finished off his glass of whiskey.

"I'd say Jed has finally met the perfect woman." Cash leaned his chair back on two legs and grinned insanely.

"Perfect woman?" Jed snapped. "Did you hear a word she just said?"

"She was angry," Rico said sensibly. "With good reason."

"And she was right about one thing, pretty boy," Reese said, clapping Rico on the back before turning about. "I'm going home."

"Me, too," Sullivan said.

Jed was left alone with a smug Cash and an almost drunk Nate.

Cash pointed a finger at Nate. "You gave me an idea. I think I'll call this place The Sun and the Moon."

"Funny name for a saloon," Nate muttered.

"Unless something else comes to me," Cash said, quickly losing his enthusiasm for the name.

He pinned his black eyes on Jed. "Calm down. You hurt Hannah's feelings and she lashed out. It's not all that unusual for a woman."

"I didn't hurt her feelings," Jed said defensively. "She doesn't have feelings. She has . . . She has . . . temper tantrums. Talk about a spoiled brat!"

But he did wish she hadn't heard what he'd said. He'd meant every word. But then again . . . "Just a spoiled brat," he reiterated, more for himself than for Cash or Nate. "A brat who's too used to getting her damned way. She'll be fine in the morning."

Cash shook his head. "If you didn't see the hurt in her eyes," he said, "then you don't deserve her. Leave her alone and let her go."

"That's exactly what I intend to do," Jed muttered as he headed for the door.

Well, she'd been so sure Bertie and Oliver Jennings made an impossible couple, but they stood before her looking shy and sweet and very much in love. Oliver even seemed quite contrite about his earlier behavior.

Hannah's heart sank. She'd always known that one day Bertie would find herself a husband and settle down. But she had never expected that her maid and companion was so brave as to turn her back on the only life she knew, to tame a rough cowboy and make him . . . sweet and malleable. Mousy Bertie had been able to accomplish what Hannah herself had not.

Jed's words from earlier that day came back to haunt her. How close was he to the truth?

"When are you going home?" Bertie asked.

Standing in the general store, long after closing time, Hannah was glad of the darkness. A single lantern lit the room, so it was no chore to stay in the shadows.

"Next week," she said. "Probably the day after Christmas." By then she would have proved Wyndham guilty and her usefulness here would be done. Time to go home. Why did her heart feel small and cold at the thought?

Oliver shuffled his feet and tried to smile. There was a vague sort of handsomeness to him, when the light hit him just so. Hannah could see why Bertie was smitten with him.

"I really am sorry you and I got off on the wrong foot," he said.

"There's no need to apologize." Again. "I suppose I was out of line with my personal questions."

Oliver's smile faded. "Everything's all right now. That's all that matters."

Bertie wrapped her arm through his and grinned. "We're getting married next month," she said. "I wish you could stay for the wedding."

Hannah shook her head. Another month in this place? She would die. "I would love to, but I'm afraid that's impossible."

She gave the young lovers a nod of her head as she turned away and headed for the stairs. An evening with Franklin and Jackson was preferable to watching this tender scene. It reminded her of what she didn't have. Love. Happiness. A man to lean on.

She didn't need any of that, she reminded herself as she climbed the stairs and braced herself. She never had and she never would.

* * *

Jed gratefully took a break from working in Cash's saloon to give Teddy the lessons he'd promised more than once since arriving in Rock Creek.

They stood by the river, a target of bottles and cans set up a good distance away.

Teddy took careful aim and fired, finding his target. Damn, the kid had been good from the first time he'd held a rifle, and he got better every day.

"Not bad," Jed said. "But you could be faster."

"Why?" Teddy asked solemnly.

Jed grinned. "Don't tell your mother I said this, but the truth of the matter is, you don't learn to handle a rifle to shoot at bottles the rest of your life. You learn so you can defend yourself and those you love from danger."

"And bandits won't stand still and wait for me to take aim," Teddy said.

"That's right."

He hoped with all his heart that Teddy would never have to fire a weapon at another person. He wanted the kid to be spared war and heartache and danger. That wasn't likely, though, and it was always best to be prepared.

"You take the three on the left," he said. "I'll take the three on the right."

Together they raised their rifles and fired. Explosions filled the air as Jed dispatched his three targets quickly and efficiently. Teddy lagged behind, but not by much.

"Good," Jed said as he lowered his weapon. The air still reverberated with the sounds of rifle

fire. Everything around them shimmered, alive
with the fading vibrations.

Yep, he'd always been brutally honest with himself and those around him. There was no use pretending that life was pretty all the time, that Eden
and Sullivan could keep all these kids safe forever.

Just as there was no use in pretending he and
Hannah could make what they had work. Unless . . .

"When are you leaving?" Teddy asked softly.

Jed looked down into deep, brown eyes that saw
too much. "Did my eyebrow twitch?"

Teddy nodded.

"Damn."

Hannah threw herself into the repair of what
would soon become Cash's saloon. She cleaned,
repaired the odds and ends of furniture they
would start with, and saw that the men were fed.
Eden did the cooking, and Hannah made the de-
liveries.

Jed worked hard but steered clear of her. She
did the same. She didn't mourn what she had lost
or thrown away, but accepted this debacle of a
love affair the same way she accepted everything
else she destroyed. Chin high and denial firmly
planted in her mind.

It would take three days to get the place up and
running, not two, and as they entered their last
day of work she felt a great sense of satisfaction.
They had taken a ramshackle old building and
made it into something. . . . She glanced around
at the mismatched tables and the long polished
bar, the shelves of whiskey and the large mirror

behind the bar, the amateurish portrait of a very nude woman at the back of the room. . . . Something quite decadent.

"This is no Golden Palace," she muttered as she stood, hands on hips, and surveyed her surroundings. "It's more like a tin shack, or a copper hovel. Cash, I fear your saloon will only be a palace to rogues and ruffians."

He grinned, that sardonic smile that did not touch his eyes. "Thank you, Hannah. Rogue's Palace it is."

Jed joined them, and for the first time since Hannah had called him a spoiled brat, among other things, she looked him in the eye. If only she didn't love him, still! He was an impossible man, insulting and demanding and . . . and too much like her in too many ways. When two people who refused to compromise came together, there could be no good end to the affair.

"So, what's the plan?" Jed asked.

"I'm still working on it," she admitted.

"Wyndham will be here tonight to play poker. When are you going to let us in on this scheme of yours so we'll know what to do?"

"There's no need for you to do anything," Hannah said primly. "I'll handle it. I just need you and your friends nearby to detain Wyndham once I have his confession."

Jed put his hands on his hips. "You plan to be here?" He shook his head in denial. "I don't think that's such a good idea."

"I got us this far. I intend to see this through to the end." She nodded her head in dismissal.

She expected an argument. What she got was a soft hand on her cheek. "I just don't want to see you hurt," he said lowly. "If you're right and Wyndham is a murderer, I don't want you anywhere near this place."

Cash quietly excused himself and headed out, for a breath of fresh air, he said. Nate, however, had claimed a seat in the corner and showed no intentions of leaving.

Jed took her arm and pulled her toward the stairway. Together they climbed to the top and sat there, side by side and looking down over the Rogue's Palace.

"We've said some harsh things to each other," Jed said softly. "But I care about you, and I don't want to see you hurt because you got yourself into something you can't get out of."

Oh, no wonder she had fallen in love with Jed. Maybe he was an ill-tempered ruffian, but he was *her* ill-tempered ruffian, and beneath that rough exterior there beat a heart of gold. She knew it, if no one else did. If only she could truly trust him. If only she could relax her guard, just a little.

She leaned over and surprised him with a kiss on the cheek, directly on his endearing dimple. "You're a very sweet man, Jed Rourke. With you and Cash and Nate standing by, I have no fears about tonight. I'll be fine."

He cupped her face and pulled her to him, for a real kiss this time. With slightly parted lips, he tasted and teased her. He stirred her blood and made her feel as if there were nothing in the world but this: the two of them and the way they came together.

"I've missed you," he whispered against her mouth. "The last couple of nights, I just lie in bed and think about you. You're making me crazy, Hannah."

"I can hardly sleep at all," she confessed. "But Jed, I don't think we can make this work."

He grinned at her, took her hand, and pulled her to the top of the stairs. There he pulled her into a dimly lit hallway. "Maybe we can," he said. "I was down by the river with Teddy this afternoon, and I had a thought." He hesitated, almost as if he were nervous about what was to come. "Don't go back to that plantation in Alabama. Stay here with me."

"Until you get itchy feet and hit the road again?" she teased, not for a moment taking him seriously. "What kind of a woman do you think I am?"

"My kind of woman," he said. "Maybe when I hit the road, you could hit it with me."

My kind of woman. Oh, she liked the sound of that. "I have a better idea," she whispered, grabbing his shirtfront and pulling his face down to hers. "Come home to Alabama with me. If your itchy feet can carry you all over the country, why can't they carry you there?"

"And stay?" he asked, incredulous. "What kind of a man do you think I am?"

"My kind of man," she whispered.

He kissed her, cupped her bottom, and pulled her against him. The evidence of his arousal pressed insistently against her.

Jed was in her blood; he reached inside and grabbed her heart and made her crave this. And more. With his mouth he devoured; with his hands he caressed and claimed her. She opened herself to him, completely. She loved him. She trusted him.

She had always had power, a power that came from her money or her family name, but she had never felt this kind of force. A personal, intimate power over a single strong man, while she herself was helpless against the need that grew inside her.

Jed backed her up against the wall, forcing her legs apart with his knee. Her heart skipped a beat.

"I need you," he whispered in her ear, lifting her leg high to bring himself closer, more intimately against her. His hand slipped beneath her skirt, pushed it high and tugged at the waistband of her drawers. She heard a small tearing sound, as a few stitches popped.

A moment ago she had been filled with passion and need and even that elusive bliss, but suddenly something was wrong. Something was very, very wrong. She smelled . . . horses. Panic rose in her throat, choking her. She froze.

Jed was so much bigger than she was, so much stronger. She had never been as aware of that fact as she was at this moment. His muscular arms trapped her here; his broad body blocked her escape. She couldn't breathe.

He kissed her throat and worked one hand beneath her wide-legged drawers. With insistent, strong fingers, he touched her. He pinned her to the wall and stroked her in the most intimate way possible.

"I love you," he whispered huskily.

Yes, Hannah realized with mounting terror, she definitely smelled horses, manure, hay, and the musky odor of the animals themselves. Somewhere in the back of her mind, she heard one whimper. With Jed pressing against her, she should be hot. But she wasn't. She was cold. Heaven above, she'd never been so cold.

Pulling herself together with great effort, she put her hands against Jed's chest and pushed as hard as she could. "Get your hands off of me," she said, the words choked and raspy. He did as she asked, dropping his hands and backing away from her one step. "Men, you're all alike! You think you can push a woman up against a stable wall and rip at her clothes and lie and tell her you *love* her, and she'll fall at your feet and do anything you ask."

He looked like she'd slapped him, like she'd plunged a knife into his heart. She didn't care. "I thought you were the one person in the world who would never lie to me." Tears stung her eyes. It was the smell of the horses, she reasoned, that made her eyes water this way. "I thought I could *trust* you."

She turned and ran, trying to escape the smell of the horses and the panic in her chest and the helpless feeling of being pressed against a wall with her skirt around her waist and a lying man whispering *I love you* into her ear.

Twenty

Jed walked calmly down the stairs, surrendering a little with each step.

He'd tried, hadn't he? He'd been understanding and forgiving and . . . and damn it, neither of those attributes came naturally to him! Truth of the matter was, he'd been right all along. Loving Hannah was just too damn hard.

Just his luck. The first time in his life he breaks down and tells a woman he loves her, she bolts like the devil is on her tail.

"Pour me one of those, will you?" he said, nodding to the bottle near Nate's hand.

Nate obliged, pouring a healthy shot into a freshly washed glass. Jed took the whiskey and threw it back, then set down the glass for a refill.

He had the urge to bolt himself, just stuff a change of clothes into his saddlebag and hit the road. So what if he'd told the kids he'd be here for Christmas? So what if he left Hannah to finish this stupid scheme to catch a killer on her own?

Cash came waltzing through the front door, his black gaze landing immediately on Jed. "What the hell did you do to that woman?"

"Not a damn thing," Jed growled as he lifted the second glass to his lips.

"Bullshit," Cash drawled.

Jed slammed his glass down on the bar. He was not about to tell these two that he'd made a fool of himself over a woman and she'd fled. That he'd gotten sappy and told Hannah he loved her and she'd pushed him away in horror and run like hell.

"She's crazy," he said calmly. At least, he tried for calm. He felt anything but. A muscle in his cheek twitched; his fingers drummed the bar nervously. Inside he was wound so tight he felt like he was about to rupture. As he glared at the other men leaning on the bar, he began to unwind. Cash understood women. More than Jed did, anyway. If he kept this inside he just might explode.

"Crazy how?" Cash pressed.

Jed wasn't looking for sympathy, and he sure as hell wouldn't get any from these two if he were, but he did need to get this off his chest.

"Try to be nice to the woman, and she turns around and gets agitated for no good reason," he said, taking one more sip. "One minute everything's fine, and then she starts talking about lying men, when I never lied to her, and stables, when we weren't anywhere near any stables. . . ." He shook his head and stared into the glass of whiskey, noting the color and swirl of the liquid there. "I just don't get it," he said softly. "I don't understand women at all. Why do I even try?"

Cash placed his hands on the bar and leaned forward. "You're making this more difficult than it has to be," he said, going for a reasonable tone of voice that didn't quite work. "So what if you don't understand women? To be honest, I don't think we were meant to understand. I don't think they *want* us to understand. If we understand them, they lose some of their appeal."

He didn't think Hannah would play that kind of game. She'd always been so straightforward and honest. But then, he really didn't know her. Not like he'd imagined he did. "But she just didn't make any damned sense."

Nate mumbled something low and indistinct. Jed and Cash both turned their heads in his direction.

"What?" Jed asked.

Nate lifted his head and set bloodshot eyes on Jed. "I said," he repeated, enunciating each word clearly and precisely, "maybe she wasn't talking about you."

For a moment everything was still and quiet. *Push a woman up against a stable wall and rip at her clothes . . . Lying men . . .*

Richard. "Oh, shit," Jed muttered, shoving his unfinished whiskey back. "Hannah's not the dimwit here. I am." He mumbled a few choice words, the obscene insults directed at himself, this time. "Where did she go?" he asked, glancing at Cash. "You saw her leave, right?"

Nate had already returned all his attention to the bottle he kept close.

"She ran to the hotel."

Jed combed back his hair with the fingers of both hands, grabbed the walking stick Hannah had propped against the bar when she'd arrived that morning, and stepped outside. He didn't know if he could fix this or not, but damn it, he had to try.

A cold wind lashed at him as he crossed the street and headed for the hotel. The few people who were out hurried to their destinations quickly, heads down and coats buttoned tight.

The hotel lobby was deserted, and he sprinted up the stairs two at a time. Tempted as he was to bust down Hannah's door, he didn't. He rapped lightly with the head of her cane.

"Hannah?" he called softly when he got no response to the knock. "Open the door."

Maybe she wasn't here. Maybe after she'd run from him she'd kept on running. Through the garden, away from town. He didn't think so, but the very thought of her standing out there in this wind, alone and upset, chilled him to the bone.

He laid his hand on the doorknob and turned. It wasn't locked. The door swung open to reveal Hannah, sitting on the bed with her head down and her hands clasped in her lap, a half-packed trunk at the side of the bed and a bulging smaller tapestry bag at her side. She'd been packing, getting herself ready to keep on running.

Closing the door behind him, Jed placed her cane aside, leaning it against the dresser near the door. He never took his eyes off Hannah, and she didn't lift her head.

He lifted her tapestry bag and placed it on the floor, noting as he moved it aside that her things were stuffed and dropped into the case with no care at all, as if she'd thrown her belongings into the bag in a panic, frantic to get away.

Maybe she was frantic to get away, but not like this. He wouldn't have it. He sat on the bed beside her, placed his hand on her chin and forced her to look at him. She didn't resist.

Hannah's gray eyes were filled with tears; her face had gone deathly pale. Her lips trembled when she whispered, "I'm sorry."

He pulled her head against his shoulder. "You don't have to apologize to me, darlin'."

"I do," she whispered. "I don't know why I . . . why I got so . . ."

Rocking gently on the bed, he comforted her. She relaxed against his chest, eventually. Wrapped her arms around his waist and held on tight.

He could let it go, pretend nothing had happened back at Cash's place. Holding Hannah, comforting her, would be enough. But he had a feeling—no, he *knew*—that if he didn't take care of this problem here and now it would continue to come back and haunt them. Again and again.

"You said Richard didn't force you," he said lowly. "Son of a bitch, I'll kill him."

She shook her head. "He didn't. He just . . ." She sighed, took a deep breath, and expelled it against his chest. "I wasn't ready. I didn't want . . . I did tell him no, at first. But he told me he loved me, and at that moment I wanted to be loved more than anything in the world, so I . . . I didn't say no again. I stood there with my back against the wall and let him do exactly what he wanted because I was such a pathetic, lonely, wretched . . ."

"Stop it," Jed ordered in a low voice.

Hannah took another deep breath. "Of course he was lying," she continued, her voice calmer. "He wanted to marry my father's fortune, and I guess he thought if we'd sealed our betrothal with an act of intimacy there was no way I or my father could refuse him." She shuddered. "He was wrong."

Jed tightened his arms around her. She had never seemed so tiny to him before, so fragile. Not his Hannah.

"When he walked away," she whispered, "I felt like the world was crumbling in on me. Nothing happened the way it was supposed to. And then my father had to have his say. He looked at me and knew what had happened." She sniffled and buried her head against his chest. "I decided it was better to let him believe I was a slut than to allow him to find out what a desperate misfit I had become."

Her hair was in a tangle, so he let it down, taking out one pin at a time. "You are not now, nor have you ever been, a desperate misfit," he said angrily. He combed out the dark red tangles with his fingers. "And I'd still like to kill Richard, that lyin', scheming, sweet-talking son of a bitch."

Hannah lifted her face to look at him. Her eyes were still damp, but no more tears fell. A touch of color had returned to her cheeks. More than anything, he wanted to take away the pain he saw there.

"I don't know what happened to me back there," she whispered. "That night is just a bad memory. I never think about it, I never dream about it, but . . . but today I smelled the stables when you touched me, I heard the horses, and when I looked at you I didn't see you. I saw *him* and I panicked."

"It's okay."

"It's not okay," she answered quickly, a hint of anger creeping into her voice. "I'm not supposed to have any weaknesses. I'm not supposed to be deathly afraid of something that happened eight years ago."

He held her head in his hands. "You don't have to be fearless, Hannah," he said, watching her eyes closely.

"I do," she breathed.

He lowered his head to kiss her softly, gently, his mouth barely brushing hers. "Then be fearless," he whispered. "I love you."

She stiffened, but didn't bolt off the bed.

"See? That wasn't so bad." He threaded his fingers through her long hair.

Hannah shook her head gently, in denial. Jed couldn't love her. He might like her on occasion, and he did want her, but he couldn't possibly *love* her. She waited for the onslaught of panic, the assault of odors and noises that did not belong in this time and place, but all she smelled was Jed, the scent of his skin near her nose; all she heard was the wind buffeting the hotel.

"What if it doesn't stop?" she whispered.

"We'll make it stop," he said, leaving no room for argument.

"But . . ."

He silenced her with a kiss, and her heart lurched. All her life she'd been hiding from this, afraid of surrender, afraid of offering her heart to be battered and broken. And cherished. "I love you, too," she whispered when he took his mouth from hers. "So much."

Jed smiled at her, and she knew, at that moment, that he wasn't lying. He truly thought he loved her. She was still afraid.

"Make love to me," she whispered.

He answered with a kiss that shook her to her bones, a deep, searing kiss that sealed their vows of love indelibly.

They fell back on the bed, kissing, touching, taking it slow. Everything—every touch, every kiss, every heartbeat—was slow and sweet. Her body pressed against his, and still she was unable to get close enough.

Jed laid his lips on the pulse at her throat, holding his mouth there, sucking gently while his hands danced over her body. He knew where to touch her—a flick of his fingers here, a heated brush of his palm there. Soon her body cried out for his, tingling and reaching.

But the memory of the moment in the hall stayed with her. She couldn't completely shake off the panic, the disorientation. The terror of being yanked back to another time and another man.

Slowly, she disengaged herself from Jed's warm embrace, pulling back her arms, rolling back her legs, scooting off the bed. Jed didn't try to drag her back. He just watched with smoldering eyes as she lifted her skirt and unbuttoned the drawers, letting them fall to the floor to be kicked aside. She crooked her finger at him, and he came.

She took his hand and led him to the wall beside the dresser, placing her spine against the wall, pulling him in to her, and lifting her face for a kiss.

"Are you sure this is what you want?" he whispered.

"Yes." He said she didn't have to be fearless. Deep in her heart she knew that wasn't true. She *did* have to be fearless. Brave. She could harbor no weaknesses. How else could she survive? If anyone could exorcise this particular fear, it was Jed Rourke.

Jed kissed her again, deep and arousing, while he lifted her skirt. He slipped one hand under her thigh and lifted it, hooking her leg around his thigh, bringing them closer together. She closed her eyes and rested her head against the wall, as he kissed and touched her. His hand caressed her hip, her thigh, and then he laid his fingers on her intimately, stroking gently until her body cried out for him to join with her.

"Open your eyes," he whispered hoarsely.

She obeyed, looking up into the fiercest, most beautiful blue eyes she had ever seen.

"If you feel even one second of doubt, all you have to do is say stop," he said, his voice low and rumbling. "I don't care where we are or what we're doing. You say *stop* and it's over."

She nodded.

Jed lowered his head to kiss her neck tenderly again, sucking against the flesh until her entire body throbbed in time with her heartbeat. Warm and gentle, tenacious and tender, he aroused her more with every touch, with every seductive brush of his lips. There was nothing so beautiful as the feel of his mouth against the side of her neck, nothing so fine as the way he sucked and nibbled and kissed the column of her throat.

The hand he caressed her breasts with was demanding without force, stimulating with every stroke. Her nipples hardened at his touch, her breasts grew heavy and tender. He unfastened the buttons of her bodice and slipped his hand inside to touch her bare breasts, and she sucked in her breath at the sensation of those large, tender hands caressing her. Arousing and readying her.

He lifted her skirt to her waist, shoved it impatiently aside. His arousal pressed against her belly. He made sure she felt it as he freed himself.

With a gentle heave he lifted her off her feet, dragging her up and across his hard body. She wrapped both legs around his hips. The arms around his neck tightened as she held on. His erection touched her. One small push and he would be inside her. But he looked her in the eye and waited.

"I love you, Hannah," he whispered.

She smelled his skin and hers, felt their heartbeats increasingly pounding, heard the sounds of their labored breaths mingling. Nothing more.

"I love you," she answered, threading her fingers through the hair at the back of his head, holding on for dear life.

He pushed inside her, and she dropped down slightly in response. His unhurried penetration stretched and filled her, took her breath away.

She held on tight and swayed in to him, as he made love to her. Slow and sweet at first, hard and fast when her body rebelled and she could take no more of his gentle restraint. There was love here, yes, but there was also an unleashed primal force that ruled their bodies. Love, and power, and need. An aching, urgent need that only Jed could satisfy.

She grasped him even tighter when the climax undulated through her body, then grabbed her so hard she cried out. He moaned and shuddered in her arms, pressed her hard against the wall and buried himself deep inside her as he found his own release.

Urgency gone, need satisfied, she expected Jed to let her go, to gently place her on her feet and step back. But he didn't. He held on to her and crushed her body against the wall as he gazed unflinchingly into her eyes and said it again.

"I love you."

And she believed him.

"You're not wearing *that*," Jed said in horror, as Hannah laid a white silk dress on the bed. Even spread innocently across the bed he could tell it was low-cut, and the skirt was too short, and . . . and it looked like something a New Orleans hooker would wear.

"Of course I am," she said, not so much as slowing down as she collected stockings and a white garter from her drawer.

"You are not," he said again.

Hannah turned about to smile at him. "Are you putting your foot down?" she asked sweetly.

He narrowed one eye. "Well, no." That hadn't worked well the last time. "It's just . . . just . . . Hell, Hannah, that dress is downright decadent. I don't want you showing everything you've got to Virgil Wyndham or anyone else."

"All right," she said, giving in much too easily. "If it truly bothers you I'll find something else to wear."

"You will?" he asked suspiciously.

"Lily loaned me a few things. I'm sure something else will suffice."

She went to her wardrobe and removed a selection of unsuitable gowns. They were all too low cut and decadent, and he found himself scowling down at the colorful options spread across the bed. He finally chose a green silk gown that seemed to have a longer skirt than the others, and he rummaged in the wardrobe until he came up with a concealing shawl she could wear with it.

He sat in the single chair in the room and watched her dress. "You sure caved easy on that one," he said suspiciously.

She smiled at him as she pulled on one black stocking, chosen to match the black lace in the green gown. "Which gown I wear is not terribly important, and I don't want to purposely annoy you."

"Since when?" he asked with a grin.

She ignored him. "But if I wear my usual clothing in Cash's saloon tonight, I won't exactly blend in."

"You'll be the only woman there," he muttered. "There's no way you'll *blend in.*"

She pulled on the other stocking and secured it with her red garter, giving him a seductive smile as she slid it into place. "Besides, I think it's rather sweet that you're jealous."

"I am not jealous," he said, sounding peevish.

"Protective, then," she offered, crossing the room to sit on his lap and wrap her arms around his neck. Wearing a corset and those stockings and that damn red garter. And nothing else.

"We're going to be late," he whispered.

"We have plenty of time," she said, leaning forward to kiss him.

"Not if you don't get off my lap, we don't." He pulled her close. "As a matter of fact, I think we should let Cash and Nate and Sullivan corner Wyndham. What do they need us for?"

She slithered off his lap, trailing her fingers over his neck as she withdrew. "I figured out who did it; I get to catch him," she said.

Jed leaned back and watched her slip into the green gown. As it fell into place and she began working the fasteners up the side, he was distressed to see that even though the gown he'd chosen was more demure than the others, it still offered a view he'd rather not share. The swell of her breasts, the column of her throat, the feminine and alluring curve of her bosom to her waist.

It occurred to him that she was being awfully agreeable tonight. What did he have to lose?

"What if I put my foot down and order you to stay here tonight."

She came closer and leaned forward. Damn, he definitely did not want another man getting this view! He'd never felt proprietary about a woman before, and he found it was an oddly helpless feeling.

"I love you," she whispered. A grin bloomed on her face. "But don't push your luck."

Twenty-one

There was a small commotion going on, as he stepped down the stairs and into the hotel lobby. The kids were running about, excited about the Christmas Eve feast Eden had prepared and the Christmas morning that would soon arrive. Reese and Mary were there, with their little girl, and so was a familiar young lady, surrounded by luggage and a mob of people, Rock Creek citizens who remembered her well.

"Josephine," he said with a grin as he recognized her. "Hell, you've grown up."

Jo Clancy, the Reverend Clancy's daughter, stepped away from the crowd to give him a hug and a small smile.

"I came as soon as I heard the news about Father."

"I'm sorry," he said. "It was a sad thing to happen."

Jo knew what her old man had been like, but he was her father, nonetheless. He could see the grief in her eyes, but there was a touch of relief, too. To be home, maybe. To be free of Maurice Clancy's direction and discipline.

"You look wonderful," she said warmly.

"So do you." He returned the compliment with a friendly wink, noting the unusually short length of her dark hair. "Who gave you permission to grow up?" Jo was still a little thing, delicate and pretty, but she wasn't a child any longer.

"Who gave you permission to cut your hair?" she asked with a grin.

"We'll call it even," he said softly, leaning down slightly.

"Where's Nate?" Jo asked, her eyes widening, her voice a little too casual. "I've asked around, but no one seems to know where he is."

Jo had always had a soft spot for Nate, their own fallen preacher. There had been a time when she'd practically followed him around like a lost puppy. She hadn't been much more than a kid at the time, as he remembered.

"I might be able to round him up."

"Thank you," Jo said softly, just before yet another old friend arrived and she was swept away.

When Hannah came sauntering down the stairs, Jed almost picked her up and carried her upstairs to change clothes. Shawl or no shawl, she looked too damn good. He didn't want any other man to see her this way. But when she smiled at him, it didn't matter anymore. She was his, and his alone. She loved him. He had no idea where they would go from here and at the moment he didn't care. He only cared that the woman he loved looked at him this way, her heart and passion for him lurking in her eyes.

Jo had been swallowed up by another round of newcomers who'd heard of her arrival, so Jed took Hannah's arm and escorted her from the hotel. There would be time for introductions later.

The afternoon wind was calmer than it had been in the past few days, but the chill remained. Hannah clung to her shawl for warmth as they hurried down the street. Down the way and across the street, before the newly opened Rogue's Palace, Nate was saddling up his horse.

Together, he and Hannah increased their pace.

"Where you headed?" Jed asked.

"Don't know," Nate said, without looking up from the task of filling his saddlebag with a bottle of whiskey.

"You can't leave right now," Jed said. "Jo's here. Jo Clancy."

"So I heard," Nate mumbled.

"She wants to see you."

Nate stepped into the stirrup and lifted himself into the saddle. "Maybe next time." He tipped his hat to Hannah and, without another word, turned his horse about and headed out of town. At a walk at first, then at a gallop. What the hell was his hurry?

"How odd," Hannah said as Jed led her into the saloon and out of the cold.

Jed stepped back and glanced down the street, narrowing his eyes, but Nate was already long gone.

Rogue's Palace. It was the perfect name for the perfect venture. His own place, at last. He'd need new furnishings, some paint, and nails, and more wood, but eventually . . . Eventually this saloon would be home. He hadn't had a place to call home in so long, he could barely remember what it felt like.

Nate was gone, had lit out of here so fast you'd think the devil himself was on the preacher's tail. Daniel Cash wasn't one to get attached to people, but he'd miss Nate. They'd been through some bad times together. A few good times, too. Why the hell couldn't he remember the good times?

He and Nate had ridden together for what seemed like forever, first with the others and then just the two of them. At the moment he felt strangely betrayed by Nate's sudden departure.

Cash sipped at his whiskey and watched Jed and Hannah. They sat side by side at a table in the corner, backs to the wall and chairs as close together as possible. They were probably holding hands beneath the table. He withheld a disgusted snort.

Whatever problem the two of them might've had earlier in the day had apparently been resolved. Hannah was relaxed and happy and more beautiful than he'd ever seen her, and Jed . . . Rough, crude, wild man Jedidiah Rourke had been tamed, and he didn't even know it yet. What a shame. What a waste.

Since it was too early for the night's crowd to have gathered, Cash sauntered over to their table and joined them. As he sat down across from the lovebirds, their conversation ceased. What *had* they been talking about?

"I hope you don't mind if the . . ." He glared at Hannah. "What am I? The stupidest man on the planet or just in Texas? I don't recall. Anyway, I hope you don't mind if I join you."

The woman had the decency to blush. "I didn't

mean that," she said. "Oh, I do hope you know that when I lost my temper the other day I was lashing out at Jed, not at you."

He liked Hannah, as well as he could like any woman he'd never bed. She wasn't gentle like Eden, one of the few women he could honestly say he admired, but Hannah had backbone and intelligence, fine qualities in a man. Fine qualities in a woman, too, he supposed, as long as she wasn't his. He liked his own women submissive and no smarter than they had to be.

"Of course," he said smoothly. "All is forgiven."

Yes, he was quite sure they were holding hands beneath the table. How disgustingly sweet.

"As a matter of fact," he said, feeling contrary at the moment, "I'd like to offer you a job."

Hannah's eyebrows shot up. "A job?"

He winked at her. "Every decent saloon needs a beguiling redhead in residence to make it complete. You can serve drinks, dance on the tables. . . ." He shrugged his shoulders. "You can do whatever you damn well please."

Jed's agreeable air faded, and his clean-shaven jaw clenched. "You son of a bitch. I'll . . ."

But Hannah smiled as she interrupted. "Cash is just kidding, isn't that right? Why, he made it clear from the beginning that there would be no women in *his* saloon." She glared at Cash with those intelligent eyes. "He's just trying to rile you, Jed."

"Jed riles easy," Cash countered. "It's not much of a challenge to get his hackles up."

"Leave my hackles out of this," Jed mumbled. But he didn't curse, and he didn't come across the table to do his best to kick Cash's ass.

Nate was gone, Jed had been tamed, and nothing was as it should be. Cash grinned. But he had his saloon, by God. He took a quick glance around the rustic place. Yep, he was home.

A small crowd had gathered for the opening night of Rogue's Palace. Cash, of course, who no longer seemed determined to pick a fight with Jed. Jed and Sullivan, sticking close and talking like good friends—or cordial brothers-in-law. And a group of locals. Hannah had spoken to several of the men during her investigation, but knew none of them well.

One of the Rock Creek residents in attendance was that skinny young man, Oliver Jennings. What would Bertie think of her fiancé spending his evenings in a place like this? Every now and then Oliver shot Hannah an anxious and curious glance, but he had not approached her to speak.

Hannah stood at the bar, the finest men of Rock Creek surrounding her. Still, she remained alone. If anyone approached with interest in their eyes, they were quickly and quietly warned away.

Jed, Cash, and Sullivan rarely spoke to her directly as the evening wore on. When her quarry arrived, she had to be prepared.

Virgil Wyndham came through the door at precisely nine o'clock, a half hour before the set time for the poker game Cash had invited him to join. The gambler looked around, liked what he saw, and took a seat. Hannah waited only a moment before heading his way.

"What'll you have to drink?"

He looked her over lasciviously, all but licking

his fat lips. When his wandering eyes landed at long last on her face, they widened in surprise.

"Miss Winters?"

She nodded and smiled.

"What are you doing"—he looked around suspiciously—"in this place?"

"One moment," she said, cocking her head and then turning slowly away.

At the bar, she grabbed a bottle of whiskey and two glasses. Jed glared at her with narrowed eyes; Cash lifted his eyebrows. Sullivan remained annoyingly stoic. How could she be afraid of what was to come when these men were watching and waiting to come to her aid?

She turned her back on them all and returned to Wyndham's table. Unfortunately, she still didn't have much of a plan. Gain his confidence and see where that took them. Was that a plan? Jed would likely think not.

She placed the glasses and bottle on the table, and Wyndham stood quickly, in what she imagined he thought a gentlemanly manner. He even pulled out a chair for her. She took the offered chair, and he reclaimed his seat directly across from her.

"What am I doing here?" she repeated, as Wyndham filled both glasses to the rim and placed one before her. "Cash needed help with his new business and I offered my assistance. It's as simple as that."

"When I met you on the stage, you didn't strike me as the kind of woman who would take a job as a saloon gal," Wyndham said suspiciously.

Hannah smiled. "I've taken the advice St. Ambrose gave to St. Augustine. '*Si fueris Romae, Ro-*

mano vivito more.' When in Rome," she translated, "live as the Romans live."

He lifted his glass to take a sip, easily accepting her explanation. "Wise advice."

She lifted her own glass and smelled the whiskey as if she were afraid of it, as if she were having second thoughts. As if what was to come was her very first taste of whiskey.

"Oh, I really shouldn't drink such strong spirits. I'm not at all accustomed to its inebriating effects."

"But when in Rome," he urged.

She straightened her spine, and Wyndham's eyes immediately drifted down to the exposed swell of her breasts. "You're right," she said, lifting her glass and taking a small sip.

Hannah was more certain than ever that this was the man who had killed Clancy. Oily, unctuous, repulsive Virgil Wyndham. She could definitely see him plunging a knife into the heart of his lover's husband. In spite of this certainty, she kept her smile in place.

After taking a few more sips of whiskey and listening intently to Virgil's braggart tales of his current lucky streak, she leaned across the table and lowered her voice. "You're so brave to go on with your life as if nothing has changed. Why, I still have nightmares about the day we were robbed," she said, as if confiding a secret. "For a while I just wanted to get away from this awful place where such things happen."

"I know what you mean," Wyndham said with a nod of his head.

"But that harrowing incident made me realize

that life is too short to waste a single minute," she said, wide-eyed and innocent.

His eyes lit up, the cretin.

"But Rock Creek is hardly the place to . . . to carouse."

"Rock Creek, small and plain as it is, has its finer points," the gambler revealed.

"Perhaps, but I have not been able to uncover them. Why do you stay here?" she asked, taking another sip of her whiskey, pretending it burned her throat, and fanning the air in front of her face. "I mean, a man such as yourself surely has better things to do than to hang around this awful little town."

"I have interests here," he said lowly.

"Interests," she repeated. "How fascinating."

"What keeps you here?" he asked.

Hannah sighed. "My sister. You know her husband was accused of murder, and I tried desperately to clear him." She threw her hands into the air. "And then the judge gives him a ridiculously light sentence, proving to me that my time and efforts were completely wasted."

"I heard you and Jed Rourke were stepping out," Wyndham said, his eyes boring into her.

Hannah took another drink and waved her hand dismissively. She wanted to be Wyndham's confidante, his friend. She wanted him to trust her. Too much to hope for, she imagined, but what else did she have? "Jed? Oh, we did share a meal together once or twice, but I must tell you"—she did her best to act as if the little bit of whiskey she'd consumed was affecting her, already—"he's a bit crude for my liking. I prefer a man who knows how to dress," she said, taking in Wyndham's atrocious checked jacket and bowler hat, the oddly yellowed shirt. "A man with a little"—she waved her hand in his direction—"style."

Wyndham beamed. "Well, if you're free this evening, I can skip the poker game and we can . . . find ourselves another, more private form of entertainment."

Hannah smiled. "I'd love that, but you see I heard a little gossip about you, too. I heard you were seeing the widow Clancy. I am not the kind of lady who moves in on another woman's man." She brought her hand to her breast in mock horror.

"Where did you hear that?" he asked, no longer smiling and happy.

"Oh, around," she said, waving her hand as if the subject meant nothing.

He reached across the table and grabbed her wrist. Out of the corner of her eye she saw Jed move. She also saw Sullivan discretely hold him back. As long as Wyndham didn't notice their interest, as long as he kept his focus on her, all would be well.

"Tell me something," she whispered, looking the gambler in the eye. "Do you love her?"

He shook his head.

"I can see why a man would fall in love with Sylvia. She's attractive, and . . . and she needs someone to take care of her. Someone strong and valiant." She shook her head slowly. "From everything I've heard, the departed Reverend Maurice Clancy had been blessed with neither of those traits."

"He was a jackass," Wyndham breathed.

Hannah didn't try to pull her hand from his, but leaned forward slightly. "He didn't deserve her," she whispered.

Wyndham shook his head.

"Is that why you killed him?" she asked in a confidential tone.

The gambler dropped her hand like he'd been burned.

"I don't know what you're talking about," he insisted indignantly.

She was right! Wyndham was about to panic. His eyes and the flush in his cheeks told everything. He'd been caught and he knew it.

"You loved Sylvia, so you killed her husband. I can understand that." She batted her lashes in pure Sylvia fashion. "It's actually very romantic."

"You don't understand anything," he said lowly. "Sylvia? I didn't love her. Most of the time I didn't even like her."

"But . . ." Hannah began.

Wyndham glared at her. "That bastard Clancy seduced my wife, years ago. We lived in Webberville, and Clancy used to . . . travel through on a regular basis. She confessed to me what had happened and asked me to forgive her, but I couldn't stand it. I couldn't bear knowing he had touched her, that she had given herself to him, so I ran. I left Laura and our baby and I started a new life. By the time I came to my senses and decided to go home and try to make my marriage whole again in spite of what Clancy had done, it was too late. Laura was dead."

"What happened?"

Wyndham's lower lip trembled. "She caught pneumonia, and I wasn't there to take care of her.

A family had taken in my son and were raising him as their own. They weren't living in Webberville anymore, so I couldn't even see him. I didn't know where Clancy was or I would have tracked him down and killed him then."

Heavens, she could actually feel sympathy for Wyndham. He'd lost everything because of Clancy.

"A couple of years ago I came into Rock Creek purely by accident, and there he was."

"So you've planned all this time to kill him?"

He shook his head. "No. I'm not normally a violent man, Miss Winters. And what happened to me happened a long time ago. But when I saw Clancy I wanted to take his wife from him the way he took Laura from me. I wanted to take what was rightfully his and then rub his face in it." His face softened, fell. "But Sylvia was lonely, an easy conquest. I thought Clancy would care, but . . . he didn't. I set it up a couple of times for him to catch us, but he never did. At least, I thought he didn't. Turns out he liked to watch, too."

"That's terrible," Hannah whispered.

"How do you hurt a man who has no heart?" he asked quietly. "I had decided there was no way I could hurt Clancy. I had almost . . . given up. But that morning I passed your sister, Rose, on the street. I'd seen her leave the rectory in a hurry, and she was so upset I knew something was wrong. I had come to town to see Sylvia, and . . . no, I didn't love her, I didn't like her, but I did care about her. I was afraid she might have been hurt." The gambler swallowed hard as he remembered. "I went inside and found Clancy wounded, and without a second thought I took the knife out of his hand and finished the job."

"Does Sylvia know?" Hannah whispered.

Wyndham shook his head. "No. I couldn't bring myself to tell her. I had just arrived in Rock Creek, on a horse I had won in a Ranburne card game that time, instead of by stage, and no one knew I was here. I killed Clancy, then turned around and rode out of town."

"Why did you come back?"

He grinned sadly. "I shouldn't have. But I wondered if your sister saw me as she ran away from the rectory in tears. I kept looking over my shoulder, waiting for a Rock Creek posse to show up with a length of rope. I worried for nothing. Your sister was so upset she didn't remember anything."

Hannah nodded. "She does remember, you know," she said, almost feeling sorry for the man. "It came to her a few days ago."

"I shouldn't have come back and I definitely shouldn't have stayed," Wyndham said with a small, defeated laugh. "My curiosity got the best of me. I wanted to see how this hand would play out."

"You really should tell the sheriff what happened," Hannah advised. "Tell them everything, how he hurt you in the past, how you couldn't control your anger."

He shook his head in dismay and denial. "Miss Winters," he said softly, "I'm sorry to say there's a derringer pointed at you, beneath this table. We're going to stand up and walk out of here, and you're going to ride with me until we're far enough away from town that I feel safe. Then I'll let you go."

"You won't get away with it," she whispered. "There are too many people here for one man to take on alone."

"I'm not alone," he said.

The other shooter. Of course he was not alone! "Who's been helping you?" she asked. "Who was with you the day you tried to kill me?"

"My son," Wyndham confessed. "I found him living outside Rock Creek with his new family a few years ago. He's one of the reasons, the main reason, I continue to come here. And we weren't trying to kill you that day. We just wanted you to . . . go away. To let things be. I thought we could scare you off. Oliver came with me that day to make sure I didn't shoot you."

"Oliver Jennings?" Her heart hitched.

Wyndham nodded his head. "Oliver wasn't even three years old when Laura died. The family who took him in gave him their name, made him their own. He tries not to say so, but I know he thinks of them as his real family, and me as a . . . an embarrassment." He pinned his eyes on hers. "But he is my son and he will help me one more time. He's going to be right disappointed to have to leave town with his pa. He's taken quite a shine to Bertie."

"But . . ."

"Enough talk," Wyndham said, rising, keeping the derringer concealed by his long sleeve and the careful positioning of his hand. "Let's get out of here. Don't make a scene or call attention to us. As far as anyone watching is concerned, we're just going out for a stroll."

Hannah rose calmly, knowing there were a number of capable eyes on her at the moment. She took a deep breath and headed for the door, Wyndham directly and too closely behind her.

"Miss Winters," Jed called out blandly, just before she and Wyndham reached the door.

She turned about to face Jed as he lifted her cane and shawl high, one item in each hand. Their eyes met briefly, and while he was outwardly calm she could see the intensity there.

"You don't want to leave without these." He shook the shawl. "It's chilly out tonight." He rounded the bar, the offered items in hand. He looked perfectly calm, perfectly natural. One would never know that he was fully aware of what was happening.

Cash moved to a position by the door, fiddling with a cigar, and Sullivan crept up on the other side. Their movements were smooth and very well planned. She saw every easy move, but Wyndham's eyes remained on Jed and Jed alone.

Jed draped the shawl over her shoulders, and held out the cane, offering it to her as if nothing were wrong.

He looked at her for a moment and then his eyes landed on the derringer, which was not quite so well concealed from his new vantage point. With a snap of the cane he continued to grasp, Jed lifted Wyndham's arm and forced it aside so the derringer was no longer a threat to Hannah. With an expert twist of the cane, the derringer went flying out of the gambler's hand.

Hannah stepped cautiously behind Jed, as he reached out and grabbed Wyndham by the arm.

"Oliver!" Wyndham cried in panic. "Help me!"

Sullivan spun on Oliver Jennings, who was, as

it turned out, no threat at all. He held up his empty hands and shook his head in refusal. "I've already helped you more than I should, even if you are my real pa. I'm not going to help you hurt Miss Hannah."

Sullivan took custody of Wyndham and led him to the door. The sheriff issued a nod and a soft command to Oliver, and the young man followed willingly, head down in shame. Oliver mumbled a soft apology to Hannah as he passed, and the three of them exited Rogue's Palace.

Hannah threw her arms around Jed when he turned to face her. "See how easy that was?" she asked softly.

"Easy?" he bellowed. "I damn near had a heart attack. He was pointing a *gun* at you."

"A little one," she argued. "Besides, that doesn't matter. He confessed."

"I guessed as much when I saw the way he was ushering you out of here."

She laid her head on his chest and relaxed there. "I was right," she whispered. "I knew Rose could never murder anyone."

She felt Jed relax, as he wrapped his arms around her. "You do love to be right, don't you," he muttered.

Hannah smiled. "I guess so. Doesn't everyone?"

"Not as much as you do," he said softly, drawing her close and holding her there.

"You two," Cash called loudly, "cut it out. This is a respectable saloon."

"There's nothing respectable about you, Daniel Cash," Hannah said as she pulled slightly away from Jed and looked past him to a grinning Cash, "so never you mind." She looked up at Jed. "Never you mind," she said again.

Jed sighed and took her face in his hands. "Tomorrow is Christmas Day, Hannah darlin'. What do you want?"

"I have everything I need," she whispered, "right here."

Twenty-two

Christmas morning in the Paradise Hotel was pure, unadulterated, magnificent chaos. Children laughed and ran and played with new dolls and wooden trains and hand-carved whistles. The adults gathered around the scrawny Christmas tree that had been erected in the lobby the night before. The tree had been decorated with colorful ornaments the children had made themselves, as well as a proliferation of red satin ribbons.

The Sullivans were there, of course, as well as the Reeses and the Salvatores. Cash was seated alone, watching silently and with a constant expression of long-suffering forbearance, and Jo Clancy was present, as well.

A turkey was roasting in the oven, and that, mingling with the aroma of pies that had been baked last night and early this morning, filled the air.

Hannah stood at the foot of the stairs and watched as Jed mingled with his nieces and nephews and the other children who had gathered here. Rico and Lily's little girl, Carrie, and Millie had their heads together, whispering and giggling as only girls of a certain age can do.

The boys stood together, the young piano player, Johnny, and Teddy listening stoically as Rafe went on and on about the rifle his Uncle Jed had given him for Christmas.

Jed sat on the floor with Georgie and Fiona both in his lap, the toddlers jumping and giggling and grabbing at his nose and ears. He smiled and let them grab and giggle, completely at ease with the children around him, so beautiful and gentle and strong.

He glanced up and his eye caught hers, and in that instant there was no one here but the two of them. She loved him, and he loved her. She knew that, with no doubts or reservations.

And her gift to him was almost ready.

She stepped from the stairway to stand over Jed, who had an arm around each of the little girls who laughed and played and teased. He started to set them aside, but a lifted hand from Hannah stopped him.

"No," she said. "Don't get up. I'm going to see Rose and her family."

"You'll be back in time for dinner, won't you?"

She smiled. Jed drew her so easily into his world. He wanted and needed her here. "I wouldn't miss it, but I did promise Rose I'd come by this morning. We haven't seen each other at Christmas for too long, and besides . . . I have a gift for her family."

He lifted his eyebrows. "What is it?"

"I'll tell you later."

This was a big step, a huge undertaking. And she wanted to have Jed to herself when it happened. "Meet me outside," she said softly. "One hour."

He was curious but did not question her. By

the time she'd greeted those in the hotel lobby and made her way outside, her hands trembled and her stomach clenched. She stood on the boardwalk in that condition for a few very long minutes, and then she proceeded.

Rose and her family were enjoying their own Christmas celebration, a quieter time but one just as lovely. They were glad to be together, vindicated and alive. It was just the four of them, since Bertie was spending the day with the Jennings clan. The parents and sisters and brothers Oliver considered his *real* family. Hannah was doubly glad she'd encouraged the sheriff, who was apparently not a moron after all, not to press any charges against Oliver.

Hannah gave everyone, even Baxter, a big hug. She was not normally a demonstrative person, but she felt the need for those hugs today. She needed to give and receive them. What she was about to do would require a tremendous amount of strength, and the hugs . . . they helped.

The boys accepted her overtures, but they had quieted, become stiff and withdrawn, the moment she'd walked into the room. She knew why. She had come too close to becoming her father, to trying to control her nephews by threatening them with the family fortune. More than anything, she did not want to be like her father.

When Rose excused herself to check on her own holiday feast and Baxter went with her, Hannah turned to the twins.

"Franklin, Jackson," she said, nodding to each one in turn. She could actually tell them apart, now. Usually. "I'm withdrawing my earlier offer."

"What?" Jackson asked. "We behaved ourselves all this time for *nothing?*"

"I knew it," Franklin grumbled, glancing at his brother. "She tricked us!"

Hannah silenced their protests with a raised hand. Amazingly enough, they responded to that silent command. "Your rights, as my nephews, have nothing to do with your behavior. I do hope you will continue to mature as you have since I arrived, to help your mother and father, and become productive, intelligent citizens. But I want you to do so because it's right, not because you think I will pay you for behaving as you should."

"What does that mean?" Franklin asked, his eyes narrowed.

Jackson elbowed his brother. "It means we get money no matter what!" He grinned widely.

Hannah sighed. Rose's battles with her boys were not yet over. She dismissed the boys from her mind and turned just as Rose and Baxter reentered the room.

"Did you manage to gather the things I asked for?" She'd stopped by last night to tell them about Wyndham, and at that time she'd given Rose a hastily scribbled list.

"Yes," Rose said softly. "But why do you need them?"

"I'll tell you in a few minutes. First," she said with a smile, "I have a Christmas gift for you." She only hoped Rose and Baxter would accept this particular gift.

Jed played with the girls awhile longer, after Hannah left, but eventually he left them to their dolls and pretend castles. He ran up the stairs, taking them two at a time, and made his way to the third floor.

He wished he'd thought to order something special for Hannah, for their first Christmas together, but . . . He pulled the magenta garter from his drawer and twirled it on his finger. . . . This would have to do for this year. Next year he'd plan ahead; he'd give her something special, something that would make her eyes light up and her face glow and her mouth curve into that enticing smile of hers.

Next year. He had never thought of a woman and next year at the same time and in conjunction with each other. He didn't doubt, at the moment, that he and Hannah would be together next year. He didn't know how, he didn't know where, but he did know that this woman was his better half. His partner for life.

Jed put the garter in his pocket and started for the door, but he stopped there with his hand on the knob. He could give Hannah something special this year, couldn't he? He knew how to make her face light up and her eyes dance. He knew what she wanted.

A half hour later, just in time for Hannah's arrival, he bounded down the steps. Millie waited for him at the foot of the stairs.

"Uncle Jed," she said sweetly, "you're purty again."

He winked at Millie and told her he'd be right back. Standing at the foot of the stairs and gathering his strength, he straightened the lapels of his frock coat and rotated his neck against the tightness of the boiled shirt's collar.

"Jedidiah!" Eden said, rising from her seat on the couch, "where are you . . ."

Sullivan grabbed Eden's wrist and pulled her

back down to his side, telling her, as only a loving husband could, to mind her own damn business.

Cash shook his head in despair.

Reese and Rico exchanged a knowing glance Jed did not want to acknowledge. Not right now.

Jed stepped onto the boardwalk and into the street. All was quiet, here, as people spent the day with their families. The wind blew, but not as coldly as it had last night, and the sun warmed the air. It was a nice enough December day.

Only one other soul moved on the street, and that was . . . He squinted and scowled. . . . Oh, what he saw was not possible. He stepped into the street to get a better view.

"Hannah?"

The buckskin split skirt was comfortable, as were the linen blouse and long buckskin coat. It was the pull of the short-barreled rifle at her back that would take some getting used to, that and the way the leather harness bit into her shoulders.

The boots were very nice, but still needed to be broken in, and the hat looked and felt much too new. It would be dusty and misshapen in no time, she imagined.

Beneath the hat her hair hung free, loose and tangled and blowing in the wind.

When Jed stepped from the hotel, right on time, her heart nearly stopped. What had he done? What on earth was he wearing?

"Hannah?" he said, hands on hips, feet planted far apart as he stood in the middle of the street and waited for her to reach him. "What's this?"

"You first," she said, looking him over from

his neatly combed hair and smoothly shaven jaw, down the length of his fine suit to the tips of his polished black boots.

He took a deep breath and stuck out his chin stubbornly. "Isn't this the way men who live on plantations are supposed to dress?"

She leaned closer and smiled widely, and inside, in her heart and her soul, she felt lighter. The world had just become a better place.

"You smell lovely."

"It's witch hazel," he admitted reluctantly, as if he were afraid someone else would hear.

Tears filled her eyes, her heart swelled, and she knew she would never love Jed more than she did at this moment. Surely more love than this was impossible. Her heart would explode with it.

"You would do that for me? You would go to Alabama with me and live on the plantation?"

"I would do anything for you."

He meant it. Hannah saw the impossible truth in his eyes.

Jed looked her up and down, his eyes raking slowly over her. "What's this getup all about?"

She rocked back on the heels of her Western boots. More than ever, she knew this decision was the right one. "Isn't this the way women with itchy feet are supposed to dress?"

Jed shook his head. "I can't let you . . ."

"*Let* me?" she interrupted.

He laid a hand on her cheek, comforting her, loving her. "I can't let you give up your home for me."

"I already did," she whispered. "I gave the plantation to Rose and Baxter, as a Christmas gift. It's not much of a gift, really. It's rightfully as much theirs as it is mine, and I . . . I'd rather be with you, wherever you go."

Jed loosened the top button of his shirt and took a deep breath. "This thing is killing me."

"I know what you mean," Hannah said, slipping out of the leather harness that held the rifle at her back. "Maybe I should stick with my cane, for the time being."

Jed took the harness and rifle and dropped it to the ground. Then he wrapped his arms around her and lifted her off her feet so they were face-to-face, nose-to-nose, and eye-to-eye. "I have a present for you," he said. "It's in my coat pocket."

She reached into the pocket and pulled out the bright garter, smiled as she twirled it on her finger. "Thank you." She kissed him soundly and returned the garter to its place. "It's lovely. I'll try it on later."

"I'll be sure that you do."

She would never forget that Jed had been willing to give up the life he loved for her, that this one man loved her not because of her family heritage and fortune, but in spite of it.

"Do you think your itchy feet could carry you all the way to Paris?" she asked tentatively.

"Paris, Texas?"

"Paris, France."

"May be."

"Perhaps we could visit both," Hannah suggested. "A kind of world tour."

"I don't know that Paris, Texas, is ready for you," Jed said lowly.

"Well, I'm quite sure that Paris, France, is not at all prepared for Jed Rourke's arrival, but I'm willing to give it a try if you are." She kissed his

neck softly, there where he'd loosened his shirt.
"I did give Rose and Baxter the plantation, but
I kept some of the money for us. I hope you
don't mind. I really would like to see Paris."

Perhaps he wasn't quite sure, because his eyes
narrowed suspiciously. "How about San Francisco
for a start? It's plenty fancy, it's far away, and we
don't have to get on a ship to get there."

"Are you afraid of ships?"

"Of course not," he said indignantly. "How
could I be? I've never been on one."

Ah, he was skeptical, whether he was willing to
admit it or not.

"Me, neither," she confessed.

"So, San Francisco . . ."

"Just think," she mused aloud, twirling one finger through his hair. "Just the two of us, all alone
in our own stateroom for thousands of miles as we
cross the ocean. Whatever will we do to pass the
time?"

"I'm sure we'll think of something."

"I'm sure we will."

She kissed him, soft and briefly. How could she
not when his mouth was so close? So tempting?

"A ship, huh," he muttered with a shake of
his head.

"A ship."

"Wily woman," he muttered fondly.

"Hardheaded man," she countered.

"Marry me."

She placed her palms on his smooth cheeks
and looked into eyes so blue they grabbed her
heart and wouldn't let go. "Yes."

COMING IN JANUARY 2002
FROM ZEBRA BALLAD ROMANCES

__THE BRIDE WORE BLUE: The Brides of Bath
by Cheryl Bolen   0-8217-7247-3 $5.99US/$7.99CAN
Felicity came to the aid of Thomas Moreland after a band of highwaymen
left him for dead. Now he's determined to convince her that there's more
to life than assembly rooms, matrons, and matchmaking. But what Felicity
doesn't know yet is that her greatest desire of all is to spend the rest of her
life in Thomas's arms . . .

__PROMISE THE MOON: The Vaudrys
by Linda Lea Castle   0-8217-7266-X $5.99US/$7.99CAN
Held captive by Thomas Le Revenant, and betrothed against her will to his
son, Rowanne Vaudry is doomed to a life of misery. Then fate—in the form
of Brandt Le Revenant—steps in, rescuing her as she journeys to meet her
fiancé. How can Rowanne know that Brandt, a knight newly returned from
the Crusades, has his own reasons for helping her?

__NATE: The Rock Creek Six
by Lori Handeland   0-8217-7275-9 $5.99US/$7.99CAN
When Josephine Clancy met Nate Lang, she couldn't help but offer her
friendship. Haunted by the War Between the States, Nate was the kind of
man who needed someone. But Jo hadn't counted on falling in love with
the hurting, secretive stranger—or the lengths she would travel to rescue
him from the melancholy that threatened to destroy him.

__REUNION: Men of Honor
by Kathryn Fox   0-8217-7242-2 $5.99US/$7.99CAN
Lauren often thought of the hardships she would face as the wife of a
Canadian Mountie. But she never imagined that her first challenge would be
her own betrothed, for Adam McPhail now seems distant and cautious. Lauren
wonders if the marriage she's dreamed of has ended before it has begun.

Call toll free **1-888-345-BOOK** to order by phone or use this coupon to
order by mail. ALL BOOKS AVAILABLE JANUARY 01, 2002.
Name_____
Address_____
City_____ State_____ Zip_____
Please send me the books that I checked above.
I am enclosing $_____
Plus postage and handling* $_____
Sales tax (in NY and TN) $_____
Total amount enclosed $_____
*Add $2.50 for the first book and $.50 for each additional book. Send
check or money order (no cash or CODs) to: **Kensington Publishing
Corp., Dept. C.O., 850 Third Avenue, New York, NY 10022**
Prices and numbers subject to change without notice. Valid only in the
U.S. All orders subject to availability. **NO ADVANCE ORDERS.**
Visit our website at **www.kensingtonbooks.com.**

Enjoy *Savage Destiny*
A Romantic Series from
Rosanne Bittner

__#1: **Sweet Prairie Passion** $5.99US/$6.99CAN
    0-8217-5342-8

__#2: **Ride the Free Wind Passion** $5.99US/$6.99CAN
    0-8217-5343-6

__#3: **River of Love** $5.99US/$6.99CAN
    0-8217-5344-4

Call toll free **1-888-345-BOOK** to order by phone or use this coupon to order by mail.

Name_____

Address _____

City_____ State _____ Zip _____

Please send me the books I have checked above.

I am enclosing	$_____
Plus postage and handling*	$_____
Sales tax (NY and TN residents)	$_____
Total amount enclosed	$_____

*Add $2.50 for the first book and $.50 for each additional book.
Send check or money order (no cash or CODs) to:
Kensington Publishing Corp., 850 Third Avenue, New York, NY 10022
Prices and Numbers subject to change without notice.
All orders subject to availability.
Check out our website at **www.kensingtonbooks.com**.